AF093816

SO RIGHT

Copyright © 2025 by Abby Millsaps

All rights reserved.

paperback ISBN: 9798990077089

No portion of this book may be reproduced, distributed, or transmitted in any form without written permission from the author, except by a reviewer who may quote brief passages in a book review.

This book is a work of fiction. Any resemblance to any person, living or dead, or any events or occurrences, is purely coincidental. The characters and story lines are created by the author's imagination and are used fictitiously.

Line Editing, Copyediting, and Proofreading by VB Edits
Cover Design © Silver at Bitter Sage Designs

Contents

Dedication	VI
Content Warning and Timeline	1
1. Hunter	2
2. Greedy	6
3. Levi	9
4. Sione	15
5. Hunter	17
6. Greedy	22
7. Kabir	28
8. Kabir	34
9. Hunter	39
10. Levi	45
11. Kabir	52
12. Greedy	57
13. Hunter	65
14. Levi	68

15.	Greedy	74
16.	Hunter	85
17.	Levi	90
18.	Hunter	96
19.	Levi	101
20.	Hunter	108
21.	Sione	114
22.	Greedy	118
23.	Hunter	129
24.	Hunter	136
25.	Greedy	140
26.	Sione	144
27.	Kabir	150
28.	Hunter	160
29.	Sione	167
30.	Greedy	170
31.	Hunter	175
32.	Kabir	181
33.	Hunter	186
34.	Greedy	189
35.	Hunter	193
36.	Kabir	203
37.	Levi	207

38.	Greedy	211
39.	Kabir	214
40.	Sione	217
41.	Greedy	222
42.	Kabir	228
43.	Greedy	231
44.	Hunter	234
45.	Hunter	241
46.	Greedy	247
47.	Kabir	252
48.	Sione	258
Epilogue 1: Kabir		263
Epilogue 2: Greedy		266
Epilogue 3: Sione		272
Epilogue 4: Hunter		278
Epilogue 5: Hunter		283
Afterword		291
Acknowledgments		293
Also By Abby Millsaps		295
About The Author		296

To the readers who have been waiting for Magnolia to get what she deserves since book one.
#YoureWelcome

Content Warning and Timeline

Content Warning

Potential triggers for So Right include breeding kink, attempted murder, actual murder, physical child abuse by a parent (descriptive flashback that occurs in a dream), mention of past emotional abuse and manipulation of an adult child by a parent, mention of past suicidal ideation and mental health crisis, and discussion of past miscarriage. Lactation kink is also featured in the third epilogue.

Timeline

Please note that the fictional Scouting Combine featured in this story occurs about a month earlier than the National Football League's annual event. This schedule change was made for continuity within the series.

Also of note: Greedy mentions the first dogwood tree blossoms in Chapter 34, signifying the arrival of spring. Although South Chapel is a fictional place, it can be assumed the flowering dogwood trees would start to bloom in Mid-March in that region of North Carolina.

Chapter 1

Hunter

"Breathe."

The low voice is sultry and comforting.

A firm knuckle of one finger smooths from the top of my spine all the way down to the small of my back. Soothing me. Grounding me. *Sione*.

Though he's only touching me with a single digit, I'm engulfed in the solace of his presence. As if he's wrapped me up in the warmest hug and cocooned me in his personal brand of sanctuary. He's the reassuring lifeline I need as my brain works triple-time to follow Spence's request and keep it together.

With a ragged exhale, I do as Sione says. I push all the air out of my lungs, then suck in a shuddering breath. Eyes closed, I allow myself one more deep breath to steel my heart. When I open my eyes, I school my expression, ready to face the alleged reality of this situation.

Both my mother and Dr. Ferguson are staring at me, shocked and slack-jawed.

They look the way I feel.

Spence just announced to all the men in my life, as well as to my sorry excuse for a mother and her husband, Greedy's father, that I'm pregnant.

I'm not.

I can't be.

My period ended a couple of days ago.

I haven't ovulated. I know this because I track my cycles closely in order to manage my PMDD symptoms.

Even if I miraculously ovulated early without experiencing any of the typical symptoms, a fertilized egg could not have implanted in such a short amount of time.

None of this is real.

The logical part of my brain knows that.

Yet...

"Take another breath," Sione reminds me, his hand now firmly resting on my low back.

I exhale in a rush, desperate to rid my lungs of the stale air I've been unknowingly holding.

It's as if I've forgotten how to breathe. I'm a mess. I don't think I can do this. If Spence honestly expects me to keep it together in light of his unexpected announcement, I fear he doesn't know me at all.

Sione rubs small circles along the base of my spine, working to unwind the unease that has me in a chokehold.

Dr. Ferguson asks a question.

I don't hear it.

Nor do I know who responds.

I can't hear over the ringing in my ears, and the way my vision tunnels makes it hard to register what's going on around me.

Pregnant.

Pregnant, pregnant, pregnant.

I was pregnant before.

I conceived a baby with a man standing in this room.

Greedy.

If this "announcement" is hurting my heart, I can't begin to imagine what it's doing to his soul. A choked hiccup escapes me as tears force themselves from my eyes.

God dammit, Spence.

I suck in another lungful of air to clear my vision so I can turn. So I can find Greedy. So I can apologize and offer comfort. Provide whatever he might need to ease the intense burning sensation that must be plaguing him the way it pains me.

Before I convince my body to cooperate so I can focus on my first love, Dr. Ferguson steps between us, arms outstretched and grinning.

"Oh, Hunter." He wraps me up in a fierce hug. "Congratulations, sweetheart."

After a moment, he steps back and grasps my shoulders. Still smiling, he squeezes them in a reassuring, fatherly way that tugs at my heartstrings.

"I'm not sure if this was planned on your end, but your mother and I are here for you. We love you, and we'll support you in any way we can."

The sincerity of his words slams into me with so much force I sway on my feet.

He believes it. They're both buying it. This is actually working?

I'm pregnant, and it's working.

The irony of this moment adds another layer of heartache, like a thick, sticky salve being sloshed on top of damp clay.

Too much, too late.

This is a moment we never got to experience the first time, Greedy and me.

Greedy.

I tilt to one side, desperate to find him, but Dr. Ferguson thwarts my attempt again by enveloping me in another hug.

When he releases me, Spence is there in my field of vision.

His usual blue-gray orbs are the color of an iceberg. They're absolutely frigid and devoid of emotion.

There isn't an ounce of sympathy in his expression. No sorrow. No remorse for the havoc he just wreaked and the chaos that'll ensue.

My vision goes red and my heart thumps deafeningly in my ears. How fucking dare he?

He told me not to overreact. He promised he had this under control. Does he have any idea what sort of pain he's unnecessarily inflicted on me? On Greedy?

Fresh tears threaten to spill over as I watch him watch me. He assesses me in a clinical way. As if I'm a specimen.

For now, for the greater good, I'll play along with his plan, but there's no easing the hurt I feel.

There's no stopping the way the wound that's never truly healed now aches.

There's no way to take away the agony surely coursing through the first boy I ever loved, who seems to always be caught off guard by Spence.

Or the pain another man in this room must be experiencing. A man I care for so deeply now. The man who held me through the tears and physical aches I suffered during my miscarriage years ago.

Pain, pain, pain.

All I feel—

All I am—

All I ever seem to cause is pain.

As I pull out of Dr. F's arms and gingerly wipe at the moisture on my cheeks, I turn toward my mother.

Despite the hurt, the pain, the emotional damage spreading through this room like wildfire, I know damn well that Spence's plan is designed to cut Magnolia out of the equation once and for all.

I steel my spine and face her head-on. This can't be for nothing.

Spence's plan will work. It has to. Some kind of reward has to come from all this pain.

Chapter 2

Greedy

Pregnant.

Hunter's pregnant.

Kabir's got the fucking blood work to prove it. We've all got the proof, now that he's shared it with all our devices.

I blink at the report on my screen, my heart stuck in my throat.

Fucking line sixteen.

I know enough about hCG levels to know what these numbers indicate. If Hunter is pregnant, she's only five weeks, six at most.

I force my attention up and search for her, desperate to understand what's going on. Did she know? If so, how could she have kept this from me? *Again*?

When I find her sobbing in my father's arms, shoulders shaking, the truth is plain as day.

Spence's announcement is news to her.

Which means he and I will be having words—at minimum—as soon as we leave this house.

Pregnant.

Pregnant?

Is it even possible?

Hunter started her period the day before Magnolia took her. If her cycle started just over a week ago, there's no fucking way she could be pregnant. Right?

Unless, of course, the bleeding was caused by something other than her period.

With a long exhale, I recall all the times we've been intimate since then. When she was riding my face and Leev was sucking me off a few days ago, there wasn't any blood.

Are her periods always that short? Or could the blood have been from implantation?

I've only encountered one maternity unit in my pre-med classes thus far, but according to texts, a woman can spot or even bleed for any number of nonemergency reasons.

If that wasn't her period...

If that was implantation bleeding...

Fuck.

Molars grinding, I do my best to recall each of our encounters over the last several weeks.

None of the timing makes sense.

Though she has been with Kabir.

Levi, too.

I made love to her the night her mother came back to town about a month ago, but I didn't come inside her. Neither did Levi.

We had intercourse up at the cabin last week, but even if her bleeding wasn't caused by menstruation, if the number on line sixteen is accurate, that was too recent. She couldn't have gotten pregnant then.

Pregnant.

A sob snags my attention. My father is still cradling Hunter in his arms.

Hunter is looking at Kabir.

If she's pregnant, she's most definitely having another man's child.

My heart plummets to the floor.

This is our second chance. This is our shot.

She can't be fucking pregnant.

If she is, we're about to have a mini–British Invasion on our hands. Or a little blond-haired, blue-eyed baby Levi.

This can't be happening.

If anyone was going to get her pregnant, it was supposed to be *me*.

Chapter 3

Levi

"Darling… I don't know what to say." Magnolia has one hand splayed over her chest. The other grips the edge of the kitchen table. "How long have you two been together?"

She's looking at me.

Magnolia St. Clair-Ferguson is speaking to *me*.

My stomach twists painfully.

Spence just dropped the biggest bombshell, and he's got the blood work to prove his claim. And based on the way Magnolia is looking from me to Hunter, then back, it's clear she thinks I knocked her daughter up.

The question hangs in the air, and now Magnolia isn't the only one looking.

One by one, each person in the room homes in on me wearing expressions of varying levels of surprise, shock, and disdain.

Emotion, confusion, and dread churn in my gut and force bile to rise up my esophagus. It hurts. It burns. I swallow down the acrid taste and stand straighter.

Before I can come up with a response, Hunter sniffles. "We got together as soon as Levi came back to town." Her voice is shaky, but she speaks loud enough for all of us to hear.

I want to go to her. Comfort her. Wrap her in my arms. Selfishly, I also want to demand to know what the hell is going on.

How pregnant is she? How the hell do we figure out who the father is? Could it be me? G? Sione or Kabir?

I don't know shit about pregnancy or lab results, but I do know that I should follow her lead.

Dr. F and Magnolia think we're dating.

Shit.

We *are* dating, but they think we're exclusive.

So in their mind, if Hunter's pregnant, I must be the father. It's possible, sure, but fuck if I know how accurate that assumption really is.

With a grimace, I lower my head and focus on the floor.

If I look at any of them, the bewilderment I can't reel in may give us away.

Spence said he had a plan.

This isn't a plan. This is a fucking onslaught.

How long has he fucking known? How long has he let us all walk around thinking all was well and that he had it handled?

A little heads-up that his brilliant plan involves a fucking baby would have been nice.

Fuck. A baby.

I can't have a baby. I don't even have a fucking job.

My blood turns to ice, and dread transforms into panic.

I can't do this. What the fuck do I even say?

I don't want to look up.

I don't want to see Spence. I don't even want to hear his fucking name.

Hunter. She's still sobbing. My heart sinks. I can't look at her. I can't stand to think that I'm the one who did this to her.

I don't dare look at my best friend. My... what? Boyfriend? Lover?

Fucking hell.

If this baby is mine, Greedy is going to be so fucking pissed.

"We should do lunch," Magnolia declares. "You, me, Levi, and his mother."

I snap my head up, the force of the move making my neck crack.

All signs of shock and disbelief have disappeared from the woman's face. She's standing straighter now, gripping the back of a kitchen chair, and her eyes are sharply focused on her daughter.

As I take her in, my hackles rise.

All concern for myself evaporates when I see the way she's leering at Hunter.

Without a second thought, I stride over and throw one arm around my girl's shoulders. "No."

All my fears, worries, and agitation dissipated the moment she brought my mother into the mix. There's no fucking way I'm letting that woman get anywhere near Hunter.

"No?" Magnolia lets out a breathy laugh. "You can't deny the future grandmothers an opportunity to get together. We have so much to plan."

Her tone may be pleasant and sweet, but it's in stark contrast to the revulsion in her eyes.

"How far along do you think you are, darling?"

When Hunter doesn't reply, I tighten my grip around her frame and place a soft kiss atop her head. "I'm here," I murmur. She might feel powerless in this moment, but she's not alone.

Magnolia huffs, her chin raised higher. "Hunter. Answer me."

Hunter sobs, the cry so violent her entire body shudders.

Fuck. She's shutting down. We have to get out of here. I can't help but hold her closer. Though my muscles are wound tight with tension, I hope our proximity is at least a little comfort.

"Those hormones are certainly doing a number on you already." Magnolia drops a hand to her hip. "When is your due date? When will you start to show?"

Even if Hunter wanted to respond, her mother asks the questions too quickly to allow for answers.

"I deserve to know whether I'll live long enough to meet my first grandchild."

Hunter's body locks up. Then she's teetering into my side. I catch her around the waist before she can fall and hold her tight, giving her hip a reassuring squeeze.

This is too much. For all of us. I have to shut this down before we find ourselves buried beneath a mountain of pain and uncertainty.

Straightening, I clear my throat. "We aren't ready to share that information with anyone just yet."

I peer down at Hunter, hoping she'll nod. Hoping she's at least breathing.

"Clever girl." A peal of humorless laughter escapes Magnolia. "Of course you shouldn't confirm anything until after you two are married."

Hunter lets out a strangled sound, then breaks into a coughing fit.

Sione appears on her other side and places a hand on her back as she tries to control the outburst.

When I'm sure he's got her, I cross my arms and look from Magnolia to Dr. F, who hasn't added a damn thing during Magnolia's entire tirade.

"No one said anything about marriage."

"Of course not," the evil woman quips. "No one has to. It's implied. If a young woman from a good family finds herself with child, she's either sent away or quickly upgraded to Mrs."

My blood pressure spikes. There's no fucking way I'll let anyone force Hunter into anything.

As I open my mouth to explain that, Magnolia cuts me off at the pass.

"We'll plan an early spring wedding. Keep things quiet for now. Though you can't keep this from your mother, Levi. Especially now that I know."

The words are sticky sweet, and yet the statement sounds like a threat.

I bite my tongue to keep from spewing anything that could complicate this situation.

Fuck. Maybe I've already made it worse. Maybe I should have let one of the other guys take point.

But there was no way I could deny Magnolia's claim about the child being mine.

I couldn't leave Hunter to deal with the scrutiny alone.

And the only relationship her mom and Dr. Ferguson know about is the one she and I share. It's annoying at best and dubious at worse. Don't they think it's strange that Hunter's accompanied by an entourage of men at all times?

Spence steps forward, his hands in the pockets of his trousers. "We all must be going now. We have an appointment to get to."

The words are casual, as if he didn't just shock the shit out of all of us and upend our entire lives.

With a squeal, Magnolia claps and bounces on her toes with fake-as-hell and over-the-top enthusiasm. She's not actually excited about any of this. Though she does know how to put on a show.

"Is it a doctor's appointment? Oh, I cannot wait to go with you to all your ultrasounds."

Hunter goes ramrod straight beside me.

Why does everything out of this woman's mouth sound like a threat more than any version of motherly love?

Maybe it's just me. Maybe I'm particularly sensitive because my mom pulls this kind of shit all the time.

My girl clears her throat and opens her mouth. But before she finds her voice, Spence interjects.

"No, no. It's business-related. You of all people should know I'm a very busy man, Ms. St. Clair-Ferguson."

Magnolia's nostrils flare as a flick of agitation mars her expression.

Dr. Ferguson circles the table and places an arm around her. God, the man is far too kind for this viper.

"We must be going." Spence extends an arm, gesturing to the door we entered through. "We just wanted to stop by and provide moral support for our... friends. And ensure we're all on the same page about Hunter's inability to provide a partial transplant, full stop."

A somberness falls over the room at the reminder, though as Magnolia zeroes in on her daughter, she looks more pissed than disappointed.

"Of course we understand, right, sweetheart?"

Dr. F's words jolt Magnolia from her trance, and she plasters a smile on her face once more.

"Your health and the baby's health and safety are the top priority, Hunter. Please don't stress about your mother. I'll keep pursuing alternative options."

Hunter nods mechanically.

Dr. Ferguson drops his arm from around Magnolia and shuffles closer. Greedy intercepts his dad, speaking in a hushed tone I can't make out.

I'm torn between staying to make sure he's okay and getting Hunter as far away from Magnolia as humanly possible. Ultimately, I choose to make sure she's okay, knowing that's what G would want.

I grip my girl by the shoulders, turn her toward the door, and march forward, determined to get the hell out of here.

As we navigate through the house and out through the garage, we're silent. We don't speak as we climb into the car or buckle our seat belts. We don't even speak as Gerald pulls out and heads back to the marina.

Chapter 4

Sione

Hunter isn't pregnant.
   It's not physically possible.
   I've had her menstrual cycles memorized for years.
   Her cycles are synced with that of the moon.
   I know when she ovulates.
   I know when she bleeds.
   I know exactly when she would be considered fertile.
   She is on day one of the follicular phase now.
   She hasn't even ovulated.
   There's nothing to fertilize.
   Yet I fear the rest of this group doesn't understand that. Not if the charged energy and intense animosity vibrating amongst them as we trudge toward the waiting car is any indication.
   The Brit must have tampered with the lab results.
   And clearly he didn't fill anyone in before he broke the news.
   The Brit asked us to trust him.
   He assured us he had a plan. That he had it handled.

But I can't begin to understand how he thought that this end, the palpable pain and heartbreak, could possibly justify the means.

It's cruel, knowing that Hunter has been pregnant before.

Knowing that for a very short time, she carried a beautiful soul in her womb.

A soul that was inspired by love and created from passion.

Kabir must have known that she and Greedy created life once before. That the soul of their baby moved on from this world before she left for London.

How he could drop a bomb so devastating to both Greedy and Hunter is beyond me.

His actions have amplified her pain and weaponized their collective heartache.

I am devastated for the both of them.

Levi's energy is off, too. He's agitated, panicky, and reeling. Rightfully so. Based on that encounter and his reaction, he assumes he is the father of a child that doesn't exist.

As we approach the vehicle, Gerald opens the door for Hunter. I position myself so I am directly behind her, first with a hand on her back, then her hip as she climbs in. She takes the bench seat in the third row, and I slide in beside her, effortlessly moving her body toward the window so I'm positioned in the middle, where I can protect her energy most successfully. She's suffering enough without factoring in the other auras in our proximity.

She needs space.

She deserves peace.

Most importantly, she requires clarity. She needs to know why the hell the Brit thought that with all his schemes and connections, *this* was the best way forward.

Kabir has some explaining to do.

And not just to Hunter.

Chapter 5

Hunter

We drove home in silence, the weight of today's events heavy enough to suffocate us as we individually stewed with our thoughts.

Greedy tried to initiate conversation the moment we pulled away from his dad's house, but Spence quickly shut him down with a pointed look and a softly whispered "later."

If I know anything about Spence, it's that if he's not ready to talk, there's no point in trying.

Trouble is, I don't think any of us truly understand what just happened. Or why.

I'm not pregnant. I can't be. Do the guys know that, though?

We need to talk. All five of us. We all deserve the truth, as well as an explanation for Spence's declaration and master plan.

As we step into the main living space of the Crusade Mansion, I inhale, ready to get this conversation started, but noise from the kitchen catches our attention.

My best friend is perched on the island, a mixing beater in hand. "How'd it go?" She swipes a glob of brownie batter from the utensil and pops it into her mouth.

Wordlessly, I walk toward her, snag it out of her hand, and lick one side of the paddle.

"Tem. You shouldn't eat raw batter if—"

"If *what*?" Eyes narrowed on Greedy, I take another slow, languid lick to prove my point.

I'm not pregnant. He should *know* I'm not pregnant. Greedy wants to be a doctor, for crying out loud.

Joey bumps her hip into my shoulder. "That good, huh?"

I peer up at my best friend, fighting back tears and resisting the urge to grab her hand, race up the stairs, and lock myself and her in her bedroom so I can tell her everything.

I'm tempted to go as far as to make a No Boys Allowed sign and stick it on the door. That's how over it I am.

But I can't do that. Not until Spence explains himself. Not until I know all my guys are okay.

As if she can read my mind, Joey pulls me into a hug. "Want to go up to my room?"

The offer makes me even more emotional. A major dish session with my bestie would be so good for my soul.

My throat tightens, and pressure builds behind my eyes. I'm upset, sure, but I'm also so damn angry. I hate crying out of anger.

"I have to talk to them first," I choke out.

She looks around the room, expression calculating, as if she's trying to deduce which of my guys made me this upset. I know that look, because it's the same look I gave Decker for weeks after the stunt he pulled last semester.

"Come find me when you're ready," she eventually murmurs.

"I'll text you." It's the easiest way to track her down in this enormous place.

"Decker would probably love the chance to take a swing at Greedy. If you needed backup, I mean."

I can't help but smile a little at that. Old rivalries die hard. I doubt Decker Crusade or any of Joey's guys will ever forgive the South Chapel football team for abducting her during Shore Week. But Greedy didn't do anything wrong. Not then and not now. He's just as much a victim of today's surprise announcement as I am.

With a deep breath in, I spin on my heel and come face to face with all four of my guys. I look at Spence first. "We need to talk."

He nods once in acknowledgment, his expression resigned.

Good.

At least he has the decency to understand the gravity of what he did.

"I assume Crusade's quarters are private and secure?" he asks Joey.

Brows arched, she assesses him, then shrugs. "Sure."

Frustration flares behind Spence's eyes. He doesn't care for her flippant response.

I know exactly what Joey's doing.

She's a mastermind when it comes to sassing back, pulling pranks, and riling up her men. At this point, she and the guys mess with Decker for sport. Clearly, she has no qualms about messing with Spence either.

I purse my lips, fighting a smile. It's difficult to do, watching the way she keeps staring blankly at him, silently daring him to push her. Greedy and Levi are smirking at one another, obviously understanding what she's doing, too.

With a step back, I pluck the other beater from the bowl. Then I promptly stick it in my mouth, just to keep myself from laughing.

"Jo."

The single syllable startles us all. When Kylian stalks into the kitchen and snatches the utensil from Joey's hand, the tension he brought with him eases quickly.

"Hey," she protests. "I wasn't finished with that."

Kylian inspects it, glaring at it as if it personally offended him.

"You should have never started with this," he says to her, his blue eyes piercing behind his glasses. Without looking at me, he holds a hand out.

Sighing, I relinquish my beater. He turns on his heel, strides to the kitchen sink, and squeezes dish soap along the prongs and shaft.

When he turns on the water, Joey huffs. "I'm gonna start calling him Daddy Buzzkill."

He turns the faucet off with more force than necessary and drops the metal beaters into the empty sink with a clatter.

"Would you like me to share the statistical probability of contracting a foodborne illness from consuming raw brownie batter, Josephine?"

I almost snort when he uses her full name. It's rare Kylian goes full Daddy on Jo in front of an audience. Suddenly, I'm more interested in how this will play out than I am in getting our group conversation started.

As expected, my best friend doesn't back down. She crosses her arms under her boobs, propping them up, and sits straighter. "You eat undercooked eggs all the time."

"The eggs aren't the only issue here, Jo. E. Coli. Listeria. Salmonella. All can be contracted from raw flour. Look." He stalks closer and picks up the empty brownie mix box. "It says right here. In Bold. 'Warning: Do not eat raw batter. Cook before enjoying.'"

He slams the box onto the quartz countertop as if he's successfully made his case.

Smirking, Joey slides a little closer to him. "Maybe I just wanted to lick something tasty."

One of my guys—Levi, I think—snorts behind me.

Kylian pulls out his phone and types out a message, all without breaking eye contact. Once he's finished, he glances at the screen, then pockets the device again.

"I'll give you something tasty to lick. Upstairs, Jo. *Now*."

She gives me a salacious grin, then she hops off the counter and murmurs "yes, Daddy" as she saunters out of the room.

Kylian looks at me, then gives the guys a single nod before he takes off after his woman.

At the bottom of the stairs, Joey spins on her heel. "Wait! The brownies. They're still in the oven."

"I already texted your husband," Kylian quips with a smack to her ass. "He'll handle the brownies while I handle *you*."

Cackling, she turns and bolts up the stairs. "Hunter!" she calls when she's out of sight. "Text me when you're done."

The reminder instantly dampens the lighter mood her antics brought with them.

SO RIGHT

I look to each of my guys, then start the trek to our wing of the house, a.k.a. the primary bedroom. "Come on. Let's get this over with."

Chapter 6

Greedy

"Explain yourself."

The gruff demand is one I was prepared to make myself, but Sione beats me to it.

Levi closes the door quietly, turning the lock, then joins us in the middle of the room so the five of us are standing in a loose circle.

Eyes cast down and face screwed up in contempt, Kabir shoves his hands into the pockets of his dress pants.

He almost appears remorseful. Though it doesn't excuse the way he blindsided us or the information he manipulated to do it.

After a few seconds, he blows out a breath and stands tall. As if a switch has been flipped, he goes into CEO mode—straightening his spine and looking directly at each of us before he clears his throat. "Right. An explanation. I want to start by sincerely apologizing for the emotional turmoil I caused today."

His words are for all of us, but his gaze lingers on me a little longer than anyone else.

"I modified test results and withheld information to garner authentic reactions. Hunter—" He shifts so he's facing her directly.

It takes more strength than it should to fight the urge to step between them. To shield her from him.

"You are not pregnant, love."

She nods, eyes glassy and shoulders slumped. "I'm not pregnant," she repeats, wrapping her arms around her midsection as the truth sinks in.

She knew that, I'm almost sure.

I sure as shit didn't, but she did.

Regardless, it's obvious she's still hurt by Spence's scheming, just like I am.

Sione sidesteps until they're inches apart and grasps her hand. Instantly, tension ebbs from her body. He extends his arm, and as if she's a puzzle piece slotting into place, she nestles into his side and rests her cheek against his chest.

Satisfied he's got her, I study Levi.

He's standing eerily still, his face ashen. "I'm sorry," he chokes out, his focus fixed on me. That simple phrase is far more contrite and sincere than Kabir's attempted apology.

I open my mouth to reassure him, but then snap it closed. I was confused and livid at my dad's house. Did Levi pick up on that? Is that why he's apologizing? Because he thought he knocked up the woman we both love?

Fuck this. I refuse to let him beat himself up over a contrived, fictional situation that's not even happening.

And fuck His Royal Highness for putting us all through this.

Kabir's not my concern right now, though. Hunter is okay, too. Levi, though? He needs me.

It takes three strides to reach him.

Two seconds to wrap my arms around his broad shoulders.

One exhale to pour out all the assurances I can offer. My lips find the scruff on his jawline. I trail my mouth along it until my face is smashed into the crook of his neck.

"It's not real," I whisper, for his sake and mine. "It's not real." Swallowing my pride, I straighten but keep my head close to his. "And even if it were—if she was pregnant, and the baby was yours—that would be okay, too."

I sneak a glance at Hunter, who's watching us from the crook of Sione's arm.

"It would be more than okay, actually," I say before turning my attention back to Levi. "Because I love you."

He pulls back, startled, his eyes welling. When he blinks, one single tear falls. I catch it with my thumb, then cup his face and step in closer.

"I love you, Levi."

I hold him steady. Force him to look me in the eye and feel my sincerity.

"There's nothing you could do to change that. *Nothing*." I grit out the last word, then pull him into a suffocatingly tight hug.

Our breaths match. Our heartbeats, too. We stay like that until there's a tug on my arm.

Tem.

She's right there, wanting to love us and accept us for who we are.

Leev and I break apart, but we only put enough distance between ourselves to let her in. We hold each other like that, comforting her, comforting one another, after the absolute shit show we've just endured.

A quick glance at Si confirms he's fine. He's standing tall, arms crossed over his enormous chest, glaring. The expression isn't aimed at the three of us. His gaze is firmly set on Kabir.

"Why?" he pushes, his tone angry. For a man who exudes calmness and serenity in almost all circumstances, he's alarmingly irritated now.

This is a side of Sione I wouldn't have guessed existed. Even I'm intimidated by his sharply worded demands.

Spence holds his gaze for a beat, then turns to the three of us. "I did it to buy us time."

"Bullshit." Hunter's curse escapes with a slight twang, her southern temper momentarily busting through.

I smooth my hand down her back like Sione does sometimes. She softens slightly, but she remains focused on Spence.

"You bought a month or two, tops. Magnolia and Dr. F will want to see ultrasounds. They'll expect my stomach to grow."

Levi slips his hand up her back, brushing over mine as he moves it from her hip to the base of her skull. Gently cupping her nape, he murmurs, "It's okay, pretty girl. We'll figure it out."

Kabir's jaw ticks, his eyes stormy. "It should be all the time we need. Over the last several days, I've put multiple measures in place to monitor Magnolia's behavior. In doing so, I uncovered plans that were already in motion. Arrangements that had been scheduled and confirmed."

It's on the tip of my tongue to ask if he put a tracker inside her. But we're dealing with enough turmoil right now without bringing that up.

"Texts. Calls. Appointments," Kabir says, ticking each word off on his fingers. "It's all available to us now. We need to be a step ahead. We can't rely on anticipating what she might do or reacting to the bullshit she pulls. We need to know her next move before she makes it."

That makes sense, but I still don't understand why only buying us a month or two was the right move—

"She has a pre-op appointment scheduled for Tuesday."

My gut sinks.

Pre-op.

Pre-op?

A palpable anxiety thrums between us, thickening the air in the room.

"Tuesday, as in, a few days from now?" Levi has unwoven himself from our embrace, but he has one arm draped over Hunter's shoulders, and with that hand, he's cuffing the back of my neck.

The heat of his palm there, along with Hunter's warmth at my side, brings me at least a modicum of comfort.

Kabir nods. "Surgery is planned for Friday."

Hunter emits a high-pitched yelp. I go rigid, my body instinctively preparing for a fight. Levi tightens his grip, keeping me from physically charging toward Spence.

"No fucking way." I shrug off Levi's touch and pace toward Kabir.

Halfway there, I remember: He's just the messenger.

As that thought hits me, I turn on my heel and stride back toward the others, then circle around again.

"She hadn't even agreed," I mumble, scuffing the floor with my pacing. Every stride feels more taxing than the last. "She hasn't consented to *anything*."

Fury erupts inside me. I'm so fucking pissed I could bottle up this feeling and fuel a weapon of mass destruction. Every cell in my body is on fire with the need to protect, to avenge. To stop Magnolia St. Clair-Ferguson once and for all.

"What were they going to do? Coerce her? Guilt her? Kidnap her *again*?"

Spence regards me, his gaze piercing. "If I had to give it my best guess, I'd say all of the above."

A high-pitched whimper pulls me out of my rage spiral. I whirl around. Hunter hasn't moved. Neither has Levi, but Sione has stepped into my place, and the two guys are comforting her.

Sniffling, she lifts her head and looks first at me, then at Kabir.

"She's never going to stop, is she?" Her voice is hollow and thoroughly defeated.

She slumps against Levi, the movement so abrupt it causes him to stumble. Sione steadies them both, then the three of them ease into a sitting position—Si cross-legged on the floor with Hunter in his lap and Levi sitting with his legs spread wide.

"This was a mistake. We can't stay here. She won't stop." Hunter's breathing is shallow, her sharp inhales coming too quickly. I open my mouth to remind her to *breathe*, but Sione is right there and gets to her first.

He rests his hands on her collarbones, his palms and long fingers covering from her shoulders to the hollow of her throat.

"Exhale for four," he instructs. He pulls his shoulders back and demonstrates what he wants her to do.

Her eyes well with tears, but she listens to him, intentionally focusing on her breath and visibly calming.

He's got her. Sione. Levi. They've got her. I suppose, in his own domineering, not always forthright way, Kabir's got her, too.

We've got each other. All of us.

Not for the first time today, I'm so fucking glad my boys are by my side. That none of us have to navigate this alone.

At the sound of a quiet chime, Kabir pulls his device from his pocket and smirks at the screen. "Pre-op and surgery appointments have been removed from Magnolia's calendar."

Hunter releases another cry, this one filled with relief.

The instinct to fight and defend ebbs from my body, but my anxiety is still raging.

Kabir steps toward Hunter and crouches, cupping her face in one hand.

"I'm sorry for the pain I caused." He brushes his thumb over her flushed, tear-stained cheek. "But I'm not sorry for what I did. There was an imminent threat. We needed a full-stop solution to derail a plan that was already in motion."

He looks to each of us then, his expression resolved but also remorseful. "I'm deeply sorry for the stress and heartache I may have caused. But today's announcement bought us the time we need. For that," he rises to full height, smooths his hands down the front of his trousers, and straightens the collar of his shirt. "I'll never apologize."

With that, he turns and walks out the door, leaving the four of us silent and dumbfounded.

Chapter 7

Kabir

There's still work to be done.

My agitation is at an all-time high, causing words on the page to blur together and images on the screen to dance each time I try to focus.

I need a break.

I need a glass or six of whiskey, neat. A long pull of my own proprietary blend from my hookah. Perhaps an intense, physically demanding scene that lasts for hours.

Any of my vices would do. Most, however, are not an option tonight.

Hence why I've relegated myself to the hot tub I found on a lower-level deck of the Crusade Mansion.

I'm ruminating, sulking over the pain and frustration I caused Garrett, Levi, Sione, and Hunter. Licking my wounds as I give them space to process today's events and how my actions affected them.

I expected their individual ire.

What I wasn't prepared for was the soul-crushing weight of their collective pain. The combined anger and disappointment directed at me is a burden I wouldn't wish on most of my enemies.

On Magnolia, surely. In a heartbeat.

But no one else.

I've been ostracized from the group by my own actions. But what's done is done. I stand by my choices. Though I admit I had not considered Levi's mother into the equation.

Perhaps it was shortsighted to assume Magnolia wouldn't adapt so quickly to what should have been startling news. I'm loath to think that I underestimated her, and yet she barely faltered when I dropped the bomb about Hunter's blood work.

The woman is cunning. A worthy opponent if I've ever encountered one.

No matter. The game has truly just begun, and I never initiate without full confidence in my ability to win.

Commotion on the staircase pulls me from my thoughts. A man's voice cuts through the night air first, then a woman's. My heart does not react to either of them.

Nevertheless, I hold my breath and wait, hoping in vain that another member of my cohort is looking for me.

Hunter's best friend Josephine and her husband appear on the landing, and I exhale, defeated.

As he rounds the corner, Decker's steps falter, and he instinctively throws a hand out to halt Josephine as well. He observes me through the dark, and I stare right back at him. Once he discerns that I'm not a threat, they resume their approach, murmuring quietly to one another.

"I'm just finishing up," I call out, drifting through the bubbling water toward the side. I find my footing, and as I emerge, the cold night air transforms the water into icy-hot trails sluicing down my torso. Just as I reach for a towel, Decker steps closer.

"We're the ones interrupting you," he says. "Don't leave on our account. We don't mind if you stay." Jaw clenched tight, he glances at Josephine for confirmation.

With her hair piled high on top of her head and one hand resting on a popped hip, she raises her eyebrows at her husband, then turns to me and scowls.

Clearly, Hunter has spoken to her friend about today's happenings. Yet another shortsighted choice on my part, agreeing to live at the Crusade Mansion. I had not previously considered the consequences of cohabitating with individuals who do not have the kind of foundational trust in me as the members of my cohort do.

"It's fine," Joey relents, the two words dripping with disdain.

She makes quick work of pulling off the oversized red jersey she's wearing. As she drops it to the deck in a heap, I glide back to my original seat and settle into the corner to survey the lake.

With a hiss, Josephine lowers herself into the water.

"Want me to turn it down, Siren?"

"No," she assures her husband. "I just need a minute to get used to it."

Decker divests himself of his T-shirt, then takes great care to fold it and place it on a chair near the towels. His swimming trunks are fitted, with a five-inch inseam that shows off the exquisite angles of his body. Even in the dark, with only the light of the moon and the glow from the hot tub lights, I can appreciate the sharp edges and perfect planes of his form.

He's as fit as Garrett and Levi, maybe more so. It's surprising and impressive, since the man no longer plays football. According to Hunter, he sacrificed what had the potential to be an extremely successful professional sports career in order to protect his family. I admire that level of dedication.

For several long moments, the churning water and whirring of the jets are the only sounds.

Once she's used to the water, Josephine nestles into Crusade's lap, her back against her husband's frame with her head tipped to the side so it rests on his shoulder.

My chest tightens as I observe the ease with which she gives him her full weight. What I wouldn't give to hold my girl like that tonight.

After a few minutes, she lifts her head. "So," she starts, a glint of mischief in her eyes. "Are you out here all alone pouting?"

"Josephine," Decker hisses, his lips ghosting the skin of her neck.

"What? We all know what happened earlier. And I'm not convinced he understands just how badly he hurt them."

Decker lets out an agitated grunt, but I'm not sure if it's directed at me or his wife.

"I can assure you," I begin, examining the water bubbling between us, "I knew the consequences well in advance of dropping the news on Hunter and our boys."

"*Your* boys?" Josephine mocks.

Lungs seizing, I drag my focus up to her. "Yes," I confirm. "*My* boys. I care for them all very much."

Josephine shrugs, a single shoulder breaching the surface of the water. "I guess we all have different ways of showing it."

I close my eyes for a beat. Then another. Gods help me if this woman doesn't send me over the edge. I can practically feel my pulse in my own ears. With a cleansing breath in through my nose, I will my heart rate to steady. I hold the air in my lungs, then breathe out for a count of ten.

Once I'm certain I can reply without flying off the handle, I meet her gaze.

"I strategically plotted every possible path forward before landing on the chosen tactic. Hell, I even considered some very backward ideas in my effort to protect my people. I ran the numbers. I did the math. I went as far as to recruit Kylian to play devil's advocate and help me analyze the risks associated with each plan."

Josephine's brows lift into her hairline at the mention of the leader of her cohort. Decker has straightened, as if invested in this conversation now, too.

"Despite today's outcome, I did not act with the intention of harming any of the people I love. My top priority was preservation for all of them, but most importantly, preservation and protection for Hunter."

For the space of several heartbeats, Josephine scrutinizes me with narrowed eyes. Eventually, she tucks her chin and glides a hand over the surface of the water. "Even if that's all true, you should have told her ahead of time."

I absorb the suggestion and let it sink all the way into my bones. I considered it time and time again, and I'll likely question my decision not to for a long time, despite all the logic and reason behind why I didn't give Hunter the choice.

Straightening until the chill of the air inspires goose pimples all over my exposed chest, I assess Decker. There is a chance what I'm about to say will earn me a black eye. My ego and my heart are hurting enough tonight. The last thing I need is a shiner to accompany the mental beating I've given myself. But it's important I make this point.

"You are Hunter's best friend, are you not?"

Josephine nods indignantly.

I don't give her time to add to that response. "As such, it's safe to assume that you know her heart. Her spirit. The goodness inside that not only makes her so incredible but allows her to sacrifice herself time and time again to protect those she loves."

She tips her head back and forth, shoulders slumping. She knows I'm right, even if she doesn't want to admit it.

"Today was about putting her first." I clear my throat and swallow down the pain I've inflicted on myself. "Yes, I could have clued her in."

I skim one hand over the surface of the water, leaving a path of bubbles in my wake.

"But tell me. Do you think for one moment, had Hunter known in advance, she would have let me hurt Garrett that way?"

Decker humphs, his reaction jostling his wife.

Josephine opens her mouth, closes it, opens it, then snaps it shut.

"I hurt everyone, I know. But Hunter didn't have to hurt *anyone* because of my choice. And that's exactly what it was: my choice. I made the call. I stand by my actions, even if you hate me, the boys hate me, or, gods forbid, she hates me. I put her first, knowing damn well she may not have put herself first if given the opportunity."

There's nothing I wouldn't do for my woman. Now, apparently, there's nothing I wouldn't do for our boys, either. The ache in my chest intensifies so greatly I have to resist the urge not to press a hand to my sternum.

"Everyone is hurting tonight, but everyone is safe. The imminent threat has been handled. We now have time and space to figure out our next move. Most importantly? None of them had to hurt another in the process."

I slump back in my corner, well and thoroughly defeated by this day.

Truth be told, I hate myself for what I did. Yet I would choose to do it again and again if it meant preserving the love, trust, and growth that our group has embraced over the last few weeks.

"I get it."

The simple statement startles me. Blinking, I shift to face Decker once more. There, in his eyes, I see his truth. My words have resonated with him. He understands my motivation.

For the first time all day, the hard shell of my exterior flexes ever so slightly. Despite how heinous today's events were, someone else acknowledges my actions were not in vain.

Nodding once, he kisses the top of Josephine's head. He whispers something low I cannot hear, and she nods.

Wordlessly, she rises, steps over the ledge, and snags a large towel.

Decker rises to follow, but instead of exiting the hot tub, he strides forward, grasps my shoulder, and offers a reassuring squeeze. "Eventually, with time, they'll get it, too."

Chapter 8

Kabir

I pad up the stairs, quietly making my somber retreat to the second floor. I typically find solace in alone time. I'm usually content with my thoughts.

Tonight, I can't keep my mind from racing.

Once I've secured the bathroom door behind me, I unwrap the robe from around my body and step out of the wet swimming trunks I borrowed from Kylian. He's leaner than me, but the plain navy blue shorts served their purpose.

I turn on the shower and adjust the knob as far as it'll go. Without giving myself too much time to think, I step under the spray and let the scalding water drown out all the noise in my head.

Hunter.

The boys.

The pain I caused.

Despite it all, I'd do it all over again.

This scheme has given us much more than just the time we need to hatch a more permanent solution. It's given us distance from Magnolia and stopped the unannounced surgery scheduled for this week. We've received confirmation that Dr. Ferguson understands and respects the situation and have created boundaries that cannot be crossed. Because despite Hunter's mother having no regard for her daughter's well-being, common sense and southern manners prevent her from attacking a pregnant woman. At least physically.

It worked.

It was awful. I loathe what I did and how I hurt all of them in the process. But it's over, and it worked.

I lather up and scrub my skin raw, desperate to wash away this day and the fallout of my actions.

My arms, chest, and back are covered in bright red splotches when I emerge from the shower. My physical container is well and truly spent. It's unlikely I'll have any trouble sleeping tonight. Thankfully, I had the foresight to reschedule all meetings and other work obligations originally set for tomorrow.

I don't bother flicking on overhead lights. Instead, I make my way to the bed in the dark. As I pull back the sheets, the outline of a person becomes visible.

I freeze, and my heart takes off.

Small frame. Soft curves. A halo of golden hair arranged on the pillow under her head.

She reaches out one hand, silently inviting me to join her.

My Firecracker.

I'm a clumsy mess of emotion as I scramble to join her.

She's here. With me. For me.

Or is she here to confront me once more? To demand answers? To ream me out for hurting her, and for hurting them, too?

Slower now, and with my stomach churning, I sink into the mattress. I take my time arranging the sheets before rolling to one side and tentatively smoothing the back of my knuckles over her cheek.

"Are you well, love?"

She shakes her head.

No.

I gulp past the trepidation that comes with the knowledge that I'm seconds away from the scolding I'm owed. If unleashing on me will help her cope, then by gods, I'll gladly spend all night on the receiving end of her wrath.

"What do you need?" I press.

Her small hand captures mine and holds it to her face. She nuzzles against it, then peels my fingers off her jaw and kisses the center of my palm.

"I don't need anything. I just want to be here for you tonight," she whispers into the darkness.

My body locks up, the breath in my lungs catching and taking up residence until my chest burns.

Finally, I exhale loudly. "You're here for me?"

With a nod, she kisses my fingertips. Then she slinks close and snuggles into me.

I wrap my arms around her on instinct, my skin searing hot in contrast to her bare legs and shoulders.

Her mouth finds my chest, her lips covering me in soft, wet kisses. She trails between my pecs, then creates a path up my throat.

When we're face to face, she pauses.

"Thank you for what you did today." With each word, her lips brush against mine with tenderness and care.

I curl my hands into fists, agitation and anger prodding at my insides. She shouldn't be thanking me. She shouldn't even be here.

As if reading my mind, she smooths a hand up my neck and grazes my nape with her nails. She places a barely there kiss on my lips, then cranes back a few inches to meet my gaze.

In the moonlight, there's no mistaking the sincerity shining in the mossy green windows to her soul.

"I trust you. I love you. What happened earlier..." She trails off.

I stay quiet, granting her the space she deserves to process.

She deflates a little. "I don't understand it," she finally admits. "But I know you, and I know you did it for me. For them. For us, and for the vision we share for our future. I told you I didn't want to run anymore. You found a solution that makes it possible for us to stay. So... thank you."

My body sags in exhaustion and relief. With a groan, I loop both arms around her and hold her close, savoring the reprieve of this moment. Until now, until her comfort was readily available, I had not allowed myself to acknowledge how deeply I needed it.

A shuddering exhale escapes me.

It's met with a small sniffle.

"Hunter—"

She shakes her head, denying me the opportunity to explain or to attempt to comfort her in return.

"I don't want to talk about any of it tonight."

I adjust my hold on her, clinging even tighter, desperate for her to feel my sorrow. To understand how sorry I am for the way I hurt her. I'm chomping at the bit to further explain. To apologize again. To beg for her forgiveness.

"Tonight, I just want to hold you. Comfort you. Care for you the way you always care for me." Her breath is warm against my neck, the words taking on a life of their own as she speaks peace into the air around us. "You're so good at taking care of me. You're so good at taking care of all of us," she amends. "Thank you for loving us so well."

Her words wash over me, gratitude and comfort I don't feel worthy of accepting blanketing us in a quiet stillness.

She nuzzles into my shoulder, and I position my chin atop her head. With every exhale, I soften, and with every intake of breath, I allow her words to seep a little deeper into me.

Loving her is my greatest accomplishment. Caring for her and all of our boys is a privilege I hold in the highest regard.

Despite the pain I caused and the havoc I wreaked today, she's still here. Our love endures. Hope for the life we're building together sustains us.

"I love you," I murmur into her hair, allowing my eyes to finally close on this wretched day. "I'll make this up to you, and I'll make it right with the boys."

"I know you do, and I know you will," she murmurs back. "Greedy especially needs the assurance. Promise me you'll talk to him?"

I still.

"Levi will be fast to forgive," she explains, still nuzzled against my chest. "Sione will come around in his own time, regardless of what you do or say. But Greedy..."

I nod in understanding, my chin rubbing the crown of her head with each pass.

"You blindsided him once before, just like this."

I think back to my unceremonious arrival in South Chapel. Was that really just weeks ago?

"An explanation would go a long way in ensuring he's okay. And Spence?"

Sighing, I pull her closer. "Yes, love?"

"I need you two to be okay. You can't be at odds with Greedy and claim to fully love me, because he's a part of who I am."

Her words sink in and settle in the pit of my stomach. I'm aware I owe Garrett a myriad of apologies. Hearing her express the same sentiment further confirms what I need to do. I'm a stubborn bastard, though. It may take a bit of time for me to muster up the courage and tact required to truly get through to Garrett in the way he deserves.

"I love you, Spence. I want to love you forever."

"Endgame," I whisper. "We always have been and always will be."

Chapter 9

Hunter

I creep down the stairs, grazing my fingertips along the handrail as I go. The sun has barely started to rise, the soft morning light the only thing illuminating my path to the main level of the house.

I couldn't sleep last night. Not until I knew Spence was okay.

Yesterday was a whirlwind, and each of us was weighed down with shock and stress. Despite the ire he caused, I believe in my heart of hearts that his intentions were pure.

I love him. I trust him. After yesterday's upsetting events, I needed him to know that.

Mission accomplished. It soothed my soul as much as his to lie beside him all night. We needed that connection: that reminder of who we are, together.

Now I'm on to my next challenge: helping Greedy, Levi, and Sione deal with the fallout and come around to some semblance of peace around what happened.

Spence explained himself. He had information we didn't have. He made a choice that we, as a group, may not have been able to make.

What's done is done, and to his credit, the plan was a success. Magnolia's appointments have been cleared for this week. For now, I'm safe. Thanks to Spence.

I pad through the kitchen, mulling over exactly how to pacify the others. I don't want any of us to be at odds when a much larger threat looms over our happiness.

As I pass by the great room, the soft light streaming in through the floor-to-ceiling windows calls to me. I allow it to draw me in, positioning myself so close to the panes I feel the chilly morning air seep through the glass.

It's probably best if I talk to the guys individually. Spence's surprise deeply affected Greedy and Levi, and it pissed off Sione in a way I never thought possible.

I stifle a laugh when I think about just how angry he was. Although he remained cool and collected on the exterior, fury simmered just beneath the surface. To his credit, he knows my cycle better than even I do, so he didn't believe for one second I was actually pregnant.

Pregnant.

The very idea shakes up a flurry of emotions inside me.

There's fear—so much fear. Fear fueled by anxiety and grief. Fear that stems from experience. From having already suffered such a painful, unexpected loss.

A whole other kind of fear regarding what kind of parent I might be blossomed yesterday as well. How can I possibly be a good mother when my own mom is so self-centered and uncaring?

Magnolia is wretched and relentless in her selfish pursuits. She doesn't deserve the title of mother. I detest her behavior, but I am her child. What if I'm more like her than I think? What if the evil living inside her, the traits that make her so ghastly, is a part of my DNA, too?

I shudder at the thought. With my arms wrapped around my torso, I focus on the soothing ripples of the lake and breathe evenly to clear my mind of all things Magnolia.

As I banish them, new, unwanted thoughts arise. My father loved me when I was a child, yet he abandoned me. Left me with my mother. Did he allow his disdain for Magnolia to tarnish his view of me as I got older? If so, I'm not sure I can ever forgive him.

A few angry tears escape from my eyes without my permission. He wasn't an awful parent. He just... didn't stick around. Maybe I'm just not worth sticking around for.

Because everything I love leaves.

No. I shake my head. That's not true. Not anymore. There are four amazing men under this roof who have stayed. Who have stuck by my side. Who've fought for my healing and for our chance at making a good life together.

They won't leave.

And I won't run.

In my darkest moments, those are the truths I cling to.

In this moment, as I think about being pregnant, fear isn't the only emotion brewing under the surface.

I'm curious, too. Intrigued by thoughts of how my body will change. Eager to discover what sort of joy might accompany all the stressors of parenthood.

I'm also hopeful. Hopeful that I can get pregnant again someday, and that the experience may help me heal wounds that still ache deep inside me. Hopeful that I will be a good mom. That my child will never know a day without love and laughter in their life.

Fear. Curiosity. Hope. They're all there, under the surface.

Most prominently, though, there's a desire that lives deep in my chest, where nothing and no one can change me. It's the desire to experience pregnancy. The desire to create and grow new life. It's a desire so biological, inevitable, and cosmological, it feels like destiny. Like it's part of who I am, who I'm meant to be.

I want to carry a child. Multiple times. I have faith that the hopeful, positive, beautiful dreams inside me are strong enough to banish the fear. If they're not, then my guys will be here to help. To remind me of how capable I am and how much love I have to give. They'll help fill in the gaps when the world feels like it's too much.

"You're up early."

With a shriek, I slap my hands to my mouth and spin.

As I come face to face with Decker Crusade, my heart hammers triple time in my chest. "*Jesus*. You scared the shit out of me, Cap."

He offers me a rueful grin. For a moment, he looks just like the boy I grew up with. "Sorry. I stomped through the kitchen, figuring you'd hear me. I thought maybe you had headphones in."

Shaking my head, I will my pulse to settle. "No. Just lost in my own head," I admit, returning his smile. "Why are you up so early?"

"Had a few calls to make." He holds up a cell phone and tilts it back and forth. "I got Levi into Lake Chapel U on scholarship, if he wants the spot. Now I'm working on getting him an internship or practicum for the semester."

My heart, which has only now slowed, trips over itself. "Really?"

Decker nods, his dark eyes somber. "Josephine doesn't need a scholarship anymore. I paid her tuition for the semester and made an extra donation in her name. Once that processed, I emailed admissions with my second choice for the Crusade Scholarship." He shrugs, as if it's no big deal. "Do you think he'll go for it? I wasn't sure, with his injury and all, how he'd feel working alongside the football team and athletes. But they're always looking for student athletic trainers, so I figured—"

"Decker." I rush to him and throw my arms around his neck. "Thank you. Thank you so much."

He pats my back a little awkwardly, then gingerly extricates himself. His rueful, boyish grin is back as he says, "five second rule," with a knowing smirk.

I huff out a laugh. "The five second rule? That applies to food on the floor, Cap. Not hugs."

He nods solemnly. "You're right. We should probably implement a three second rule to appease His Royal Highness."

I swat at his arm. "Don't call him that." Not because Spence would be insulted by the nickname, but because it would absolutely feed his ego.

He smirks. "The man's intense. He's like Kylian with an added dose of privilege and an overinflated sense of self-regard." Between one blink and the next, the humor disappears from his expression. "He loves you, you know. So damn much. Even if his methods are unconventional. Even if they don't make a lot of sense on the surface—"

"I know." I give him a small smile, amused but also surprised by his words. The last thing I expected this morning was for Decker to come to Spence's defense, but here we are. "I've never questioned his devotion. He did what he did yesterday from a place of love. I get it."

With a quick nod, I step back. I don't want to get into the whole ordeal. Experiencing it once and then dealing with the fallout last night was enough for me. I'm ready to move forward and desperately hopeful that my guys will follow suit.

"Right." The hint of gentleness in his tone has disappeared. "There's one more thing."

Instantly, I go on alert. I don't know how Joey does this all the time. Decker has the uncanny ability to go from playful to concerningly serious in the blink of an eye. Cautiously, I ask, "And what would that be?"

He inspects me, his obsidian eyes unblinking. "I want you to stay here. All of you. Indefinitely."

I open my mouth, but before I can utter a word, he continues.

"We have more than enough space. And more importantly, the security is unmatched. I can't promise you're completely out of harm's way here." He stretches out and pops his neck, as if the idea is painful. "But unless your mom commandeers a Sherp, she's not getting on this fucking isle."

I snort, but quickly school my expression. I honestly wouldn't put it past Magnolia to find an all-terrain vehicle that'll make it through swamps and even float like the one Decker and his crew possess.

"Stay." He takes a step closer, his head bowed as he makes his plea. "Stay here for the semester. Longer if you need to. You'll be safe—all of you. Josephine will worry less. And I'll feel like I can actually help this time around, instead of sitting on the sidelines. Instead of being complicit."

"Decker..." My heart aches as I study him.

This is a sentiment he's shared before. I've known him and his friends since childhood. We grew up together, our lives intertwined because of football and cheerleading. But there's no way he could have known what went on in my home when I was younger. Hell, I didn't even really begin to process it until my dad left during my senior year of high school.

"Just think about it." He wraps me up in another quick hug. "You're more than welcome here. You're wanted."

With a loud exhale, he releases me. Then he gently taps his knuckles on my chin.

"Work on Levi for me, too." With that, he strides away. Halfway across the room, with his phone out and his thumb hovering over the screen, he turns. "Oh, and since classes start tomorrow, we're doing family brunch today. Make sure you and the boys are in the dining room by eleven. Kylian hates when we start late."

I stifle a laugh, knowing damn well that *Decker* is the one who hates when a family meal starts late and that *Kylian* follows a very specific routine on Sunday mornings that has little to do with eating brunch and a whole lot to do with consuming Joey.

"Whatever you say, Cap."

Chapter 10

Levi

Leg day is always a beast. Tapering the effort on my bad leg is the most difficult part. I would kill to feel the burn from a set of Hungarian split squats right about now. I don't dare put that sort of isolated tension on my still-healing quad yet, so I've settled for elevated goblet squats instead.

"Can you handle more weight?" Locke catches my gaze in the floor-to-ceiling mirrors that line three of the walls of the in-home gym. The setup here is sick. They've got all the most up-to-date equipment, including a few selectorized machines I've never seen before. The space is clean and bright, and the sound system is chest-poundingly loud.

I give him a nod, then watch as he strides over to a shelf and picks up two pieces of fabric.

"Try these." He stretches one of the bands.

I work my hand through the cuff at one end, and he adjusts it until it covers from wrist to elbow. When Locke releases the tension, the weight hits, and my entire arm sags.

"What the hell?" I marvel at the thin fabric that has to weigh at least twenty pounds.

"Cool, right?" He grins. "The metal in it is twice as heavy as lead."

"Damn." I hold out my other arm so he can sheath that one as well. "I've never seen anything like this."

Locke straightens, his shoulders pulled back. "Kylian invented it."

A sharp exhale escapes me. "He *invented* it?" I knew the guy was smart, but I thought he was computer smart. A gadget geek.

"Yes. He created them for me. I have rheumatoid arthritis. Sometimes, when it flares up, I can't even grip a barbell or wrap my hand around a set of free weights. But I can wear these and at least get some semblance of a workout in." His tone is casual, like rather than a hardship, his RA is just a fact of life. "Sometimes I use them to add weight to my regular routine. Try it." He steps back, his hands on his hips, and dips his chin.

Heels repositioned, I squat low. Instantly, my thighs burn more deeply than before.

"Shit. That's fantastic."

"What's fantastic?"

I whip around and momentarily lose my footing. Locke catches my elbow and steadies me. Once I'm sure I won't topple, I properly turn to Spence, who's sauntering across the gym.

Swallowing past the anger and frustration I've been harboring, I greet him with a nod. "These weighted sleeves Locke let me try. Apparently, Kylian made them."

"Then of course they're fantastic," Spence remarks.

Right. I forgot about the affinity he has for all things Kylian Walsh.

Spence is dressed in matte navy blue athletic shorts and a fitted tech T-shirt on top. I'm not sure I've ever seen the man in anything but a three-piece suit or his birthday suit.

My balls zing as I drink in the sinewy, defined angles of his body. Every inch of his brown skin is flawless. Despite being here to work out, his hair is coifed and he's perfectly put together.

"I'm hitting the showers." Locke thumps me on the back. "Just hang those up over there when you're done."

I nod absentmindedly. I don't have the wherewithal to be embarrassed that he caught me ogling the man across the room.

My focus stays fixed on Spence's back. I'm jonesing for him to lift his head and meet my eyes in the mirror wall.

He doesn't.

Instead, he selects his weights, carries them to a bench, and places them on the floor.

Only then does he give me his attention.

With a jut of his chin, he asks, "Are you well, Champ?"

His tone is too cool, the words too even.

He's all business, wearing the façade of the unfazed CEO. Hiding behind the mask and the battle armor the world requires of him.

Until yesterday, he'd stopped wearing the mask with me.

Muscles tense, I shuck off the bands, then I stride toward him.

I lock eyes with him in the mirror before I slowly, deliberately, rest my chin on his shoulder and hug him from behind.

He goes stiff in my arms.

Rather than back off, I hold him closer, letting his warm, spicy scent overwhelm me.

"I'm still working through things," I admit. "But I'll be okay. Right now, I'm more concerned about how you are."

His breath catches, his rich brown eyes wide and searching as he examines my reflection. I splay my palms against his abs and gently press my fingertips into the fabric of his shirt, pouring into him every ounce of support I can dredge up. He needs to know I'm here.

I've got you.

I'm not going anywhere.

We'll be okay.

After a few breaths, he covers one of my hands with his and intertwines our fingers. We stay like that, breathing each other in, silently soothing the aches and fears.

"You're not upset with me?" he eventually asks, his expression still puzzled.

I scoff. "Fuck yes, I'm upset with you."

He jolts and shifts, as if to spin out of my arms.

I tighten my hold on him. When I'm sure he won't dart away, I smooth my palms up his abs and rest them on his chest.

"I'm upset, but that doesn't change how I feel about you. About... us."

His throat dips with a long swallow. "And how do you feel about us?" he asks, tone low and husky.

I drag my hand up his sternum and over his pecs until my palm rests at the hollow of his throat. Gently, I tip his head to the side, then dust my lips over his neck.

"Like you're one of the most important people in my life."

He inhales sharply. The reaction shoots straight to my groin, all warm and heavy.

I kiss his neck again. "Like I want to keep exploring where this goes."

He stifles a grunt. It's the sexiest sound I think he's ever made.

I lick the stubbled skin beneath his jaw. "Like if you feel the same way, I want to keep you forever."

As I place a final kiss below his ear, his eyes flutter closed and he sighs.

"Spence." I grasp his shoulders and turn him so we're face to face. I'm painfully hard, aching for him. But before I can give in to the sensation, he needs to understand that this—us—is so much more than physical.

Swallowing, I frame his face with my hands. I need his attention. More importantly, I need him to really hear what I'm saying.

"Yesterday was awful, but it's over now. It happened, and it was a success. I know you're used to running the show, and most of the time, I'm okay with that. But know this: when it all feels too heavy, I'm here. We're all here. You don't have to fester in the heaviness of this on your own."

"Did you just use the word *fester*?" He arches a brow, his expression cocky.

I snort. "Guess Sione's rubbing off on me." Arms wrapped around him again, I pull him in until our chests are pressed together.

On his exhale, he sinks into my touch. The movement is minute, but it's enough. He hears me. He feels me. And he's absorbed at least some of what I'm saying.

"You don't have to do any of this alone."

He sinks into me further, leans on me more, and buries his face in the crook of my neck. "I'm sorry, Champ," he mutters, his lips ghosting over my skin. "I was sure I had thought of everything in advance."

Confusion threads through me. What does he mean by *everything*?

"Your mother," he clarifies, as if he's read my mind. "I didn't account for your mother."

Talk about a boner killer.

Sighing, I pull back and stretch out my neck. "Yeah, she's going to be a complication."

He drops onto the bench and crosses one leg over his knee. "Perhaps we could eliminate that complication?"

My stomach twists painfully. "Spence, no."

He looks up at me, brows furrowed and lips turned down.

"My mom... leave her be. I can deal with her. She's not evil like Magnolia. She's misguided and narrowminded, but she would never try to physically harm anyone."

He straightens, his expression smoothing out. "You see the difference, then?"

I frown. "Yeah, of course I do. My mom..." I trail off. I've yet to delve into the complex, mostly negative relationship I share with my mother with Spence, and now is not the time. "Just—let me handle her. I can set and hold boundaries. She's a nuisance—"

"But she's not pure evil," he finishes for me. "Fine." He nods succinctly. "My sole focus will be Magnolia."

Anxiety churns in my gut. Not because I care about Hunter's mom, but because I care about the fallout of what he might be planning.

I focus on my feet, scuffing my sneaker against the matted floor. "Spence—"

He snatches my hand in his, startling me.

When I meet his eye, there's nothing but unwavering determination there. "As long as Magnolia is breathing, Hunter is not safe. Until she's handled, Hunter cannot be free."

I tug my hand from his hold and run it through my hair. I don't want him to get hurt or involve himself in a crime, or to be tied up in something he might regret someday.

He rises to his feet, slow, steady, and sure, and pulls me into his body, encasing me in his firm embrace until I relax and hug him in return.

"Shh," he soothes. "I don't want to talk anymore."

I open my mouth, then snap it closed and inhale harshly, trying to breathe through the tightness in my chest. Whatever he's planning... whatever he thinks he has to do to get rid of Magnolia...

"You don't have to—"

They're the only words I can choke out before he slams his mouth to mine.

The kiss is fierce from the start, his tongue pushing between my lips and demanding entrance. He licks and nips and devours me until I'm breathless.

Fuck. He's intense.

Hands, tongue, and teeth claim me. Kneading, stroking, and clashing with an undeniably ferocious hunger.

"No more talking," he grunts between kisses.

His stubble scratches against my face as he ravishes my neck, and though we're separated by two thin layers of fabric, the heat emanating from him soaks into me. It takes all my willpower not to rip off both our shirts so I can feel him for real.

With his hands twisted in the hair at my nape, he backs me up toward the wall without mirrors.

"Where—"

"Cameras." Without further explanation, he dives back in, kissing me like his life depends on it.

When I slam into the wall, he lines up with me and grinds his pelvis into mine.

"Fucking hell." I close my eyes and let my head drop back. I can feel every inch of his erection dueling against mine.

"You like that, Champ?"

My only response is a whimper. It's all I can muster.

He rolls his hips again and again until precum seeps from my tip.

Then he's encasing my length with both hands. He doesn't falter. Doesn't ease me into it. He jerks me fast, hard—so fucking hard—then, abruptly, he stops.

"I want you on your knees. I want my cock to find its home in your throat as deep as you can take it."

Fuck. I want that, too.

A surge of adrenaline shoots through me. The sensation is almost identical to the feeling that used to hit me when I made a perfect catch and tore down an empty field.

"Yes, sir." With a teasing nip of his lips, I reverse our positions and press his back into the wall.

With my fingers trailing along the waistband of his athletic shorts, I bend my knees, ready to drop to the floor and take his pants and boxers with me.

Before I can, he grasps my wrist. "Wait."

I still, and when I register the deep concern radiating from his blue-gray eyes, my heart constricts.

"Your leg." That's all the explanation I get before he tilts to one side, snags a short stack of yoga mats, and places them between us at his feet.

Warmth blooms in my chest and filters through my extremities. *This man.*

I can't fight my grin as I lower myself, taking care to position my knee on the center of the mats and ensure my leg is in a decent lunge.

I'm so moved by his tenderness I'm almost embarrassed to look up and let him see how much he affects me.

Thankfully, Spence doesn't let the moment linger.

With a hand buried in my hair, he tugs my head back. His irises have gone fierce, stormy when I finally make eye contact.

"You remember what Hunter taught you, Champ?"

Licking my lips, I tip my head back farther. Hell yeah, I do. I can't wait to fucking rock his world.

Chapter 11

Kabir

"Open."

With a quick swallow, he obeys.

"Stick out your tongue."

Jaw relaxed, he opens wider, keeping his bright blue eyes locked with mine.

"Hold it." I make quick work of dropping my athletic trousers. Then I bend low, grip his chin to position his perfect face right where I want it, and spit directly into his mouth.

A sound somewhere between a moan and a whimper escapes him and travels right to my groin.

Dear gods.

This boy's needy little noises will have me coming without contact if I'm not careful.

I restrain from telling him as much. If Hunter is not with us, it's technically not a scene, and I will always respect his limits. Levi may be on his knees for me—he may be my undoing—but he is in every way my equal in this moment.

As I straighten, I savor the sight of my wet wad coating his tongue as he waits for further instruction.

"What are you waiting for, Champ?" I tighten my hold on his hair. "It's not going to suck itself."

Without a second's hesitation, he springs into action: gripping my base with one hand while fondling my sack with the other. When my sheathed head breeches his mouth, we both moan.

He's sensational.

I fight the instinct to close my eyes. I don't want to miss a moment of this show.

He's beautiful. Rosy cheeks. Puffy lips and wide eyes. Exertion causing sweat to bead at his hairline and his blond curls to stick to his skin.

Our shared saliva drips down his face as he makes a fucking feast of my tip. He pulls back my foreskin, lapping ravenously at my glands, and pumps me harder. Harder. Faster.

My cock twitches eagerly.

The intensity is divine. The roughness. The depth at which he takes me. The way he maintains eye contact as he pulls back, then catches the string of saliva connecting us and smears it over his prominent Adam's apple.

"That's it, Champ. Paint yourself with us."

He's a sight. He's my sole focus and total fixation.

Back at it, he sucks harder and bobs faster. Fuck. This is, without a doubt, the sloppiest, sexiest blowjob of my life. I love it. I crave it, as proven by the precum leaking out of me.

"Okay?" I ask, gripping his curls with both hands and steering him closer.

He nods, and the sensation causes my knees to quiver.

Repositioning myself, I look down at his gorgeous face, stuffed full of cock and cradled in my hands.

He's gorgeous. So brilliantly beautiful. But together? We're a masterpiece: flushed skin and puffy pink lips stretched around my cock, his pale face framed by my darker hands.

"I want to fuck your throat so deep we can't tell whether it's your tears or my cum seeping out of you."

He pops off my cock. "Fuck. Yes. I'm ready."

Repositioning himself, he takes more of me.

"Relax for me, Champ." With two fingers, I trace his throat from chin to chest.

He exhales through his nose, his jaw dropping farther.

When my crown meets resistance, I bite back a moan. "That's it," I encourage. "Clear your mind. Swallow, Levi."

He does.

I almost combust.

"Keep swallowing," I grit out.

With each contraction, my cock creeps farther down his throat. Connecting us. Forging a path I never want to stray from, in this lifetime or in any of the rest.

Filling...

Filling...

So fucking full.

When my pelvis grazes his face, I'm home.

When I meet his eager gaze, I'm reborn.

When I cup his cheeks reverently, then use my thumbs to wipe away the tears leaking from both eyes, my lust reaches its peak, boiling over, spilling out. Transforming to love.

"Swallow again for me, Champ. I'm there. I'm right there, but only you can push me over the edge."

With obvious effort, he works down a thick swallow.

The slight contraction and the sight of him send me toppling. Spinning. Crashing. Coming.

Becoming.

I roll my hips back, easing up a fraction as I spill my seed down his throat.

"That's it. Fucking perfect. Such a good boy, taking me all the fucking way."

We're both panting when we break apart.

Quickly, I clutch his face. "Don't swallow the last of it."

His eyes spark as he presses his lips together to seal me in.

"Rise."

Carefully, he pushes himself to standing.

When he's on his feet, I hold a hand out beneath his chin. "Spit."

As soon as I have the wet wad, I turn him and shove him against the wall.

With my mouth at his ear, I whisper, "Now turn your head toward the mirror and watch."

"Fuck." He's still panting as he rests his cheek on the wall, then meets my gaze in the mirror across from where we stand.

With my free hand, I caress the globes of his ass, then tease the seam between them through the mesh material covering him. "May I enter?"

He nods.

"Words, Levi. I need your words." I grind my pelvis against him. "I want to finger your ass, massage your prostate, and jerk you to completion. Do I have your consent?"

"Yes." The word leaves him in a rush of air. He clears his throat, and this time, when he speaks, his tone is firm. "Fuck yes."

"Watch me as I work you over, Champ. See for yourself just how ravenous I am for every piece of you."

After I've tugged his waistband past his knees, I toy with his ass, smearing his spit and my cum around his puckered hole before pressing one finger inside him. I fist as much of his cock as I can handle with my other hand while using my weight to keep him firmly against the wall.

I ease into him a few times, stretching, prepping, and playing. Committing this moment to memory. It's the first time I've breached him. The first time he's allowed me inside.

I kiss his neck and lick the sweat from his skin.

Sighing, he lets his head fall forward, though his eyes stay fixed on our reflection. I add a second finger, quickly find his prostate, and caress him from the inside.

The moan that escapes him is instantaneous.

I capture his mouth in a kiss and jack his cock in time with my more subtle movements inside him.

When my lungs are starved for oxygen, I break off the kiss and suck in a breath.

"Levi." My chest tightens, despite the deep inhale. Nerves steal my resolve as an overwhelming sensation—part peace, part fear, part excitement—washes over me.

His breathing increases, his entire torso heaving, his lower extremities tense. "Spence."

In that moment, all fear leaves me.

"Levi," I croak out. "I love you."

As if in response to my declaration, he shouts, contracts around my fingers, and spills all over my hand.

I work him through it—caressing and stroking with the gentlest of touches, cognizant of how sensitive he must be.

With his chin tucked to his chest, he forces a harsh inhale, then releases a deep, satisfied sigh. Then he lifts his head and finds my reflection once more, a glazed, satisfied smirk on his face.

"Did you just tell me you love me while playing me like a fiddle?"

I guffaw, trying to place the word fiddle. It's an instrument, I believe. Similar to a viola?

"Hey." He laughs, though the sound is a nervous one. "I'm teasing." He turns, slumps against the wall, and pulls me into his arms.

"I..." He swallows hard, searching my face.

In return, I search his, pouring every drop of sincerity and reassurance I can muster into the look.

"I love you, too." He lowers his forehead to mine and rests it there. "I love you so much," he repeats with a heavy sigh. Quieter, he adds, "I hope it feels like this forever."

I shake my head, my forehead rubbing against his. "It won't."

Rearing back, he locks questioning eyes on me.

"One day soon, we won't have to worry about Magnolia. We'll be in our own home. We'll be together—all of us—and it'll feel so much better than we could have ever imagined."

The power of his dreamy smile hits me like a metric ton to the gut. I'll do everything in my power to make him smile like this for the rest of our days. I'll stop at nothing to make him happy—to care for all of them. With everything I am, I swear to gods, I'll focus all my energy and commit every dollar in my name to delivering on my promise to this man.

Chapter 12

Greedy

"I think we're about to get brunch *and* a show."

Levi smirks in agreement.

Decker's trying to cling to his final threads of patience, but he's clearly losing. I've played ball against him since we were kids; I've watched enough film to know his tells. His dark eyes are narrowed in agitation and a muscle in his jaw spasms at regular intervals that coincide with the opening and closing of his hands. Each time he balls them into fists, his knuckles blanch white with effort.

He's moments away from going off.

Our cohort isn't causing the chaos, which makes the whole situation funnier.

Locke is talking a little too loudly to Si and Hunter across the table, all while shoveling huge bites of food into his mouth. Kendrick is wearing earbuds and staring at his phone, mindlessly drumming on the dining room table, adding to the growing noise level of the room.

Mrs. Lansbury comes in every minute or two, each time muttering "excuse me! Pardon me!" and adding fresh waffles to the stacks. Then she sets to topping off our drinks unnecessarily, paying extra attention to Spence's valet, Gerald. She goes as far as to place more sausage directly on his plate before setting the serving platter down for the rest of us to access.

Each time she does something for Gerald, he sputters assurances that he can do it himself and asks her to please take a seat. She's technically working, so she insists she's fine, but carries on paying special attention to him and nervously chattering to no one in particular.

Spence is positioned across from Decker, at the far end of the table. He's been quiet since entering the dining room promptly at 10:59 a.m., but his shoulders aren't quite as slumped this morning.

He keeps making googly eyes at Levi when he thinks no one is watching. Can't say I love that. Conceptually, I'm fine with sharing. More than fine. We're better together. I know it, yet I can't banish the hot prod of jealousy that forms deep in my belly when I think about anyone else possessing Levi or Hunter in the way I crave to possess them.

I'm a man obsessed. I accepted that long ago. Is it asking too much to hope my partners are equally obsessed with me?

A sharp scraping sound cuts through the chatter. Decker has pushed away from the table and is rising to his feet.

I press my lips together, stifling a laugh. Levi play-punches my arm, which only makes it harder to keep my shit together.

"Where the hell—"

"Here! We're here!" Joze breezes into the dining room, cheeks flushed and her hair a tangled mess.

Kylian strolls in behind her, looking completely unbothered, with his gaze fixed on his phone. He takes the empty seat beside Locke and snags several pieces of crisp bacon from the serving plate in the middle of the table without ever looking up from the device.

Joze is singularly focused on Decker, whose jaw tic is more pronounced now. He's clearly still perturbed. She glides around one side of the table as if there's an invisible tether connecting them, pulling her to her husband.

Before she can get to him, though, Kendrick scoots his chair back, blocking her path, and pulls her into his lap. He braces both hands on her back so she's locked in his hold, straddling him. With his mouth at her ear, he speaks, the timbre too low to make out. She bites down on her bottom lip, eyes twinkling, and the tension between them sizzles so hot I turn away, not wanting to intrude on their private moment.

"Family brunch was set to start at eleven, Josephine." Decker is still on his feet, hands braced on the edge of the table.

My spine stiffens, and I straighten. I was hoping for a classic Crusade tantrum, but definitely not at Joze's expense.

With an exaggerated roll of her eyes, she slinks off Kendrick's lap. Then she flips her hair over one shoulder and sashays toward her husband.

The moment she winds her arms around his neck, his scowl softens significantly. She cups his cheek and murmurs low, offering him a semblance of peace I swear only she seems to be able to provide him.

As if she's cast a spell, Crusade settles. His hands abandon their grip on the table so he can hold her hips. His scowl continues to fade until his face is even and unbothered, smooth and stoic once more. For him, it might as well be the equivalent of a smile.

"Sit." His one-word command is harsh.

It would be very on brand for Josephine Crusade to do the opposite of what he wants, just to rattle him further. Instead, she pecks him on the lips, smiles demurely, brushes past him, and takes what was his seat at the head of the table.

"Okay." Decker blows out a centering breath. "School starts tomorrow," he announces. As if that's news to any of us. "I'd like to discuss how we can best coordinate our schedules and ensure maximum security in terms of access to the isle."

I sit up straighter, ignoring the plate of half-eaten food in front of me. Across from me, Kabir does the same. A coordinated safety plan? Decker Crusade is speaking our language.

"We'll travel to and from the isle in groups when possible, and we'll have set launch times for the pontoons that travel between here and the marina. Kylian." Decker nods at the man who, for the first time since entering the dining room, is looking up from his phone.

"I'm AirDropping a color-coded schedule of everyone's on-campus commitments, as well as the proposed transportation schedule. It's prioritized by safety, sustainability, and convenience. You'll see three established round-trip launches per day, organized by color. I've also created recommended transportation plans for each person based on their schedules."

Pings and vibrations ring out around the table, a cacophony of electronic noises.

"I did not include Sione or Kabir in these plans." He turns to speak to them directly. "Should you wish for me to create individual schedules for you, send me a list of your off-isle activities. Additionally." He turns my way, though he's focused on his phone again. "I elected not to obtain access to Garrett Reed's schedule in the South Chapel University system. You can provide that to me if you wish, and I will create a schedule for you as well."

I scroll through pages and pages of data. Sure enough, he's listed the names of almost everyone around the table, with times highlighted in either red, blue, or purple to coordinate with the boat each person is supposed to be on each day.

Still scrolling, I note one name and freeze. "Wait. Why is Levi on here so much?"

"That was my doing." Decker clears his throat and sets his sights on Levi. "I meant to talk to you about this earlier, in private, but you were otherwise occupied this morning..." His cheeks go pink as he shifts his gaze from Levi to the table.

"Decker got you in on scholarship at LCU, Duke," Hunter says, her voice full of hope. "If you want the spot."

Her smile is radiant, her excitement palpable all the way from across the table.

Levi stills beside me. He locks eyes with Hunter, then unblinkingly turns to Crusade. "What's the catch?"

Decker crosses his arms and regards him, brow furrowed. "What do you mean?"

Levi huffs, his leg bouncing. I grip his knee in silent support. Instinctively, he shifts back in his seat, but on the next breath, his body relaxes and he grasps my hand and weaves his fingers with mine.

"The catch," he repeats. "What—what do I have to do to apply? Am I even eligible? Because of my injury, I had to withdraw from my classes last semester, so my grades—"

Decker shakes his head. "There's no catch. The scholarship was Josephine's, but she doesn't need it anymore."

"The hell?" Joze shoots up straight, giving Decker a fierce scowl.

He takes a step closer and puts a hand on her shoulder. "I paid your tuition outright, Siren. I figured if someone else could benefit from the Crusade Scholarship, it was the right thing to do."

Expression instantly morphing into one of admiration, she settles back in her seat.

"You can just do that?" Levi challenges. His accent is thicker than usual when he speaks, a sign that he's either nervous or apprehensive. Or both. "You can just say, hey, it's gonna go to this guy?"

With a snort, Locke shovels another forkful of food into his mouth. He hasn't stopped eating since he sat down.

"The Crusade Scholarship is part of an endowment left by my mom," Decker explains, his tone contrite. "As the sole heir to her trust, I can do whatever I want with it."

Joze takes her husband's hand in silent support.

"As for classes and such, I may have used Kendrick's name for that one."

Kendrick zeroes in on Crusade, looking just as surprised by this news as the rest of us.

"LCU has two players headed to the Combine in a few weeks." A bitter frown tugs at Decker's face, but it's gone as quickly as it appeared. "Because of that, the athletic training team has a few additional spots to fill for practicum students. One spot is yours if you want it. You'd have to work in the field house this semester, assisting not just the football team, but any team that needs it. You'd be doing a lot of hands-on rehab and recovery with other students, but it's worth twelve credits."

Shit. This really does sound too good to be true. But Crusade threw this all together without Levi's knowledge or consent. He's not going to like this.

While Levi blinks rapidly, stunned and taking in all the information, Hunter stands and circles the table. Wordlessly, she slides into his lap, wraps her arms around his neck, and burrows into his chest.

She's positioned in his lap so she's facing me. But all her focus is set on him.

"Come to LCU with me, Duke. Please?"

My concern dissipates the moment her words register. I know before his head even moves that he'll agree.

Way to go, Tem.

They're so good together. It warms me from the inside to witness the way she handles his heart with such loving care.

"This family breakfast is getting a little too mushy for my taste," Joze quips from the head of the table.

Hunter's blond hair whips Levi in the face as she turns to look at her friend.

Locke snorts. "Says the girl who was late because she was spread wide like an all-you-can-eat buffet up in the Nest."

Joze lifts her hand to her chest in mock-outrage. Kendrick chuckles, and Kylian grins.

Decker is the only member of their group not amused. His face is fixed in a seething stare as he looks from one person to another.

"We have guests." He nods at Gerald.

The poor man is pink from his chin to the tips of his ears.

Locke drops his fork to his plate with a clatter. "Oh, shit. Sorry, my guy."

"*Your* guy?" Kabir goes rigid.

Gerald is Kabir's valet. By pure definition, he is actually *his* guy.

"Just an expression," Sione assures him.

"Levi, let me know by this afternoon what you decide. Okay. Last order of business," Decker announces, calling all our attention back to his side of the table. "The Combine is two weeks away." There's a pinch between his eyebrows. Another clenching of his hand into a fist. They're subtle changes, but they're telling, nonetheless.

The NFL Combine is the annual gathering of potential draftees. It's a multi-day event where coaches, teams, and prospective players congregate and the players have the opportunity to show off their skills and vie for the most coveted places in the draft.

Decker Crusade was slated to be a first-round pick. He's professional football royalty, with the arm, stealth, and adaptability of the very best veteran quarterbacks in the league.

But he's not attending the Combine, and he won't be going pro. Instead, his football career ended before it could begin.

I didn't understand it at the time—what he did, all he gave up, and why he did it.

Now that I've found my people, it makes absolute fucking sense.

Still. Staying behind while Kendrick heads to the Combine can't be easy for him.

"I'm still planning to go with K," Joze announces, although there's not a whole lot of conviction to her statement.

"Good," Kylian says, glancing at her over his glasses. "He needs you there."

Kendrick lifts his head and turns toward the head of the table. "Not just need, Mama. I want you there, too."

Joze nods, her movement tentative as her eyes dart up to Decker.

Ah. It hits me then. Her hesitation has everything to do with him. That makes me feel for him even more.

"Cap, Kyl, and I will be at the cabin that weekend," Locke announces. "So you all will have the place to yourselves."

My chest expands. Excellent.

Before my imagination can get the best of me, Joze speaks up.

"Wait. You should come with us."

Her attention is fixed on Hunter, her eyes dancing with renewed excitement. "I'll be in the stands or at the hotel most of the time anyway. It'll be the perfect opportunity for girl time."

My hackles instantly raise. There's no way she can travel out of state.

Hunter peers at me from under her lashes and squirms in Levi's lap.

"I'm not sure it's safe for me to travel right now." Her entire demeanor has changed, face sullen and shoulders slumped in defeat.

"Do you want to go, Firecracker?"

She shrugs at Spence, then makes eye contact with Sione and Levi before focusing on me again. "Does it matter? It's not an option thanks to Magnolia."

I lock eyes with Kabir, finding his face etched in the same kind of frustration plaguing me. Not an option, my ass.

"I assure you, love. There'll be no threat to your safety should you wish to attend."

Hunter's eyes spark with hope.

"Levi and Garrett have class, and I'm in the midst of a project I really cannot leave on the back burner," he explains. "But perhaps if Sione is amenable to going, too, and it's not too much trouble for you to miss your classes, it would be okay."

"Si?" Hunter straightens in Levi's lap, arms still looped around his neck.

As if it's even a question. It wouldn't be, for any of us. Anything for our girl. Anything to make her smile.

"If it is not an intrusion or hardship, I would love to attend."

Kendrick rises, taps his knuckles on the table twice, and strides over to Joze. "It's settled, then. Kylian can send you the itinerary, and we'll get the arrangements taken care of." With that, he grabs his woman's hand and guides her out of the room.

Chapter 13

Hunter

"You're sure you know how to drive this thing?"

It's not that I don't trust my bestie. It's just that on the first night we ever hung out, she confessed she'd never even been on a boat. Now she's cruising across Lake Chapel with total confidence and a decent amount of speed.

"Yep." Joey centers herself behind the helm of the smaller speed boat, headed toward the marina and the first day of spring semester.

It's just the two of us.

Sort of.

Kylian is already at the marina, awaiting our arrival. The guys are on the pontoon not far behind us. It doesn't surprise me in the least that within twenty-four hours of the unveiling of Decker and Kylian's transportation schedule and proposed plans, Joey convinced them that we needed girl time and would be taking a boat just the two of us.

I giggled when I saw *Little Green* added to the color-coded schedule this morning.

"Hold on, babe. I don't know who we're racing, but I fully intend to win."

Joey thrusts the throttle forward, and the boat jerks. She screams with glee as the wind makes an absolute mess of her hair. Thankfully, I opted for a beanie today.

As my eyes water and the wind stings my cheeks, I laugh, weightless and free. I love new beginnings.

Fresh starts.

This is exactly how the first day of school is supposed to feel.

When my phone vibrates in my pocket, I pull it out, and when I catch sight of Spence's name on the screen, giddiness surges through me.

> **Spence**: You appear to be traveling at a much faster pace than the rest of our cohort, love. Care to explain?

Explain, I won't.

I do, however, sidle up to Joey, hold out my phone, and take a quick selfie of her windswept hair and my wild, gleeful smile.

> **Firecracker:** I can't help it if the boys can't keep up.

I follow that up with a serious text, not wanting him to worry.

> **Firecracker**: The guys are behind us. Kylian is waiting at the docks. Joey got her boating license a few months ago. We're good!

> **Spence:** A few MONTHS ago?

Whoopsies... I didn't think that one through.

> **Spence:** I suddenly have the urge to make Gerald acquire a boating license and escort you to and from class each day.

> **Firecracker:** Unnecessary. Besides, the guys are with me.

> **Spence:** But if it were Gerald with you, you wouldn't be trying to ditch him.

He's got me there.

> **Firecracker:** Why don't YOU get a boating license? Then we can race each other next time.

> **Spence:** I can think of many, many creative things I would like to do with you on a boat, Firecracker. Racing is quite low on the list.

"Earth to Hunter."

"Sorry, sorry." I stash my phone, cheeks heating, and give Joey a sheepish smile. It was rude of me to ignore her when she specifically wanted to have a little time for just the two of us.

"Don't ever apologize for being *that* happy, babe. I don't know who you were messaging or what they were saying, but I'm not sure I've ever seen you smile that wide."

The heat in my cheeks spreads down my neck and to my ears. She can tease me all she wants, though. She's my bestie, so it's her God-given right.

Besides, she's not wrong.

Despite everything we've endured and the fact that my mother is still a menace, I've never been this happy in my life.

Chapter 14

Levi

"Library. Science building. Humanities center." Locke sweeps his tatted hand around the imposing brick structures surrounding us as we wander through the quad.

Shortly after we arrived on campus, Decker, Kylian, and Joey headed off to their respective classes. The rest of us have a little time to kill, so Locke and Kendrick offered to show me around beforehand. Hunter could have done it, but since she's only been here for one semester, they know more of the ins and outs and finer details.

Locke continues playing tour guide, and beside me, Hunter squeezes my hand. I can't help but grin at our laced fingers. When I came back to North Carolina, I couldn't have begun to dream that my life could look like this.

"Performing arts center over there. Math building, which has the best coffee cart on campus, according to Joey. Then over there's the business school."

I repeat the name of each building as we go, trying to commit them all to memory.

"This will be your home base. At least for this semester."

We stop in front of the massive state-of-the-art field house situated on the west end of campus.

My gut hollows out. Fucking hell.

Decker not only got me in and had the Crusade Scholarship reassigned to me, he went as far as to secure a twelve-credit-hour practicum for me.

My life has changed completely in the last twenty-four hours, but here we fucking go.

"I'm heading in for speed drills and PT," Kendrick tells me with a clap on the back. "I'll get you where you need to be."

After I give my girl a quick kiss, I follow the big guy inside.

Curtis, who's a massive hulk of a man with blond hair formed into a sharp buzz cut, is the teaching assistant for my practicum. He's newer to campus, too, having transferred from a school up in Northeast Ohio last year.

He originally planned to go into marketing, but then had a change of heart. He's technically in the first year of the athletic training grad program here, despite being in his mid-twenties.

As he shows me around, pointing out offices and supply closets, he goes over the procedures for signing student athletes in and out of the clinic.

"You'll need this on you at all times." He holds out a red and black lanyard. I lift the plastic tag at the end to inspect it, shocked to find it already has my name and student ID along the bottom.

"Curtis, my man. What's good?" A beast of a guy enters the clinic, signs in, then hops up onto a table and whips off his shirt.

"Hey, Jackson. I've got a new student trainer with me today, showing him the ropes. Okay if he observes while I tape your shoulder?"

The rest of the day flies by. I stick by Curtis's side, except after lunch when he needs a specific waterproof kinesiology tape for a female swimmer. I remember seeing it in one of the closets earlier, so I offer to grab it, proud as hell when I find it behind the second door I try.

"And that's the day," Curtis announces.

Though it feels far earlier than four p.m., the next shift has already arrived, fresh faces of students and supervisors ready to take on the needs of the student athletes after practice and evening lift sessions.

"Do you have somewhere to be?" Curtis asks. "A few of us from the club hockey team are heading to the Outpost for a drink. You're welcome to join us."

The offer almost bowls me over. Fuck, it feels good to jump back into life again, to meet new people and experience new things.

Going out with them isn't an option tonight, though. Not with the way my body vibrates with excitement to get back to the mansion and tell the others about my day.

Even so, I'm curious about the club he mentioned, and I definitely want to be invited out again. "I've got plans tonight. But I'd love to join you another time. What's club hockey?"

"LCU doesn't have a full hockey program, but I was on the team at my old school, so when I transferred, I got together with a few other guys and got the club set up here. We have to drive out to Farquay to practice at their rink, but it's worth it."

A club team. I didn't even know that was an option.

"Are there other club sports at LCU?"

Curtis claps me on the shoulder. "Yeah, man. They've got just about everything you can think of."

My lungs seize up, but I force my next question out. "Football?"

"Yep. Dodgeball and rugby, too."

Realistically, I won't ever play football at the collegiate level again. But that doesn't mean I can't play for myself.

Club football. I didn't even know that was a fucking option.

There's no stopping the smile that erupts and there's no schooling my expression when I clock out and exit the building. I'm all tingly inside as I stride down the sidewalk. Today was... Hell, it was so much more than I ever thought it could be.

I'm walking aimlessly, too pumped to consider where I'm supposed to be going, when my phone vibrates in my pocket.

> **Daisy:** Meet me in the library. Third floor. Turn right at the top of the stairs. Botany and entomology section.

A huff of a laugh escapes me. That's an extremely specific request, but I'm happy to oblige.

I find the library without a problem, thanks to Locke's thorough tour, then take the stairs two at a time up to the third floor.

Pulse thrumming in my veins, I weave through the stacks, scanning the space for my girl. I'm a bundle of nerves and anticipation when I finally spot her. She's pretending to search for a text on the highest shelf. She's a terrible actress, her whole face scrunching up as she tries to fight back her smile.

She turns just as I approach.

I scoop her up and plant a wanton, love-drunk kiss on her lips. Gasping, she grips my face. I lean into her and press her back to the shelves, thanking god I found her in an end aisle conveniently supported by a wall.

She melts into me, giving as good as she gets, stoking the fire that's ignited low in my stomach. Lips parting, she slicks her tongue against mine. I fight back, meeting her stroke for stroke.

Fingers tangled in the hair at my nape, she drops her head back and moans. "Levi."

I kiss and suck along her jaw and down her neck. "I know, pretty girl. I know."

Nudging the knee of my good leg between her thighs, I take her weight, pulling a whimper from her. God bless thin leggings and oversized sweatshirts. I kiss her harder, feeding her my tongue as I savor every sweet, delicious taste she allows me to take, and encourage her to grind down against my thigh.

Fuck, I want to make her feel good. I'm practically soaring already. Getting her off in a semi-public place would be the ultimate cherry on top of my day.

At the quick vibrating sensation between us, I jolt.

Hunter breaks away, breathless and giggling. "Uh, Duke? Did you bring accessories for us, or…?"

Embarrassed, I jam my hand into my pocket and pull out my vibrating phone. "It's probably Greedy, wondering if we're on our way home." I grimace. This detour was her idea. If he's upset that we're late, she'll be the one answering to our boyfriend.

Except when I glance down, I see that it's not Greedy.

It's much worse.

My hard-on instantly deflates when the name on the screen registers.

"It's my mom." I show Hunter the phone. I'm well-versed in ignoring her calls from my years out in California. Hell, I've probably interacted with her more over the last few months than I have in the last three years. Maintaining boundaries and keeping her at arm's length will be imperative now that it's not just me I'm worried about protecting.

But then Hunter catches my wrist before I can hit Ignore. "Wait." Stepping closer, she worries her lip between her teeth. "No more running, remember? Answer it now. We're both here. If she's anything like Magnolia, she's not going to give up easily. Let's just get it over with."

Fucking hell. She's right. But this is far from the way I wanted this little encounter in the library to go.

With dread swirling in my gut, I slide to accept the call. "Hello?"

"Levi Moore. I have it on good authority you got a girl—" She chokes, then hiccups. She can't even say the word out loud.

"Pregnant?" I blow out an exasperated breath. I figured it was only a matter of time before my mother found out, though I'm surprised the rumor mill moved this quickly.

"Yes. *Pregnant*. We need to start planning the wedding at once."

My heart stutters and I'm pretty sure my eyes bug out, but Daisy grips my wrist gently, quickly soothing me. I shouldn't be surprised she can hear both sides of the conversation with the way my mom is practically yelling.

"That's not our highest priority right now." It's the wrong answer, but it's all I've got.

"Like hell it's not," she snaps back.

I wince. She never curses.

"I need to meet this girl. The—the mother of my grandchild. Her mother already called me. She wants the four of us to get together at the country club next week. The sheer embarrassment I felt, finding out from a stranger. And now she's invited us to share a meal! I take it you'll actually prioritize this particular luncheon?"

The horror painted on Hunter's face matches the sensation coursing through me.

Fucking. Hell.

Magnolia already got to my mom.

Hunter's bottom lip trembles. I catch it between my forefinger and thumb and give it a gentle tug. It does us no good to freak out. We knew this was a possibility.

"No more running," I mouth.

Pretty dark lashes flutter closed. Then she takes a few calming breaths. When she opens her eyes, they're filled with determination. My girl is ready for battle.

"Hunter and I will be there," I confirm. "Will you text me the details?"

Whatever we have to do to get Hunter out of Magnolia's clutches for good—we'll do it. Whatever comes next, we'll meet it head-on.

I'm ready to stand up to my mom. I'm fully prepared to stay and fight.

No more running.

We've got this.

Chapter 15

Greedy

Though I know I shouldn't, I once again study the results on my phone, only glancing up occasionally as I stalk down the long hallway that connects the primary suite to the rest of the house.

Why the fuck did I even click on the damn file? Every time my mind starts reeling or fresh insecurity creeps in, my subconscious goes for the jugular. It's happened at least a dozen times today. On the boat leaving the isle, when Hunter was on the other boat with Joey. In the car at the marina, when she and Levi and Joey and her crew piled in to Kendrick's Suburban and Decker's G-Wagon to head to Lake Chapel University. Then when I parked in front of the sciences building at South Chapel. Every one of those instances happened before nine a.m.

I'm a glutton for punishment, apparently. I should just delete this file from my phone. Several times today, I've considered it, but I always chicken out. Some sick part of me wants to stare at the lab results showing that Hunter's pregnant. Even if I know it's not true.

I breeze past the butler's pantry and the dark, empty home gym. The pantry appears to be vacated, too. That spurs a thought that, for once, I don't want to push away. I wonder how I can convince Hunter and Levi to meet me in there for round two.

As much as I hate to admit it, the Crusade Mansion is starting to feel like home.

We're together, and despite all the bullshit happening with Magnolia, we're safe.

I quietly enter the bedroom, ready to unwind. I'm anxious to be done with this day. My class load is lighter this semester—part of my plan to stave off graduation and stick around for another year. I only had two in-person classes today, plus an unofficial workout session with some of the guys from the team.

My day will start earlier tomorrow. I didn't bat an eye at the eight-a.m. lab when I scheduled it, but now that I live on an isle and my commute requires a boat ride *and* a drive to campus?

I huff, but quickly cool my attitude. The minor inconveniences of staying at the Crusade Mansion amount to practically nothing compared to the safety and security this place affords us.

A dim light is on in the en suite bathroom, but the door's wide open, so I stride straight for it.

Inside, Hunter is standing in front of the double-sink vanity brushing her teeth.

From here, she can't see me, but I can see her profile and her reflection in the mirror. I take a minute to watch her, savoring the mundaneness of this moment. Her hair is loose down her back, her posture casual. Her hips sway slightly as she shifts from foot to foot. She's already in pajamas—a pink cotton set that clings to the globes of her ass.

There's no hard exterior around her now. No faux air of loathing. No more need to keep me at arm's length.

She's safe. She's okay. Right now, in this place and this moment, she may even be happy.

I rap my knuckles on the molding to get her attention.

Her eyes widen and find mine in the mirror.

The foamy toothpaste smile that lights up her face is equal parts adorable and goofy.

She squeaks when she catches her reflection and quickly spits and rinses her mouth. When she's toothpaste free, she turns to properly greet me. "Hi."

I stroll into the bathroom with purpose, and when I'm within reach, she yanks me into her body like she can't stand the distance between us anymore.

Good. Me neither.

Crowding her space, I thread my arms low around her back and cage her against the vanity. I run my nose along her jaw, then place a kiss at the pulse point of her neck. "Hi."

She melts into me, but it's still not close enough. I tighten my hold and pour every damn ounce of desire and need coursing through me into the embrace.

It's a heady combination, what I feel for Hunter. It's lust and love, two passions personified and constantly at war for dominance.

Physically, I crave her, my body thrumming and aching to make up for lost time. I want to fuck her and claim her and make love to her like it's my sole directive. She's mine. I want to mark her and fill her up over and over again until she accepts it as her truth. That's lust.

Then there's the deeper desire beneath the surface. I love her. My instinct is to provide and protect. I want to be responsible for more of her foamy toothpaste smiles. I want her to have everything she wants and needs, even if those needs extend beyond what I can offer alone. Her happiness is my purpose. I want her to thrive in our polyamorous relationship. She's endured a lifetime without the love, care, or devotion from her family she deserves. But the guys and I can give that to her now, tenfold.

I sigh into the crook of her neck. "Missed you today."

One thing I won't ever take for granted is how effortless it is to allow myself to be vulnerable with her. Now that there are no secrets between us, I couldn't imagine not appreciating every tender moment we have together.

"I missed you more." She presses a kiss to my sternum.

Her words dull the envy that spending the day without her has caused, though I'm still a little off-kilter.

"Levi came home beaming." I drag a hand up her spine and find the tension near her neck, massaging it on instinct, eager to absolve her of any discomfort.

Sighing, she turns her head, offering me better access. With her cheek resting against my chest, she says, "He had the best day. I'm so happy for him."

I tense. "I hate that I wasn't there. With you. To see him in his element. I'm about to fucking transfer schools."

Hunter's responding laugh is breathy. "It's just for the semester," she reminds me. "Sixteen weeks. Plus, you have a lighter course load for spring, don't you?"

With a grunt, I nod.

"We'll see each other plenty," she assures me.

When I say nothing, she cranes back and searches my face.

"Greedy." She places a soft, tender kiss on my lips, then cups my cheeks. "We just have to get through this semester. If it helps, you and I can have some alone time each week. Tell me the day and time, and I'm yours."

"*Only* mine?" I definitely don't hate the sound of that.

"Only yours," she promises, bringing her lips to meet mine once more.

I capture her mouth and lick along the seam of her pretty pink lips. Immediately, she lets me in. The minty taste of her sparks a tingle in my own mouth. I take the kiss deeper, gripping her chin to hold her mouth open as I feed her my tongue.

She kisses me back, the desire in the air around us skyrocketing as she finds the hair at my nape and tugs. Hard.

On a groan, I break away, then pepper kisses along her cheek and jaw before settling into the crook of her neck.

Gently, I lick and kiss the smooth skin below her ear. When she whimpers, I bite her and suck the pleasure point with abandon.

Mine.

"Greedy." She tugs on my hair again. The sound of my name on her lips, all breathy and needy, makes me want to mark more of her.

I kiss a trail down her chest, between her breasts, and bite one nipple, then the other through the thin fabric, leaving them pebbled beneath her thin tank top.

As I sink to my knees, I smooth both hands up her bare legs and rest them on her hips, then dip my head to kiss the apex of her thighs.

Lust and love war inside me once more.

I want to lick her. Bite her. Fuck her with my tongue and shove my cock so deep into her cunt she doesn't remember anyone else exists. Kabir who?

The deeper longing is there, too. The love that lives in my soul, the connection I had to shove down for so long.

I may be a possessive, horny, red-blooded man. But the soft, vulnerable, deprived romantic in me is winning the battle tonight.

With reverence, I lift my head and lock eyes with her.

Her smile is soft as she brushes my hair off my forehead. Every time she tugs on my hair or scrapes her nails against my scalp, I wonder if she knows.

No. I don't think she understands just how desperate and unhinged I was when she left for Europe.

Slowly, without breaking eye contact, I flip down the waistband of her sleep shorts. I turn them again, and then I'm eye level with the smooth expanse of her stomach.

I place a kiss on her low abdomen, the place our baby once occupied.

"Greedy," she murmurs, her voice rife with emotion.

I know.

I fucking know.

It's torture to think of what could have been. To ruminate about what we lost. It was years ago, but grief doesn't have an expiration date.

Kabir's surprise announcement this week stirred up all sorts of feelings for me that had just begun to settle.

"I'm still mad at him." My voice is low and gravelly as I fight back the tears that want to leak from my eyes.

She cups my head, pressing my cheek against her pelvis, and sniffles. "I know. You're allowed to be."

A lump lodges itself in my throat. "I didn't get to know the first time, when it was real. Then to see those test results without being warned that it was all a ruse..."

With a growl, I push to my feet and scrape one hand through my hair. "Do you think it'll even work?" I demand.

Hunter's not the enemy here. I know that. Yet I can't temper the emotion brewing beneath the surface. We haven't had a chance to talk, just the two of us, since the incident. I've barely begun to process everything I'm feeling.

With a sad smile, she shrugs. "I honestly don't know. It's worth a shot, I think. Spence thought of almost everything, and I trust that he has a bigger plan in place."

Yeah. Another plan I'm sure he'll refuse to share.

She crosses her arms over her chest and regards me. "Levi's mom called today. Demanding to have lunch with the both of us, plus Magnolia. She wants to talk about the baby."

The reminder that everyone assumes Levi is the father is like a punch to the gut. I understand why we're going along with it, but dammit. It was supposed to be *me*.

With a long breath, I force out some of my pent-up frustration.

I'm not upset with Hunter, but this whole situation is picking at the scabs of old scars and fresh wounds alike.

I give myself another few seconds to fixate. Then, with a shake of my head, I clear my mind and let go of my anger.

"Sorry." Inching closer, I open my arms to hug her once more.

She sinks back into my hold without hesitation.

"I'm not upset with you," I assure her. "It just... hurts. The constant reminder that I didn't support you then. Knowing that I wasn't there for you when this was real."

She shakes her head against my collarbone. "You couldn't have known. Then, once we found out our parents were engaged, I wouldn't let you get any closer."

Regret and grief pour from her, all the same emotions pummeling me in this moment, too. The fact that she's hurting—that she's *still* hurting after all these years—sends my anger skyrocketing once more.

"I should have at least been there when you found out you were pregnant."

Hunter stills in my arms. "Greedy... I never found out."

I brush the pads of my thumbs along her cheekbones, aching to be the soft, gentle version of myself right now, knowing that she's grappling with the same heartache that's rooted deep inside me. "What do you mean, you never found out?"

She sniffles, the green of her eyes like sea glass behind unshed tears. "I never took a test. Never even suspected. I found out I was pregnant the same moment I was told I was losing our baby."

My heart cracks wide open. "You've never taken a pregnancy test?"

She shakes her head, blinking and releasing the tears she was holding on to.

I wipe away the moisture, then dip my head to kiss one cheek, then the other, along the path of wetness.

As I right myself and take her in, an idea sparks inside me.

A selfish, slightly unhinged idea.

I'm speaking before I can even think the question through. I can't help it. It's the test results on my phone and the residual anger still living inside me because of Spence's announcement.

With bated breath, I ask, "Will you take one for me now?"

Her breath hitches as her eyes go wide and search mine.

"Why?" The single whispered syllable is filled with pain.

I shouldn't ask her to do this. I don't want to cause her any more heartache. But now that the idea has been planted in my mind...

"You're not pregnant," I state. I know it's the truth.

"My period was last weekend. It ended a few days ago."

"And yet we have blood work that says you are. Blood work I've studied at least a hundred times since Kabir AirDropped it to my phone."

Understanding registers.

Expression resolute, she pulls my face down and presses her forehead to mine. "I'll take a test," she murmurs. "Let me see if Joey has any on hand."

Before she texts Joze for help, we peek in the cabinets, and, sure enough, find one below the sink.

Heads bent together, we read over the instructions. She doesn't ask me to turn around or look away when she sits on the toilet to pee. Her cheeks go pink when a trickle of urine hits the bowl, but I hold her gaze, hoping she can sense the immense gratitude and appreciation I have for this moment.

She caps the test. Per the instructions, I set a timer for two minutes on my phone.

Once she's cleaned up, she blows out a long, timid breath.

Throat thick, I hold out a hand. "Come here." When she sinks into my hold without hesitation, I press my mouth to hers. "Thank you," I whisper against her lips. "I love you, Hunter. I love you so much, and I'm so sorry I wasn't there for you before."

I steal another kiss before she can refuse my apology or insist it's okay.

It's not. It'll never be.

All we can do now is move forward.

I kiss her tenderly, my movements sweet and slow as I savor every second that ticks by.

When the timer dings, we still.

Hunter turns to retrieve the test, but I don't let go of her. With her hand in mine, I follow closely.

"It's negative." She holds up the stick so I can see the word for myself, her expression in the mirror crestfallen.

"We knew it would be."

I sweep her hair to the side so I can kiss her neck from behind.

"But Tem?"

I freeze with my mouth still on her skin, waiting until she looks me right in the eyes before I continue.

"One day, it won't be."

Still holding her attention, I snake one hand down her stomach, dipping beneath her waistband, and cup her sex. I kiss her neck again, sucking and coaxing until she's making little noises of pleasure. I caress one breast, toying with her nipple while the fingers of my other hand caress lightly over her clit.

"One day, your stomach will be round and full, these perfect tits heavy with milk."

She grinds her ass into me, and I press right back, nestling my length between her cheeks. Fuck. I'm already hard and aching to be buried deep inside.

"One day," I murmur, moving to her other nipple and pinching it hard. "We're going to make a baby for real. Again."

"Greedy. Please." She moans, head hung low, and squeezes her thighs together, creating an even tighter grip on my hand. Though I haven't breached her entrance yet, my fingers are coated in her slickness.

"You want that, Tem? You want me to fill this pretty cunt with cum and put a baby in you?"

She whimpers in response.

I tug on her hair, forcing her to look at me in the mirror. "Yes or no, Hunter? Are you going to have my baby someday?"

"Yes," she pants, cheeks flushed.

"That's right. I'm going to fill you with my seed. Come in your cunt again and again until it takes and you're pregnant with my child."

Her eyes are glassy with lust, her chest heaving with want. She rolls her hips forward and back, seeking me. "Greedy," she whines. "I'm so empty."

That fucking does it.

I jerk away from the vanity, turn her around, and smash my mouth against hers. The negative pregnancy test flies out of her hand and clatters to the tile as we claw at each other.

"Get on the fucking floor and spread yourself wide open."

With a whimper, she lowers herself. I follow, dropping to my knees. We're a mess of limbs, tearing at our clothes while still kissing and biting, anything to maintain contact.

This isn't just a quick tryst or a little kinky role playing. This is sexual healing fueled by biological desire.

Once she's bare for me, she does exactly as I ask, spreading her legs wide and holding her thighs open.

"Fucking perfection." Hovering over her, I line myself up at her core and drag my cock through her wetness, groaning with each pass.

"Greedy," she begs, writhing. "Fill me up. Please. I need it. I need *you*."

With a deep inhale, I plunge inside her in one smooth thrust. I work myself all the way to the hilt, grinding my pelvis against her clit and capturing her lips once more.

I hold the position, then, without pulling out even an inch, I thrust and grind against her.

"Do you feel how deep I am, Tem?"

She mewls, biting my lip, hips scraping against mine. "I'm right there. All the way in. Right at your womb, ready to fill you up and make us a baby."

She moans into my mouth, squirming, attempting to meet me thrust for thrust.

"Lay still and fucking take it." I kiss her harder, bite at her neck, nip at her breasts and suck hard, marking her so intensely she'll have bruises tomorrow.

"Harder," she pants, her hips still now as her fingers dig into my ass cheeks, urging me on. "Fill me up," she begs. "Put a baby in me," she pleads.

I pull all the way out for the first time since I entered her. She claws at my low back, marking me in this moment just like I'm marking her.

Good. Fucking claim it, baby.

I slam back into her with a thrust that pushes her along the tiled floor.

For a moment, still seated fully and with hands splayed on either side of her and my arms locked, all I can do is admire the woman who will carry my children one day.

When she meets my gaze, the most feral growl tears through me. I press my forearm along her low belly, holding her in place, then thrust forward, giving her quick, hurried, hard pumps of my cock. She's so tight. So warm. So needy and pliable as I drill into her.

"This is how I'm coming." I rut into her, my orgasm building from the base of my spine to the top of my skull and through my extremities. "I'm as deep as humanly possible, Tem. Filling you up. Right here, right now."

Flames lick up my calves and thighs until they form one combustible fireball burning bright in my pelvis.

"Greedy." She claws at my skull. "Put a baby in me," she begs, her voice hollow and far away.

That's all it takes for me to detonate. Heat spreads through my balls and low back with such ferocity I nearly topple over with the force.

"Fuck, I'm coming. Clench around me, Tem. Take it all and hold it in," I command, frantically rubbing her clit to get her there, too.

She shrieks, and as the pleasure crescendos, her walls squeezing so tightly my balls swell with another surge of cum, she lets out a long, low moan.

"That's it. Milk me. Take it all, Hunter. Take it fucking all."

When the pleasure ebbs and we're catching our breath, I study her, mystified.

I've never been that rough during sex. That intense. That demanding. But based on the way she's smiling up at me, glassy-eyed, soft, and malleable, I think she enjoyed it as much as I did.

"I love you." I drop to my elbows, careful to remain buried deep inside her, and brush my lips over hers. "I love you so much, Hunter."

She clenches around me in response.

A groan escapes me. "Fuck. That was incredible, but I'm sorry if—"

"Don't you dare try to apologize." She tightens her walls around me once more for emphasis. "That was incredible, full stop. I loved that side of you." With her lip caught between her teeth, she takes me in. "I can't wait to do it again."

Chapter 16

Hunter

I lay with Greedy for a while after we came down from the high of fucking each other senseless on the bathroom floor, cuddling close and whispering sweet affirmations.

He tried to apologize countless times, but I wasn't interested in hearing it. He had absolutely nothing to apologize for.

I reveled in the intensity. The pent-up anger. The primal, reckless dirty talk as he pounded into me. It was excruciatingly intimate and surprisingly healing for him to fuck me with the intent of knocking me up, even if it was only words spewing from him in the heat of the moment.

I never would have guessed Greedy would have a breeding kink. I'm already dreaming about when I can experience it again.

Once his breathing evened out and I was sure he was asleep, I snuck out of bed, intent on taking a quick shower and finishing my nighttime routine.

I'm blotting toner along my forehead when the bathroom door creaks open and Levi's bright blue eyes meet mine in the mirror.

"Shh," I tell him, waving him into the room.

He enters and silently pulls the door closed. "Is G asleep?" he whispers, coming to stand beside me with his back against the vanity.

I take him in from head to toe. It's been a long day for all of us, most especially him, but he doesn't look tired. In fact, he's practically glowing.

"You checkin' me out, Daisy?"

I grin. "Always. Yes, Greedy's asleep. Did you have a good day?" I toss the cotton pad I was using and quickly dab on my nighttime moisturizer.

Without responding, he watches me.

"What?" I don't ever feel self-conscious in front of my guys, but with the way he's looking at me right now...

"I had the best day." If possible, his smile widens. "But you and I have unfinished business, pretty girl." He captures me by the hips, hauls me toward him, and tips my chin up so he has better access to my mouth.

I squeal, though the sound cuts off quickly.

Oh. He's right. We *do* have unfinished business.

"We have to be quiet." I return his kiss and wrap my arms around his neck. When the brim of his ball cap hits me, I turn it backward.

He grins into my mouth, teasing me with playful strokes of his tongue. "You're so sweet, Daisy. I could kiss you for hours and it still wouldn't be enough."

And kiss me, he does.

Every caress of his tongue and nip at my lips sends glimmers of want through my stomach. Levi may be a pussy-eating prodigy, but he's also a grand master when it comes to making out.

By the time he breaks away, I'm breathless and worked up all over again.

A-plus, Levi Moore.

Ten out of ten. No notes.

When he pulls back, his cheeks flushed and his chest rising and falling fast, he smirks.

I place my hand over his heart and revel in the way it feels beating against my palm. He grasps my wrist and places the gentlest kiss on my fingertips.

It's magical, knowing that this man wants me just as keenly as I want him.

Mind, body, and soul, I want to give myself to him completely and make him pinky promise to never let me go.

Head bowed now, he peppers my neck with kisses, each one lingering a little longer than the last. I'm panting by the time he makes it to the hollow of my throat.

"You a little worked up, pretty girl?" He kisses my collarbone and trails his tongue along my shoulder as he makes quick work of undoing the belt of my robe.

He nudges the fabric off one shoulder and grabs me behind the thighs, then lifts and places me on the edge of the bathroom counter.

Straightening, he tosses his hat. "Don't need this for what I plan to do to you." Then, without preamble, he takes a knee.

"Wait." I snap my legs closed.

He swiftly pries them apart, focus narrowed on my face.

"You're going to taste Greedy if you go down on me." God, I can only imagine how swollen I am, too. Greedy fucked me so hard. I'm throbbing now, and I know I'll still ache tomorrow.

He groans and tosses his head back. "Fucking perfect." When he returns his attention to me, his eyes are burning like the hottest blue flames. He kisses and nips at my flesh, blazing a trail up my thigh. "I'm gonna eat him right out of you. Spread your legs wider and put them over my shoulders, pretty girl. I want to see for myself how pink and puffy our boy has made you."

Oh.

Fuck.

Pushing down my insecurities, I spread my legs wide for him to see.

He stares at my center, licking his lips, then dives in to make a feast of my cunt.

With both hands, he holds me open, giving himself even better access. He laps at my clit, alternating flicks and long licks in a delicious rhythm. Already, I'm dripping on the counter and a combination of my juices and Greedy's cum coats Levi's lips and chin.

"Fucking delicious." Head tilted to one side, he thrusts his tongue up into me.

It's a heady, subtle sensation. He's barely breaching me with the tip of it, but as he establishes a rhythm, my thighs tremble and warmth gathers in my core. Within seconds, little zaps of electricity start up, sizzling through my nerves.

He's so much gentler than Greedy was earlier, but he's no less effective.

My pussy spasms involuntarily. My thighs try to clench around his head, but he uses his hands to hold me open as he devours me.

With both hands in his hair, I tip my head back. Giving in to this moment. Offering him all of me, unabashed and unashamed.

The telltale tightness in my hips and thighs keys us both in to how close I am.

"Come for me, Daisy. Push out everything Greedy gave you and fill my mouth."

Fuck.

That does it.

His dirty command. His insatiable desire not only for me, but for the man we both love.

My orgasm crests, and as slow waves of pleasure undulate through my core, creating a ripple effect against the walls of my pussy, I throw my head back farther, lost in absolute ecstasy.

Swell after swell crashes over me, each one stronger than the last.

Just when I think I've peaked, another wave crashes over me.

Levi doesn't let up, lapping at every drop I give him.

Then, as he presses his thumb to my clit, I shatter.

A second orgasm stacks on top of the first, this one hot and fiery and *wet.*

So. Fucking. Wet.

"*Fuck yes.* Soak me, Daisy. Give me every fucking drop."

My mind short-circuits and my body turns to goo.

I lose sense of time and place. My breathing halts. I'm nothing but sensation. Surging, never-ending, sopping-wet sensation.

When I finally stop coming, I steady myself on my elbows and peer down.

My heart lurches when I take him in. Shit.

He wasn't joking.

His face is practically dripping, his white T-shirt so soaked I can see the distinct lines of his shoulders and upper chest through the fabric.

He's also grinning, a proud, deeply satisfied expression painted on his face. Clearly, I don't have anything to worry about. He fucking loved it.

"That was incredible." Angling forward, he places a gentle kiss between my thighs.

I scrape my nails against his head, my mind still a scattered mess after the intensity and deliciousness of my orgasms. We should clean up. I should offer to return the favor. At the very least—

"Fucking seriously?"

Levi and I both startle and plummet back to reality.

Chapter 17

Levi

Heart hammering, I scramble to my feet like I've been caught committing a crime.

"Hey, man. We thought you were asleep." I swipe at the slick evidence coating my lips and chin. Not that it matters. My T-shirt is fucking soaked from the way Hunter just squirted all over me.

"I was." He narrows his focus on our girl, who is still propped on the vanity. "But I woke to the sound of screaming and jumped out of bed in a panic."

"Oh." Hunter slides off the vanity and quickly adjusts her robe. "I'm so sorry we woke you." She hurries to him, but before she can touch him, she freezes, like she's not sure what to do.

He takes her in, glare softening, and opens his arms.

I deftly sneak forward and snatch my hat from the floor in front of him and pull it on backward. With one more swipe at my mouth, I smile, but the expression I get in return is hard and surly.

"Did you lick all my cum out of her?"

I snort, shocked by the crudeness of his question. If he wants to banter, I'm game.

"Sure did." I preen, assaulted by the memories of the way our woman just unraveled under my tongue. Fuck. She came so hard. She came twice. And she squirted all over me. I doubt there's a single drop of him left inside her pretty little cunt. "Jealous, G?"

Instantly, his face is a mask of rage.

Shit. Clearly, we're not bantering. My heart sinks and my mind spins in confusion as I try to think of what to say or do to recover.

"Of course I'm fucking jealous." He grips Hunter's arms possessively, shooting daggers my way.

Fucking hell.

He's legitimately upset? I thought we were joking around. My cheeks heat. Dammit, how the hell did I misread the situation so badly?

"*You* got to be there for her when she found out about the baby. *You* were fucking there, and I was fucking clueless. I don't know if I'll ever fucking forgive myself for not being what she needed. Of course I'm jealous. I jolt awake and come in here, only to find you eating her out, after I filled her up—"

"Whoa. G. Hold up." I raise both hands. He's talking about that summer after high school, I think, but also about what he just walked in on, I guess?

"Don't tell *me* to hold up. Maybe you should have fucking held up and thought about your actions before you went down on her while I was asleep in the other room."

"Greedy—" Hunter spins out of his arms and grasps his hands, her lips turned down and her eyes pleading.

I straighten to my full height. "You're not the orgasm police."

Eyes flaring with indignation, he sidesteps Hunter and charges toward me. Now I've gone and done it. I always did have a knack for earning myself a beating.

I'm braced for a solid punch in the gut, but Hunter utters, "*Stop it,*" and Greedy freezes, his hands still balled into fists at his sides.

With a huff, she slinks between us and puts a palm on each of our chests. "We can't do this."

"We can't do *what?*" Greedy snaps.

My hackles rise in response to his tone. He can give me whatever shit he wants to dish out, but if he thinks he's going to talk to her like that—

Hunter sighs and drops her hands, looking first at me, then at G. "This." She waves a hand between us. "We can't bicker. We can't let jealousy get the best of us or allow a simple misunderstanding to steal what little joy we have these days."

Greedy huffs indignantly, his shoulders rising and falling.

She turns to him, brows raised, and shakes her head. "I'm sorry we woke you. I'm especially sorry that we made you think something was wrong. But Levi and I are allowed to be together without you, just like you and I were together without him earlier. Just like the two of you are allowed to be together without me."

His whole being deflates. "I didn't mean you two can't be together—"

"I know." She steps closer and hugs his bicep, resting her head on his shoulder. "But Levi doesn't know what happened earlier, so he's not at fault for the, uh, mess we made just now."

G hangs his head, his defenses finally lowering.

"Let's go to bed," Hunter encourages.

We haven't technically resolved anything, but it's probably for the best. It's late. Everyone's on edge, our emotions too raw. A good night's sleep will make a difference. I hope.

We reach a silent agreement. Without a word, I let Greedy exit first, then we both follow our girl back to the bedroom.

The next blow doesn't even hurt. I'm beyond the point of no return.
Dark spots dance in my vision.
Good thing I'm already lying down.
Upstairs, Mama's praying.
She never sticks around to witness what he does.
She flees and she prays.

She prays and she prays, yelling to the heavens, adding to the chaos without partaking in the physical blows.

There's more darkness than light in front of me now.

I lift my hand. At least I think I do. I can't see the fingers in front of my face.

My wrist snaps back. Bones crush to dust, grated into the ground by the heel of a heavy boot.

Throat gargling, I open my mouth in a scream. No sound comes out. No one comes. I count backward from ten, and I pray, too. I beg and I plead and I pray that the darkness will eventually come.

"Levi!"

The sharp sound of my name cuts through the nightmare. My eyes fly open, and the first thing I do is lift my hand to my face.

Panting, I squint at the digits of my right hand. They're slightly crooked from the way they healed, but in the dark, it looks as if they're all there.

"Leev, you okay?"

It takes a few more blinks to remember where I am.

When I shove up to sitting, it finally comes to me. Crusade Mansion. Decker's enormous bed. I'm sandwiched between Greedy and Hunter. Both, I realize, are awake and staring.

"Yeah, sorry," I croak. "I didn't mean to wake you."

"We don't care about that." Greedy gently rests a hand on my forearm. "Are *you* okay?"

Hunter sniffles, wrapping herself around my bicep in a suffocatingly tight hug. "You were screaming, Duke. We couldn't wake you."

Fucking hell.

Sometimes, the nightmares trap me in my own head. It sucks, but honestly, I don't stress about them anymore. They're just a fact of life for me. Memories I'll always have to endure, made worse by how deeply I sleep.

I've always been a heavy sleeper. It started young, probably as a way for my body to protect me after a really bad night. As a kid, I passed out on the floor more times than I can count—from pain and exhaustion, mostly. It's how I coped. The only way my brain could truly rest.

Once I passed out, he would stop. Once I gave up, he'd leave me be. Deep, uninterrupted sleep was my only guaranteed reprieve, like a reward at the end of it all.

"It was just a nightmare," I force out. "Just a nightmare." I keep my tone even. I need them to know I'm fine. I don't want them worrying about me. That version of my life no longer exists. I'm safe. Loved. Even if we hit a rough patch like we did tonight, this group is solid. I think.

Greedy rolls until he's sprawled out with half his body on top of me, pressing his pelvis into mine and pinning me to the mattress. On a broken whisper, he says, "You said my name just now."

My heart splinters at the brokenness of his tone.

"I'm sorry, man." I slip both hands under my head and tilt my chin up.

"Sorry? Why are you fucking sorry?" G rolls his hips against mine.

I don't think he means to do it. It's likely a product of the way his body has tensed up. Even so, my dick twitches with interest.

I push down those thoughts and rack my brain for an explanation. "I—" I struggle to reply.

Hunter snuggles closer, and instinctively, I lower an arm and stroke her hair.

"I don't know what you want me to say," I finally admit.

Greedy is silent, his presence foreboding, looming over us like he's the king of the fucking world. He is in my book. At least one of them.

"Don't apologize," he grits out. "I'm the one who should be apologizing to you." He bends low, causing our bare chests to brush together.

The sensation of his skin against mine sends shivers dancing along my spine.

"I'm sorry I reacted so poorly earlier," he rasps. "I'm especially sorry if my reaction triggered your nightmare. Leev, I love you. I swear I'll always try to do right by you."

His nose brushes mine, his still minty breath warm on my face. His tongue darts out to wet his lips, but he doesn't kiss me. He waits for me to close the distance between us.

"I love you, too." I leave it at that. It's hard for me to accept apologies, even when I've been wronged. Probably because I was rarely shown true remorse growing up.

Now, though, I deserve his apology, and Greedy deserves to give it. So I make myself take it. Craning up slightly, I press my mouth to his and glide my tongue along the seam of his lips until he opens for me with a satisfied groan.

After a moment, I break away and turn my head to kiss Hunter, too. Her kiss is softer. Sweet and tentative. Like she wants to provide what I need but doesn't want to take away from what Greedy has just given me.

"What can we do for you?" G implores.

"Stay just like this."

He's still practically on top of me, and Hunter is curled up against my side.

"Stay like this and don't let me go."

It's the last thing I remember before drifting back to sleep.

Chapter 18

Hunter

A gentle, rolling wave washes over me as I hover in the space between sleep and alertness. Drowsiness and a deep ache in my low belly urge me to rest. To lay down my defenses. To give up the fight, at least for a little while.

It's no use.

My mind is awake, unwilling to allow the rest of me to remain in that dreamless state.

I crack my eyes open, finding a dark room. A large hand encircles my bare hip, anchoring me to the mattress as prominent hardness presses into my backside.

Sione.

Wordlessly, I weave my fingers with his and bring our hands to the front of my body. His enormous frame engulfs me. In this moment, I feel so warm. So safe. So wanted and loved.

With a sweep of my hair to one side, he kisses my bare shoulder.

"What time is it?" I ask through a yawn.

"It's the between time," he whispers back.

With my free hand, I search the mattress in front of me but find nothing but cool, smooth fabric. Greedy and Levi must be up already. They've been rising early to work out before everyone goes their separate ways for the day. Spence hasn't come to bed yet—if he plans to at all. I swear he has to be sleeping in Decker's office or maybe just sticking to the upstairs bedroom. He's barely set foot in here since his surprise reveal.

"What's the between time?"

Sione nudges his nose along my neck, cuddling closer.

"Hundreds of years ago, our ancestors slept in two shifts. There was the first sleep—the deep, restful slumber that happened around nightfall—then there was the second sleep. It usually occurred from first light to sunrise. There weren't specific times assigned to the sleeps, but they existed in all cultures all over the planet. This was before electricity and artificial light."

Levi was right—everything Si says sounds like poetry. I could listen to him whisper in the dark all damn night.

"The between time isn't widely recognized anymore. But it was universal then. It was a time for having a small meal or stoking a fire. For checking on the children. Making love in the moonlight. It was a time to connect in the ways that weren't possible during the hustle and bustle of the day."

"Do you want to make love, Si?" I ask, vulnerability coating my every word. I didn't wake up needy and wanting—I woke feeling warm and safe and loved—but if that's what the between time is for, who am I to argue?

He lifts our joined hands and kisses my knuckles. "I do not. I just want to hold you and give our souls this quiet time, when the demands of the world and the others don't feel quite so loud."

His rejection soothes rather than stings. Sione has a way of making me feel loved and cared for well beyond the physical needs of my libido.

I don't need the same attentiveness I get from Levi or the insatiable longing I feel with Greedy. I don't need him to connect with my darkness the way Spence is so keen to do. With Sione, I don't have to overthink anything. Our souls intertwine and soothe each other with little conscious effort.

I curl into him, not stopping until I'm met with the hardness of his bare chest and thick thighs. "Hold me, please."

"Always, Mahina. Always."

We fall asleep like that. For how long, I couldn't say. When I wake next, I roll over and prop my head on my hand.

Sione's eyes are still closed, but I know he's awake. Present and ever attentive.

"Can I ask you something?" I whisper.

"Of course."

"Do you like it here?"

He slowly opens his eyes, the brown of his irises so deep it's almost impossible to distinguish in the dark. "I like being with you," he says, his word choice as deliberate and thoughtful as ever.

"But not here? In North Carolina?"

He rolls his lips, considering his answer.

"This place—it feels like a stopover." He takes my hand and plasters it over the center of his chest. "Nothing is settled. The uncertainty of what lies ahead clouds my ability to like it or dislike it. I do like the people," he murmurs. "Your other men. Your friend and her cohort. I really like being part of something bigger than myself. This group dynamic—whatever we are and whatever we're going to be—I like it a lot, and one day, I may even grow to love it."

Not a single part of his confession surprises me. I expected this kind of response, though I couldn't have articulated it on my own. I can always count on Si to be fully transparent and steadfast. It's why I feel so secure in our relationship.

For long moments, we study each other in the darkness, letting the reality of the situation somber the mood. With a sigh, I roll to my back.

He follows and rests a hand on my cheek. "Please don't be upset, Mahina. It's not a good use of my energy to form feelings about something so temporary."

Without my permission, his words take root deep inside me, and dread washes over me.

"Temporary?" I breathe. I can't shut down. I won't. We need to be honest with each other now more than ever.

Despite my brave determination, a single tear still rolls down my cheek.

Sione catches it with a thumb, then pops the digit into his mouth.

"This place. These hardships. They're all temporary, Mahina. They're temporary, but they're no match for our love. Nothing could tear me away from you."

Understanding soothes the unraveling edges of my anxiety. I wiggle my way close, and he settles on his back again, holding me and letting me shed a few more tears as I come to terms with the reality that it's not over. We're not done. We still have a fight ahead of us, one way or another.

Eventually, he drags me so I'm sprawled over one side of him, his hands finding my low back, his strong knuckles digging into the tense muscles there.

Tension seeps out of me as he works. With every exhale, another pound of stress drops away. I'm not ready to rise and greet the day, but I'm not sleepy, either.

"Have you talked to Kitty lately?"

Though it's dark, Sione's entire soul lights up with joy at the mention of his grandmother. "I have. Two days ago when you were at school. My sister arrived last week. All is well, and she sends her love."

An idea springs to mind then. Something to look forward to. Something to hope for.

"Could we go there soon? All of us? Together?"

He splays a hand between my shoulder blades. "You want to go back to Lake Como?"

"Yes," I answer without hesitation. "I miss it so much."

"You are aware there's a lake right outside the steps of this house, yes?" he teases.

I nip his tatted arm, latching on and biting.

"Okay, okay!" He laughs. "Don't break the skin."

He flips me onto my back, pinning me to the mattress with his hips, and tickles me senseless.

Our caresses turn needy, our bodies reacting to one another as we twist and turn in the sheets.

"I'll take you to Lake Como this summer, Mahina. As long as the others agree." He brushes his lips against mine. He finds my neck next, then my collarbone. He peppers kisses down the center of my chest until his head comes to rest on one hip, his hand cradling the other.

"Do you require more sleep?" he asks.

I stretch my muscles, giving myself a moment to consider.

"No."

"Good." He springs off the bed and offers me his hand. "I want to walk along the beach and explore the shores of these waters."

I take his hand, allowing him to help me out of bed. "I'm pretty sure it's so early the moon will still be out." A quick glance at the bedside clock shows it's only 6:10 a.m.

"Even better."

Chapter 19

Levi

"Pass that over when you're done," I tell G as he wipes down the thirty-pounders he used for today's workout.

He holds the spray bottle out and tips his chin, gesturing to Spence, who's on the treadmill. "Should we wait for him?"

He's been doing interval sprints and fielding what sound to be very aggressive phone calls since we got here.

"I need two minutes," he announces before immediately going back to his phone call—and bursting into a full sprint on an incline.

I don't know how long I watch him before Greedy steps in front of me and presses two fingers to the bottom of my chin, closing my mouth for me.

"You're kind of a man whore. You know that, right?"

I snort. He's not wrong. With a slow, sultry up and down, I drag my gaze over his body. "I like to think of it as being generous with my appreciation."

He grins in response, his eyes dancing.

I smile right back, relishing in the much-needed lightness of the moment.

Unfortunately, the lightness doesn't keep.

"Listen, Leev." He roughs a hand through his sweaty hair. "About last night—"

"It's fine." I shrug. I'm not all that interested in getting into it with him again.

Last night, I felt like a kid who'd been caught with his hand in the proverbial candy jar, being scolded by a displeased parent. Except when I was a kid, I got beat rather than scolded. Beat for things I did wrong. Beat for things I didn't even do.

It's nothing new, a person going off on me for no rational reason, though I'd be much happier if I never had to experience that again. Especially if the lashing is coming from one of my partners.

Hunter put a stop to the bickering and called G out on his shit last night. We had our moment after my nightmare subsided. I woke up with his morning wood pressed against my ass, and he's been playful with me for the last hour.

It's over; I'm ready to move on.

"It's not fine." He crosses his arms over his chest in a way that makes his defined biceps pop. "None of my anger or frustration last night was about you, and yet you took the brunt of it. I was wrong to react that way, and I'm sorry. It won't happen again."

A weird lump of emotion lodges itself in my throat, making it hard to breathe. It's unfamiliar to me, the way he's taking responsibility for his actions. My parents sure as hell never said they were sorry for lashing out. Maybe because they weren't. Or maybe because they didn't think I was worth the effort.

I bite down on my tongue to stave off the emotion swelling like a wave inside me.

Receiving a genuine apology shouldn't send me reeling, but fuck if it does.

"Yeah. Okay. Thanks," I grit out, shifting uncomfortably from one leg to the other while trying my best to avoid his gaze.

I'm staring at my feet when he grabs me around the neck, pulls me close, and thumps me on the back so hard I wheeze.

He brings his lips to my ear, and when his warm exhale meets my sweat-soaked skin, I shudder. "You don't have to thank me, Leev. I was wrong. I owed it to you, and you deserve better than my bad attitude coming at you out of nowhere."

He licks his lips, the tip of his tongue brushing against my neck, then kisses me softly and cuffs the back of my neck with both hands.

"I won't always get it right. But I promise to apologize when I fuck up. And I'll never stop working to do my best for you and for her."

Fuck. Why is this so hard? How emotionally damaged must I be if receiving a genuine apology hurts more than letting the moment pass?

A throat clears behind us.

We break apart and find Spence stationed near the door.

"Hate to interrupt your little gym date love fest." He waves a hand flippantly our way.

Jealous bastard. As if I wasn't on my knees for him against the back wall a few days ago.

"But I'm heading out to find Hunter and get on with my day. Cheers."

Greedy shoots me a concerned look, then takes off after Spence. "What do you mean *find* Hunter?"

When we catch up, Kabir is stalking through the main living space, not bothering to acknowledge Gerald and Mrs. Lansbury in the kitchen or Locke and Joey sitting cross-legged on a couch in the great room. I wave but don't stop as I follow my guys.

"Spence," Greedy huffs.

Finally, he glances over his shoulder. "She's outside somewhere." Deftly, he unlocks a sliding glass door and yanks it open, inviting in the frigid morning air. "I just need to put eyes on her."

Fair enough.

G and I step out onto the upper deck behind him, and a chill instantly settles in my bones.

Through chattering teeth, Greedy says, "I'm gonna need a long, hot shower after this."

With a squeeze of his hip, I take a step closer. "I might need to join you."

His lips tip in a smirk, lust dancing in his eyes.

It's hard for me to accept a verbal apology. But I have no issue with letting my boyfriend show me how sorry he is in the shower.

"There," Kabir announces, once again breaking us from our spell.

Kabir Spencer is a cockblock and a flirtation killer. I'd like to believe it's unintentional, but with his attitude this morning, it's hard not to suspect that he's doing it on purpose.

I look past the yard to where he's pointing, barely making out two people walking hand-in-hand along the rocky shore of the lake.

Inching closer, I join Spence at the rail of the deck. Greedy steps up on my other side.

Silently, the three of us watch as Hunter and Sione trek toward the house.

She doesn't look like she's wearing enough layers for this weather, but I bite my tongue and refrain from making any comments.

Spence and Greedy do not.

"Where the hell is her jacket?" Greedy gripes.

"The man is not stupid." This from Spence. "They have climate in Italy. There's no way he thinks her attire is reasonable for this weather."

I roll my lips to hold in a laugh.

Greedy clutches the railing and squeezes. "We're really letting her go to this Combine without us?"

For a moment, no one speaks.

It's safe to assume we all would prefer Hunter stay close, for her safety and for our own self-assurances. But...

"She'll be with Si," I remind them. "And Kendrick and Joey. She'll be okay."

"Are we sure?" G presses.

Kabir sighs, the sound echoing the resignation I feel surrounding the situation.

"I'm not sure of anything anymore," he admits. The confession is so candid, so intimate, it takes me by surprise.

I survey him, taking in the torment, the worry, and the self-loathing he harbors behind those stormy irises.

A few beats pass, then he snaps out of his revery and reverts back into his usual self.

Shoulders pulled back and chin high, he clears his throat. "Hunter will be as safe as possible, given the situation. I've hired three investigators to tail Magnolia around the clock. I've increased tracking efforts as well."

Greedy guffaws, the sound echoing in the early air. "Did you put an actual tracker in her, too?"

It's a sarcastic barb. But, of course, Spence answers it at face value.

"Not in her, no. But I have access to her phone, car, and all her correspondence. I'm also monitoring everyone who enters your father's home and all the individuals and businesses she's interacted with since returning to South Chapel. If she leaves the house, I'll know about it. If she hires anyone to do anything on her behalf, I'll be fully aware. She will not make a move against us that we do not see coming. Not ever again."

The heavy silence returns. I mull over his confession as I watch Hunter and Sione. At this distance, I can see he has an arm around her, holding her close. She's focused on the ground in front of her mostly but looks up and graces him with a wide smile from time to time.

All I want to do is protect her. Keep her safe. Make sure Magnolia can't fucking touch her. Does Spence intend to do more than just follow Magnolia around until she dies? Are we going to keep playing defense or finally switch it up and take the offensive lead?

As if he can read my thoughts, Greedy says, "You have a plan, I assume?"

Heart in my throat, I study Spence, eager for his answer.

"I *always* have a plan."

"As one of many people negatively impacted by your most recent plan, is there anything we should know?" With fire in his eyes, Greedy stares down the man who upended our world just a few days ago. He doesn't blink, even as Spence holds his gaze and makes no indication whatsoever that he's going to open up to us.

Tension sizzles between them. I'm half tempted to take a step back and remove myself from the line of fire, but if this escalates, it might be better if I'm ready to intercept.

"Spence."

Kabir's eyes shift to me, then back to G.

"Garrett."

I smack my hand over my mouth to hide the laugh threatening to escape me.

"Look..." Spence turns and sets his focus to where Hunter and Sione are now standing in front of the house. "I've been playing it too safe. I've taken the path of least resistance, obtained the lowest hanging fruit. But now we are beyond trying to reason with or simply deter Magnolia St. Clair-Ferguson."

He braces his hands on the wooden railing and drops his head in an uncharacteristically vulnerable display and sighs heavily.

"I will not fill you in on the plan I'm devising. To tell you would be to implicate you."

He lifts his head and meets my gaze first before looking to Greedy. The storm clouds in his eyes send my blood pressure spiking.

"What I am prepared to do is not something I want either of you to have to live with."

G pounds a fist against the top of the railing, rattling the support we're leaning against. "God dammit. You don't have to do this alone. We can help."

"I'm not doubting your ability or willingness to contribute, Garrett. I'm attempting to preserve the version of you our girl loves and needs during this time."

G simpers, but he doesn't push back. These two may be at odds with one another for years to come. But there's no denying they trust one another. It's that trust that makes this family possible. I just wish Spence didn't have to carry so much on his own.

Taking a different approach, I splay my hand on Spence's lower back and move it up and down his spine in smooth strokes.

He stands taller but doesn't brush off my touch.

Warmth gathers in my chest as I take him in and wrap my head around what he's implying. "You shouldn't have to do something that will be hard to live with either."

He steps away quickly, breaking contact. "Your concern is endearing, Champ." His tone is far too nonchalant. "But I have the help I need. Have a nice day at school, you two."

With that, he turns and walks away.

Chapter 20

Hunter

"Joey, let's go."

"Coming," she calls through the closed door of the hotel room. A moment later, she curses, her voice more muffled, as if she's turned around.

Sione and I have been waiting in the hallway for nearly five minutes. I shoot him an apologetic look, but he just smiles assuredly back at me.

A crash resounds from inside the room. Ouch. That sounded painful.

"Is she always like this?" Si muses.

"Honestly? No. I have no idea what's gotten into her."

With a huff, my best friend swings open the door and shifts her clear backpack onto one shoulder. "Ready."

She's wearing wide-leg jeans and a fitted bright red crop top, her hair plaited in two French braids.

"Where's your lanyard?" I ask.

She slaps a hand to her chest and squeaks. "Shit on a crumbly cracker. Hold on..." She whips around and disappears, only to reemerge a few seconds later, lanyard in hand. "Okay. Now I'm *really* ready,"

"After you," Sione insists.

As Joey and I head toward the exit, he discreetly checks that the hotel room door is truly closed and locked.

I link my arm with my best friend's as we walk, giddy to experience this occasion with her.

The NFL Combine is a multi-day event. Yesterday, Kendrick got registered, completed a physical, and attended a mixer with other running backs hoping to be drafted. Today, he'll be on the field showing out, and tomorrow's events will take place in the weight room.

He was vibrating with excitement at the end of day one. Earlier this year, there was genuine concern he'd have to answer to criminal charges ahead of the draft. He took the fall for Locke when he was in a tight spot, despite knowing how it could affect his future.

Thankfully, no charges were ever brought up. I never pushed Joey for information, so I couldn't say whether it all worked out or whether Kylian took care of it quietly in a way only Kylian can.

Joey's cohort is a force, that's for damn sure. Between Cap's money and connections and Kylian's hacking skills and resourcefulness, they excel at getting shit done.

I'm so happy for Kendrick. I love seeing him in his element. We've heard his name whispered dozens of times since the weekend started. He's clearly one to watch. He's the running back to beat and a top draft pick contender.

Despite how incredibly this event is going for him, nerves and frenetic energy roll off Joey in waves.

"Babe. You have to chill the fuck out," I tell her, going for playful as we stride down the concourse of the stadium.

She whips her head around, her bright blue eyes widening. "Fuck. I know. I'm sorry. I'm trying, I swear." With a long breath in, then back out, she gives her head a little shake.

Flovely.

I didn't intend to make her feel bad. I thought she would laugh it off or sass me back, then finally relax a smidge. Clearly, she needs more than quippy banter in this moment.

Interlocking my fingers with hers, I give them a squeeze. "I'm sorry. I shouldn't have said that. What's going on?" I don't let go of her as we search for the seats Kylian assures us are the best to view Kendrick today.

Plopping into a seat, Joey releases a long, tortured sigh.

Sione, who followed several strides behind us, giving us privacy, coasts his hand down my arm, startling me. "I'm going to sit a few rows back, if that's okay."

I turn to take him in over my shoulder. "Are you sure?"

His reassuring smile is as brilliant as it is sincere. Gosh, I love this man. My period started two nights ago, and he's been over-the-top attentive in caring for me. His calming presence has been felt and appreciated by both Joey and Kendrick this weekend as well. He even performed reiki on Kendrick last night as a way to help him recover and mentally prepare for today.

With a nod, Sione explains, "She needs you. I'll be right up there. I'll join you when the timing feels right."

I settle in beside my friend, worrying my lip as she fights back tears and focuses on the field. "Talk to me."

Without taking her eyes off the synthetic turf, she finally says, "I can't stop thinking about Decker. He was supposed to be here, too." Head lowered, she slumps, defeated.

"Joey." I wrap my arms around her, pouring all my love into the awkward sideways hug. "It's not your fault."

"But it is. I'm *literally* the reason he's not going pro," she retorts.

Fair. Decker upended his entire life last semester when he held a press conference and outed himself for using prohibited substances to enhance his performance on the field.

The truth is that he wasn't the one using. And the people who were using peptides—Kendrick and Locke, who both suffer from chronic illness and pain—needed those therapies to stay well. By drawing the attention to himself, he ended his father's reign over his life and effectively absolved the others from ever having to deal with the fallout.

It was Decker's choice in the end, no one else's. His Big Decker Energy took control, and he did what he deemed necessary for those he loves.

Their lives are better, safer, because of it. It was the right thing to do for himself, for her, and for their cohort. Joey must understand that.

"Decker went into that press conference with his eyes wide open. He chose you. He loves you. There's no way he'd give you up or change the course of the last few months for anything, least of all football. If you called him right now and asked him, he'd tell you the same thing."

She sniffles, then cracks her knuckles in her lap. She's quiet for a long moment, but eventually, she whispers, "I know you're right. But I still can't shake this feeling."

Little by little, guys take to the field. There are hundreds of them, all dressed in fitted athletic shorts and cut-off shirts with initials and numbers across the front. Thankfully, the stadium is covered by its retractable roof today. Kendrick and Kylian researched it in advance to ensure he didn't need to request an accommodation, since sun exposure affects his chronic illness.

Whistles blow on the field, and after half a second of silence, a cacophony of sound and excitement rings out. Anticipation and eagerness zip through the air like lightning. The entire stadium develops a heartbeat, the field pulsating with energy.

I don't care about any of what's happening on the field, though. Right now, all I care about is Joey. I'm singularly focused on my best friend. I'd do anything to take away her pain.

Bumping my shoulder into hers, I try to keep her talking. "Don't leave me hanging, sister. What can't you shake?"

She sniffs again, scrubbing at her cheeks, and sighs. "The feeling that Decker's going to wake up one day and realize he gave up everything he ever wanted, and in return, all he got was me."

My chest aches so painfully I have to fight the urge to rub at the spot. Her despair is so deep, it sinks into the marrow of my bones. The idea that Decker could ever regret *anything* when it comes to his wife is preposterous. He loves her so deeply. His devotion is what romance books are made of, dammit.

Though I'm relatively certain this isn't really about Decker or what he gave up.

This is about Joey. About the value she puts on herself.

Levi is similar in that respect. He retreats into himself when he's worried he's not worthy. His insecurities and the lack of stability and love he experienced as a child still inform his view of himself and his sense of value among our group.

I rise to my feet and plant my hands on my hips. When Joey lifts her head to meet my gaze, I give it to her. "Josephine Crusade, you are the motherfucking prize. Decker didn't sacrifice his dreams for you; he leveled up, and he damn well knows it."

The smallest hint of a smile tugs at one side of her mouth. But then she schools her expression, shakes her head, and shifts her gaze back to the field. "Sit down."

"Nope." I pop the *P* for emphasis. "I can't. Sorry. I won't sit down until you claim your crown, queen."

"*Hunter.*"

"Josephine." I offer her my most saccharine smile. "You're the prize, babe. Say it with me. You're the motherfucking prize."

She buries her face in her hands and shakes her head.

"Come on," I encourage, grabbing her wrist and dragging her to her feet.

"Say it. Say it. *Say it.*"

She huffs, her expression pure annoyance. "Hunter."

This song and dance again? Fine.

"Josephine." I refuse to give up on her. Not now. Not ever.

"Jojo!"

In unison, we turn to the field.

Kendrick is in front of the section where we're seated, shifting from leg to leg as he stretches.

"K!" I call out, waving obnoxiously despite being just a dozen rows back. "Tell this woman she's a prize."

His brows shoot up, his gaze scorching as he takes in his woman. "You're not *a* prize, Mama. You're *the* fucking prize. Now get down here and let me see you."

Joey shoots me an incredulous look, then schools her features, dabs at her eyes, and jogs down the stairs.

With a spring in my step, I follow.

By the time I reach her at the railing, she's leaning over it, grinning as Kendrick whispers in her ear. They exchange quiet *I love you*s before she pulls away—but apparently, Kendrick's not done with her.

"Mouth," he demands.

She obeys quickly, and when she bends down again, he grips her face and kisses her in earnest.

"My favorite fucking prize," he murmurs before he pulls away.

By the time she rights herself, she's grinning from ear to ear.

Mission accomplished.

Linking arms once more, we take the stairs back toward our seats. Sione watches our every move. His calm, steady gaze is a gentle caress. I make eye contact and give him a small smile, but he doesn't make a move to join us just yet.

"Today is Kendrick's day," I remind my best friend as we slip back into our row. "You get to be here for him, so really be here, babe."

She pulls me in for a hug. "You're right. Why the hell are you always right?" As she releases me, she gives me a smirk, though the expression quickly softens. "You're my best friend, Hunter. I don't know what I'd do without you."

"Right back atcha, babe."

Chapter 21

Sione

I glance from my phone to Hunter and back again several times, typing, deleting, then retyping the message I intend to send to the others. They did not ask that I send status updates, but I have a hunch they'll appreciate the effort. Finally, I settle on a short, direct note.

> **Sione:** There is nothing of significance to report. All is well.

My phone immediately buzzes.

> **Spence:** Hunter has eaten? The girls are with you now?

He's a bit of a mother hen, as Hunter would say. While I appreciate his concern, it's not a great use of energy to provide solace for his overbearing nature.

> **Sione:** Everyone has eaten. The girls are together, and the athletes are taking the field.

> **Greedy:** They're together? Where the hell are you?

Sighing, I quickly snap a picture and send it to the group.

> **Sione:** I'm sitting a few rows back. Giving them space. They have not left my sight, I assure you.

> **Levi:** LMAO. What the hell is she doing?

Squinting, I study the photo I just sent. In my haste to satisfy their inquiries, I wasn't focused on what was happening. In the image on my screen, Hunter is standing above Josephine, hands to hips, like she's giving her a lecture.

She's still standing when I look at her now. Every other word or so carries up to my row. She's talking animatedly about a prize, attempting to comfort Josephine, I think. Although her methods are unorthodox, it seems.

> **Spence:** From what I can make out, Hunter is trying to cheer up Josephine.

How the hell does he know that?

A sense of foreboding washes over me. Straightening, I scan our surroundings. Spence is here. Or at the very least, he has access to this space.

> **Sione:** Where are you?

Do they not trust me? Is my attendance at this event a deceptive ruse? Just for show? I thought my purpose here was to be the eyes, ears, and general protection our cohort deemed necessary.

> **Spence:** Sitting in Decker's office. Why?

With a frown, I study his response. It's an honest reply. Despite the communication method being digital, his answer harbors no deception. But what is he playing at?

> **Sione:** Because, clearly, you can see and hear their conversation. How?

> **Greedy:** Yeah. What the hell?

> **Spence:** Settle. I simply turned up the volume on the feed Kylian provided. Decker hired protection detail. A man named Corbin. He must be wearing a camera. He appears to be to the left of where the girls are sitting.

Relief surges, but then ebbs just as quickly.

> **Greedy:** Why is protection detail necessary, and why didn't Si know about him?

Garrett's subtle vote of confidence warms me through.

> **Levi:** Shady AF. Si had us covered.

Levi's declaration causes my heart to float in my chest.

> **Spence:** I concur. I didn't know about Corbin until this morning. Kylian informed me when he sent me the streaming link. I believe it was at Decker's insistence.

Sighing, I accept the situation for what it is. Decker Crusade has his own concerns about this event. I won't sit in judgment of what he deemed necessary for his woman and his sanity.

The knowledge that amongst our cohort I was enough is like a warm, loving embrace.

During my interaction with the other men, the girls skipped down to the railing to speak to Kendrick. Now, as they flounce back up, I lock eyes with Hunter.

Love flows through her from her heart to my soul.

All is well, and all will remain well under my watch.

Chapter 22

Greedy

It takes every ounce of restraint I possess not to reach down and squeeze my throbbing erection.

Spence knows it, too, based on the way he's taunting me as he pleasures Levi like his own personal fuck toy.

He's my fuck toy, too, dammit.

"Garrett, tell him how sexy he looks, writhing in my lap while I stroke his massive cock."

I can't. I won't do it.

I bite my tongue and fight back a moan.

Shit.

I did not expect the night to take this sort of turn when Spence suggested we relax in the hot tub.

Hunter, Si, Joze, and Kendrick are at the Combine for the weekend.

Locke, Kylian, and Decker are at the cabin, like they planned. No one else is expected on the isle until Sunday. Even if someone was approaching, we'd see the lights from the boat cutting across the lake long before they arrived.

We're utterly alone.

Heat and desire stir in my core, heating deep inside me, burning hotter by the second.

Levi and Kabir are going at it like animals.

Resisting, I ball my hands into fists so tight the blunt ends of my nails dig into my palms.

Resist. Resist. Resist.

"Fuck, this throat is sexy." Spence grips Levi's curls and uses his hold on my boyfriend to turn his head to one side, exposing the thick veins and tendons framing his Adam's apple.

He licks a line up Levi's neck, his eyes locked on me as he does. "Tell him his throat is sexy, Garrett."

Levi whimpers—he fucking whimpers—and I lose it.

With an angry thrash, I clamor out of the water and sit on the ledge. Cold air licks at my skin. Shivers rack up and down my spine.

Good. Maybe the frigid air will quell the inferno searing through my veins.

"Kabir," Levi groans, making a half-assed attempt to escape the other man's hold.

They're sitting back to chest, facing me. I can't see exactly what's happening under the bubbles, but I can fucking picture it based on the way my boyfriend keeps thrusting forward.

His Royal Highness probably has his fancy ring-clad fist wrapped as tight as it'll go around Levi's cock. Does he know how much he likes having his tip squeezed? Or that if he pulls on his sac, he'll leak precum?

I should be the one pleasuring him.

I want it to be *me*.

"What?" Kabir gives Levi a mock innocent look. "Do you want me to stop, Champ?" He latches on to his neck and sucks.

I'm struck with a phantom sensation, as if he's biting me instead. In response, pleasure zips straight through my balls.

Levi groans, shutters his eyes closed, and curses. "Don't you dare fucking stop."

I should leave. Let them have this moment. Give them some privacy.

But no matter what the logical side of my brain tells me to do, I can't walk away. Hell, I can't even look away as my boyfriend and his lover work each other into a frenzy.

"Garrett."

Head snapping up, I search Kabir's face through the steam. The lights from the tub shine on it in an eerie, erotic way.

"Safe words are always available, even for an observer," he reminds me. "Say red, and it all ends, full stop."

Blood rushes in my ears.

Fuck.

I appreciate the reminder, but despite what logic tells me, I don't want either of them to fucking stop.

I clear my throat and wait until Spence focuses on me again. "And if I don't want to be just an observer?"

Levi's eyes fly open.

Spence gifts me his most devilish grin. "Why don't you swim over here and see for yourself?"

I slice through the water—arousal and desire fueling each slick step I take.

Nothing's changed. I am who I am and I feel what I feel. My attraction is solely focused on the two people I love most.

But seeing one of them being pleasured like this? By someone else? Twists me up inside. I'm aching to contribute, to make him feel good, too.

Kabir trails a line of kisses up and down Levi's neck.

With hazy eyes, Leev watches me as I approach. "You're sure?" he croaks.

"So fucking sure," I promise.

Kabir lifts his head, his brows pulled low. "Are you taking over or tapping in for a teamwork scenario?"

"Teamwork." The decision is an easy one. I want in, and I want to do it together.

"Have you let your boyfriend claim your ass yet, Champ?"

Body going still, Levi peers up at me, clarity returning to his expression. "Not yet."

"But you want him inside you, I presume?"

Fuck. I palm my cock through my swim trunks, staving off the little pulses of pleasure that are already rolling through my length.

"Have me, G. Fucking make me yours."

I step up close, pressing my bare chest against Levi's and sucking on the tender spot on his neck Kabir has been particularly fascinated with.

"You're sure?" The question is a hopeful prayer spoken directly into his skin.

He tips his head back onto Spence's shoulder and sighs. "So fucking sure."

My legs bump into the Brit's as I trail kisses down Levi's chest.

"You'll help me?" My words are quiet, tentative, but I need Spence's consent for what I have planned for our boy.

He nods, his grin mischievous, but his eyes sincere.

"I've never done this before," I confess. "I don't know how to prep him, or—"

I rear back. Shit. We don't have any lube.

"Here." Spence holds out a small plastic bottle before I can even articulate my concern.

The man came prepared. Can't fault him for that.

All the jealousy and turmoil I felt moments ago seeps out of me and drifts away like the steam rising off the tub. Levi wants me to fuck him. Spence is willing to help me.

With shaking hands, I grip Levi's neck and lean over to whisper in his ear. "Turn around, baby. Let me see the tight ass I'm about to claim."

With a fierce kiss to my lips, he stands, turns, and straddles Kabir.

Only now does it hit me that I'm going to have to get extremely close to Spence to make this work.

Surprisingly, I'm okay with that. It's reassuring, knowing he's here with us. He has way more experience with anal than I do, and I trust him for guidance if I need it.

"First, you want to play a little," he says, his hands in Levi's hair. "Tease his hole with your fingers or your tongue. Make him pucker and clench around nothing for a while."

Levi groans, and mentally, I'm right there with him. This is going to be the most exquisite kind of torture.

As instructed, I trace one finger between Levi's cheeks, making long sweeps between his legs so I can choke his cock in my fist, too. All the while, he makes sounds of pleasure, groans and grunts and heavy sighs. Each one spurs me on.

Eventually, I feel brave enough to spread the globes of his ass and swirl my tongue around his hole. With a hiss, he jolts, but a heartbeat later, he sinks back onto my tongue, desperate for more.

I take my time, teasing him like Kabir said, alternating licks and probes of my tongue with long, tight strokes of his heavy cock.

Levi clings to Spence, whimpering into his neck and occasionally kissing him on the mouth while I eat his ass. When I pierce him with my tongue and lap at his tight little hole as it clenches and opens ever-so-slightly for me, his whole body spasms.

"Fuck, G. I could come just like this."

No. No fucking way.

I abandon his ass, grip the damp hair at his nape, and pull his head to the side so I have access to his throat and mouth. "Not a chance. You're coming with my cock buried to the hilt inside this perfect ass, or you're not coming at all."

With a chuckle, Kabir snags the lube from where I abandoned it on the side of the tub and holds it out.

"Allow me to hold him open for you." Ring-clad fingers dig into the meat of Levi's ass cheeks as he spreads him wide open.

I savor the fucking sight while I coat my fingers with lube. With one to start, I ease past the tight ring of muscle.

Levi breathes through the intrusion, and Kabir murmurs praise in his ear. When he starts to rock back on my hand, I add a second finger.

Levi quickly acclimates, his curses loud and needy. "More," he tells me, voice husky, and peers over his shoulder.

Kabir continues to hold him open. I savor the sight, commit this to memory, and take my sweet fucking time swirling my fingers inside the man I love.

"More like this?" I tease. Head lowered, I run the tip of my tongue around the pleated opening. "Or more like this?" I add a third finger, then thread my free hand between his legs and gently tug on his balls.

"Fuck me, G. Please. I need more of you. I want all of you. I need you in my ass, *now*."

I pull back and peer over his shoulder. I think he's ready. I know I'm more than ready. But I don't want to rush things. I need to make sure I get this right. Focused on Spence, I ask, "Is he—"

Kabir chuckles darkly and cuts me off before I get the question out. "If he's begging for your cock, then give him your fucking cock."

Fuck. Yes. This is it.

I remove my fingers, drench my length with lube, and give it a few quick strokes. For good measure, I squirt a bit more around Levi's asshole, too.

Nerves erupt in my gut. This is a first for me, but it's not for him. Concerns about pleasing him swamp me. I just want to make him feel good—

"G. I swear to god. If you're gonna overthink it, I'll ask Spence to fuck me instead."

My gut clenches in response to his threat. Fuck no.

With more intensity than I intended, I slam into him. Those simple words were what I needed to snap out of my mini spiral and force myself back to this moment, where my boyfriend's begging me to fill his ass and fuck him for the first time.

"Is this what you wanted, Leev?" I rasp. "For me to claim you?"

"Yes. *Fuck*. Yes. Right there. That's perfect."

I pull out, then drive right back into his ass, entranced by the sight of his body taking me so well. I maintain my pace and focus on the angle at which I'm railing him. If he says it's perfect, then I won't change a thing. Each thrust of my cock into his tight channel is bliss. Every time I pull out, I miss him, miss it, miss *us*.

"You feel incredible." I slide a hand up his damp chest and grip his throat as I fuck him. "You feel so fucking good on my cock, Leev."

He clenches around me, and I see stars. Stars and moons and brilliant light.

"Do that again," I beg.

He does. Over and over, using his tight ass to choke my dick, giving me pleasure even though I'm the one fucking him.

"Baby, can you come like this?" I grit out.

I'm close. Embarrassingly close. I can't wait to blow my whole fucking load deep inside him, then watch the remnants drip out when I pull back.

He has to get there first. I'll do whatever it takes.

"Keep hitting that spot." He gyrates, matching me stroke for stroke. "I'm close."

"Want me to fill him up on this end?" Kabir asks. He could easily shift up onto the side of the hot tub and choke Levi with his cock.

A burst of liquid heat courses through me. Fuck. As much as I like the idea of spit roasting my boyfriend with his lover, I want it to be just the two of us this time.

"No. Don't touch his cock, either. I want to make him come like this."

I slam into him hard, driving as deep as I can get over and over again. Our breathing hastens. Our balls slap together, sending extra sparks of pleasure and pain with each strike. I'm dangerously close to careening over the edge, and I don't know how much longer I can hold off.

Finally, Levi whimpers, "G," and my body seizes.

"Let go for me, Leev. Come, then I'll fill you up."

He collapses into Kabir's arms, his body spasming and convulsing with pleasure.

I unload in his ass, wave after violent wave coursing through me, my desire erupting.

When we're both well and truly spent, I pull back and take in his gaping, empty hole, watch the rim of it spasm with pleasure and the first drips of cum leak out.

Palming his ass, I bend low and kiss the place we were just joined. "Hold it in for me, baby."

Instantly, he clenches.

"Good boy." I kiss his puckered hole once more.

"Got a bit of a breeding kink going there, Garrett?"

Straightening, I shoot Kabir a deadpan glare. "That, or I don't want to pay to have Decker Crusade's hot tub deep cleaned. It's a couple hundred bucks to fully drain and sanitize one this size. Did you know that, Spence?"

His eyes flare in realization.

Yeah, fucker. I saw what you did in my hot tub at the cabin last month.

"I know now," he concedes. "And thankfully, I caught most of this one's load as well." With a smug smirk, he points to a white-streaked towel sitting on the edge.

Well played. Well played, indeed.

Levi's cheeks are bright red and his eyes are shining when he turns to face me. "That was incredible." He presses a hard kiss to my mouth.

With a groan, I open and sweep my tongue against his. "Leev, I love you. I love you so fucking much."

He beams, his expression full of pride and affection. Fuck. I want to make him smile like that for the rest of our lives.

"I love you, too." The moment the last word is out, a yawn catches him by surprise.

"Come on, you two." Kabir's already out of the hot tub, a towel wrapped low around his waist. He didn't get off, I realize. But based on his calm expression, he isn't overly concerned about it. "Let's go to bed."

We sleep out of order without Hunter here. But for maybe the first time since we got here, the three of us are all in bed at the same time.

Levi barely made it out of the shower before he passed out, crashing in the middle of the mattress. I took my time washing, reminiscing about tonight and fantasizing about doing it again, but this time with Hunter, too.

Spence was last to shower and last to bed.

He crawled in on the other side of Levi and immediately unlocked his phone. From here, it's obvious he's opened the tracking app he uses for all of us.

"You really should tell her."

Hunter still doesn't know about the tracker Spence put under her skin. It doesn't sit well with me that Levi and I are aware of it, but she isn't.

With a sigh, he gives the screen one more wistful glance. Then he sets the device on the nightstand and rolls onto his side, setting his sights on me.

He brushes one of Levi's damp curls off his forehead, the gesture so tender and natural I'm not sure he realizes he did it. It calms me, knowing that Levi has him, too. Sure, jealousy rears its ugly head sometimes, and I don't always know how to navigate what we're doing, but Levi deserves this kind of love. I want him to have it all.

"You never thought of chasing after her when she left for London?" Spence asks, still mindlessly playing with Levi's hair.

A grimace crosses my face before I can stop it.

"Wait. You did pursue her, didn't you?" Kabir guesses.

"Technically, no." I heave out a long breath. "But I bought a plane ticket three separate times that fall. I sat on the bench the entire football season. I couldn't get my head in the game. I bombed two midterms and had to drop those classes to save my GPA and maintain athletic eligibility. Oh. And one night, I got piss-ass drunk, shaved my head as part of a Shore Week dare, and got a scalp tattoo."

"A *what*?" He gapes at me, wide-eyed.

"A scalp tattoo." My heart thumps painfully. Why the hell am I telling him this? Not even Levi and Hunter know my secret. "It's a scorpion. Right here." I brush enough of my hair back to reveal the hints of black ink that extend from my temple to behind my ear.

"What the hell does that have to do with Hunter?" Spence presses.

Good fucking question. It was stupid to do it, but I was young and I was so heartbroken I couldn't see straight. I didn't know what else to do with my grief. I couldn't move on. I thought tattooing a lethal scorpion surrounded by arrows would somehow give me the closure I so desperately needed.

I was wrong.

"Do you know why I call her Tem?"

"Not a clue."

"It's short for Artemis."

"The Hunter." He smirks. "Clever boy."

I fight back a smile. "Legend goes that Artemis fell in love with Orion, but mortals and gods couldn't be together, so they were doomed from the start."

"Star-crossed lovers?"

"More like the moon and her star. Artemis is goddess of the hunt, but also goddess of the moon."

Spence tilts his head and hums. "And here we have Sione calling her Mahina."

"Exactly. There are several canons of the mythology, but in one version, Artemis unknowingly strikes Orion with her arrow and kills him outright. In another, he died because he jumped in front of a scorpion to save her and her mother."

This time, Spence's reaction is much more measured. "Did you just mansplain Greek mythology to me, Garrett?"

"I mean—"

Spence eyes me playfully. "I was taught that Orion was so boastful and braggadocios, he wouldn't shut up about his ability to kill all living creatures on the planet. So Gaia sent the scorpion to eliminate him as a threat once and for all."

Damn. Of course the British billionaire with his fancy prep schools and higher education knows more about mythology than me.

"Potato, pa-tah-toe?" I offer with a shrug.

That makes him snort. "Sure, Garrett. If it helps you justify your impulse *scalp tattoo*, I'll gladly prescribe to your version of the story."

For a long moment, we're silent, nothing but Levi's soft snores rising and falling between us. I try to settle in for the night, but it's no use. I can't shake the feeling I might not have a chance like this again anytime soon, so I go for it.

"Hey, Spence?"

"Yes, Garrett?"

I lie flat on my back, keeping my gaze laser-focused on the ceiling. "I never imagined sharing her with anyone. But seeing how thoroughly and devotedly you love both of them, I couldn't imagine it being any other way."

His response is a contented hum that sends a peaceful warmth flowing through me. The love we share isn't about the two of us at all: it's about the two people we both love. I see that now. I see so clearly how we can work in tandem, support each other, and love them both, together.

Chapter 23

Hunter

Nerves skittering, I slide out of the passenger seat of the truck and smooth my skirt over my legs. In the space of what feels like a heartbeat, Levi's around the cab and by my side.

He's right there. We've got this. It's the mantra I've repeated since I opened my eyes this morning.

"If this isn't the strangest case of déjà vu." I take his proffered arm, and the two of us trek toward the entrance of the South Chapel Country Club, each step heavier than the last. We've been here before. We've walked through these doors together. Years ago, we even shared secret, silent heartbreak in this place.

Levi squeezes my arm, then places a kiss atop my head. "Except this time, we're in control. We've got this, Daisy. We know what we're facing and how this is likely going to go."

"Abysmally," I snark, unable to slow my quick breaths or calm my hammering heart.

"Hunter." Gently, he tugs on my arm and stops in front of the large wooden doors. "I love you," he tells me, brushing my hair behind my ear. He hovers close, his lips ghosting over mine. "We'll go in there and play pretend, then walk out and forget about this whole charade. Spence has a plan. I trust him, and I know you do, too. They can't touch us, baby. We've got this."

I let his words sink in and soothe the rough edges of my anxiety.

He's right. This is just pretend. It's all part of a bigger plan.

We'll get through this.

I hope.

It isn't until after formal greetings and half-assed hugs, between the hollow small talk and loaded glances aimed at my flat stomach, that I realize we've walked into a trap.

Or perhaps a series of traps.

First, there are the subtle word choices and attempts to get me to slip up, all orchestrated by Magnolia. Then we're served a four-course prix fixe menu, with courses offered at regular increments with no indication of what will arrive next.

The meal starts with a champagne toast, which I politely decline.

Then comes the baked brie wrapped in puff pastry, a personal fave that I have to pass on.

The main course consists of poached eggs and hollandaise. This one may be okay, but it feels like a gamble, nonetheless. What did Kylian say about undercooked eggs the other day?

Avocado toast covered in sprouts comes out last.

By the time a small cup of espresso is placed in front of me, I'm ready to burst.

Levi nudges me with a knee under the table. When I lift my gaze, his blue eyes swim with questions.

Swallowing hard, I slip my phone from my bag and send him a quick text.

> **Daisy:** It's a trap. Alcohol... coffee... soft cheese and drippy eggs. She's trying to catch me in a snare.

Levi stares incredulously at the device he's cradling in his lap.

> **Duke:** Or she's trying to give us all food poisoning...

Despite my panic, I snort. Quickly, I cover my mouth with my napkin to disguise the sound.

Thankfully, the mothers are engaged in hushed gossip about a man at Mrs. Moore's church that Magnolia apparently knows, too.

> **Daisy:** These are all foods a pregnant woman should avoid.

> **Duke:** Really? How do you know that?

My throat tightens. How much of the truth do I want to type out in the middle of the country club dining room? Today feels heavy enough without scouring old wounds.

Levi nudges my foot, pulling me from my racing thoughts.

When I meet his gaze, he gives me a soft smile. He won't push, it says. He's more than willing to listen, to comfort, to handle the darkest parts of me. He's here, and he's not going anywhere.

I type out my explanation and hit Send before I can lose my nerve.

> **Daisy:** After I lost the baby, I spent a lot of time reading pregnancy blogs and articles. I even downloaded a pregnancy app when I was in London. Maybe it's strange, but it comforted me, learning what I could about pregnancy and allowing myself to daydream about the what-ifs.

Levi keeps his focus fixed on his phone for an extended length of time, his eyes scanning the screen as if he's reading it over a second time and maybe even a third.

Rather than reply, he grabs the leg of my chair and pulls me over until I'm crowding his space. Then, eyes blazing, he captures my chin, tilts my face up, and kisses me on the forehead.

"I'll never forgive myself for letting you leave for London that summer, knowing what I knew." The confession is shared so quietly there's no way anyone else heard him.

Instead of arguing, instead of reminding him that I didn't give him much choice, I simply lean into him, resting my forehead against his, and breathe him in.

We're here. We're doing this. We have a plan, and it will work.

"Aren't you two just sticky sweet?" Magnolia's comment is more cutting than kind. "Do you want anything else, darling? You barely touched your food, and you are eating for two, after all."

I straighten in my chair and rest my hand on my lower abdomen. "I'm full," I declare. "Maybe even feeling a bit queasy," I add for good measure. "We should probably get going soon."

"Oh," Levi's mom murmurs. "Not yet. There's still so much to discuss."

That's what I was afraid of. Nevertheless, I plaster on a smile and sit patiently, waiting for the other shoe to drop.

"Thank you for hosting today, Magnolia," Mrs. Moore says, her hands fisting the espresso cup like it's a lifeline. She takes the tiniest sip and pulls a face when she tastes the dark roast.

"Now that we've eaten, I think we should talk about the most pressing matter at hand." She gives me a pitying look, her lips turned down, but as she glances at Levi, the expression turns to one of disdain. "We need to finalize wedding plans."

With his hand clasped around mine, he rests them on the table, squeezes, and calmly turns to face his mother head-on.

"Hunter and I don't intend to get married."

Mrs. Moore's eyes double in size. "Levi Joseph Moore," she hisses through clenched teeth. "Your intentions do not matter. If your... *girlfriend* is with child, then you will do the right thing and marry her in the church."

Lips pressed together, I breathe deeply, keeping my expression even. Levi can handle his mom without my input.

Magnolia sits back and sips her espresso as if she doesn't have a care in the world. She channels nothing but mild interest, and I suppose that doesn't surprise me. She doesn't believe she has a real dog in this particular fight, so clearly, she's more than happy to let Mrs. Moore tantrum and carry on.

"I'll do right by Hunter and our baby, but your version of what's right and my version are not the same." Levi sits up straight, his shoulders wide as he squares off with his mother.

There's nothing particularly threatening about his posture or his tone, but hot damn does his authoritativeness cause heat to pool deep in my belly. More bossy Duke, please and thank you.

Mrs. Moore clearly does not share the sentiment.

Her tone is hushed but still sharp as she cries, "My grandchild will *not* be a bastard. You liked her well enough to take her to your bed, Levi. Now be a man and take her to the altar."

Levi's bright blue eyes narrow, his expression seething.

"Watch your mouth when you're talking about the mother of my child."

Shit. Now he's being authoritative, bossy, *and* possessive on my behalf? I'm going to be a puddle of want by the time we leave this luncheon.

With a renewed sense of calm, he plainly swallows and lifts his chin. "We don't want to get married right now, and there's nothing you can say to make us change our minds."

Mrs. Moore's face reddens to the color of a cherry tomato. Hands splayed on the linen tablecloth, she angles closer. "Then you need to consider leaving town before she starts to show. People will talk." She turns to Magnolia now, her eyes wild. "Neither of us should have to deal with the shame their irresponsible, impulsive choices will bring."

Magnolia sits up straighter, her wrinkle-free face straining with fresh tension. "Hunter can't leave." She locks her deceptively bright green eyes on me. She's staring at me, through me, even. Not really seeing me at all as her mind works overtime.

For a moment, she's frozen like that. When she snaps out of the trance, she shifts in her chair, her back ramrod straight.

"Hunter won't be leaving. My husband is the chief physician at Lake Chapel General. She'll receive the very best care here. She can't leave. I won't allow it."

Mrs. Moore lets out a strangled cry. "Think of her reputation. Her *future*."

"Mom, *stop*," Levi grits out. "Hunter is my future. And I'm hers. Your opinions are just that—opinions. This is *our* life, and we'll live it how we see fit."

I reach for him, feeling surprisingly calm as the group talks about me and around me. Levi's steadiness and protectiveness bring me a shroud of peace. I don't have to run anymore; I don't have to fight alone.

Soon enough, we will walk out of here with our mothers temporarily mollified and Magnolia off our case.

"Hunter. Darling."

Soon, but clearly not soon enough. Here we fucking go.

"I don't share Patricia's sentiment that you should be shipped off because of your *condition*. But I must insist you settle back in at the house as soon as possible."

A thread of unease winds through me. "The house? What house?"

A shrill laugh escapes her. "Our house, of course."

Ah. Dr. Ferguson's house. *Flovely*.

My general unease transforms into nauseating dread as I inhale and meet her eye. Taking a page from Levi's big book on boundaries, I hold eye contact and say, "That won't be happening."

She gasps as if I slapped her. "But darling, you must—"

With a shake of my head, I stand, cutting her off. Levi quickly follows suit. "I'm good. We have a place to stay for the semester."

"The semester? You're not planning to take time off from school?" She smirks as if she's outwitted me.

Brow cocked, I stare. If she thinks she's "caught" me, she has another think coming.

"The semester is only sixteen weeks. It will be over long before the baby is born. I can take time off next year as needed."

There. That should suffice.

As if reading my mind, Levi grasps my hand and guides me away from the table. "Thank you for the meal," he says over his shoulder, always the southern gentleman. "We'll be going now. And since we're clearly not aligned about our future, there's no need to contact us again anytime soon."

Chapter 24

Hunter

Between the drive and the boat ride back to the mansion, there's no way I'll make it home without a bathroom break. As desperately as I want to get out of here, I need to pee before we leave.

I use the restroom quickly, wash my hands, then lean over the sink to snag one of the soft cotton towels. My shirt rides up slightly, and the hard, cold surface presses into my stomach, making me shiver.

I straighten, drop the used towel in the hamper, and instinctively rub one hand down my torso.

What would it feel like to have a sweet little baby growing inside me?

Emotion catches in my throat and heat gathers at the backs of my eyes.

Without overthinking it, I lift the hem of my blouse a few inches, exposing the skin of my stomach, and rest my hand above the hem of my skirt.

A baby. In my heart of hearts, I want to have a baby.

I've never let myself want this. It's always been a means of self-preservation. Though I allowed myself to ruminate on the what-ifs of my pregnancy, I never allowed myself to consider if and when I might carry a child again.

Avoiding even considering the prospect was easier than facing the pain.

Now?

Now is different.

Now is not then.

Now, when I think about being pregnant, a peaceful, hopeful warmth blooms inside me. It's subtle, almost too indiscernible to notice. If I try hard enough, though, I find it. It's there.

It's there, and day by day, as we pretend, it grows louder.

Is it foolish? To want to get pregnant now?

Despite feeling like I've lived multiple lifetimes in the last three and a half years, I'm still young. My relationship is... less than conventional, to say the least, and really fresh and new in a lot of ways.

I don't want to miss out on moments and memories with my guys. Only...

What if those moments and memories would feel even more magical with little ones to experience them with?

I'm still staring at my stomach in the mirror when a vision forms in my mind.

It's a mini Levi, with blond hair and big blue eyes, grinning and reaching up for me. Another baby toddles toward me. A sweet little girl with Sione's complexion and soulful smile. I think about what Greedy's kids might look like. I imagine a beautiful baby with Kabir's skin tone and his steely gray-blue eyes.

By the time I've envisioned all versions of our future family, there's no question left in my mind: I want it.

I want it now.

Despite the timing and the newness and all the reasons we could and should wait, I want to have kids sooner rather than later.

I could still go to school this semester and take summer classes. I'd probably need to take one or two semesters off after and consider balancing in-person classes with online when I do go back to make my schedule more manageable.

Continuing to work toward my degree even while starting a family is not impossible. People do it all the time. Others do it without nearly the number of resources I have or multiple partners to share the load with.

I want it.

I want it so badly I ache.

I yearn to see my guys as parents. They're all different, yet each brims with love. The fears about my own inadequacies around motherhood vanish when I consider co-parenting with Greedy, Spence, Sione, and Levi. Any child would be lucky to be born into our cohort.

The future isn't hard to imagine, and the yearning for it in my heart is palpable. The realization that this could be my life slams into me like a tidal wave of desperate hope.

I don't just want to get pregnant because of the situation we're in. I really, truly want this.

I'm grinning so wide my cheeks hurt. I'm energized and alive in a way I can't quell. I can't wait to get home. I can't wait to talk to the guys.

With a cleansing breath, I drop my shirt and smooth out my outfit. Then I turn on my heel. When I push through the door that leads to the foyer, I find Magnolia looming outside, lying in wait.

When she spots me, her features barely change, thanks to all the Botox she's injected into herself. But there's still a discernible antagonistic twinkle in her eye.

She opens her mouth to speak, but before she can utter a word, I breeze past her.

"Darling, wait," she calls after me.

Not a chance. I pick up the pace and round the corner, intent on leaving her behind before she can so much as get another word in.

When Levi comes into view, I exhale a big sigh of relief, then break into a smile so big it hurts. For the first time in a very long time, I'm not running from something. I'm running *to* something.

To the men I love.

To the future I want to share with them.

To my dream of growing our family and filling our lives with all the joy, laughter, and chaos that's sure to ensue.

To happiness and hope.

To a more brilliant version of my life than I've ever let myself dream of.

I don't look back or give Magnolia another thought as I take Levi's proffered hand and leave the country club with him by my side.

Chapter 25

Greedy

Despite the ball of anxiety ping-ponging against my internal organs, I'm trying to keep it together.

Subtly, I slide my phone out of my pocket, pretending to check the time. They've been gone for three hours and twenty-five minutes. That's reasonable, given the distance, the drive, and the seclusion of the isle. Nothing to worry about yet, I tell myself again.

Spence is sitting in the enormous lounge chair to my right. He's got an iPad in hand, and he's focused intently on the screen.

Sione's on my left, eyes closed and breathing slowly. He's not fidgeting or playing with his phone. In fact, I'm not sure he's even awake.

I check the time again, then give in to the urge to send Levi a text.

> **G:** You guys okay? ETA?

"Stop stressing," Spence huffs.

I shoot him a glare, but it does me no good when I discover he's still staring at the screen in his lap.

"They'll be here soon enough. They don't need any additional distractions."

"Caring about someone isn't a distraction," I bite back.

He turns and arches a brow. "Tempting them to read and reply to a text when they're en route is the definition of a distraction."

Frowning, I rack my brain for a retort, unwilling to admit, even to myself, that he's right.

Sione snickers, his lips curving up into a smile while his eyes remain closed. "If you have the tracking software pulled up, at least let Garrett see the screen, too."

Spence's eyes flare in indignation. Looks like I'm not the only one obsessing about their whereabouts.

As he tilts his iPad screen toward me, my phone buzzes against my thigh.

> **Leev:** Docking now. We'll be there in 2 minutes.

Though relief floods my system, I still can't resist checking the radar on Spence's device.

On screen, six beacons glow, all in close proximity, rather than the one I anticipate. Three of them are right on top of each other; the other three are approaching the mansion.

The key on the side of the screen reveals who's who.

Pink for Hunter.
Blue for Levi.
Purple for Sione.
Green for me.
Red for Spence.

The one labeled "Internal" is black. I can only assume it's the tracker Hunter still doesn't know about.

At the thought of it, disquiet filters through me. He's got to tell her.

A minute later, the door to the media center opens, and Hunter bounds into the room.

Instantly, I'm on my feet, sweeping her up in my arms and willing my nerves to finally settle.

"I'm so happy you're back," I say into her hair, tears of relief flooding my eyes. I cup her wind-kissed cheeks, warming them with my palms. I kiss each one, then her forehead, her nose, and her lips. Then I pull her in tight once more.

I hadn't fully realized how keyed up and anxious I was until now.

But they're here. They played their parts perfectly. They're home, and now they're safe.

A few feet behind Hunter, Levi stands, his hands shoved into his pockets.

I drag Hunter with me as I lunge for him. Cuffing the back of his neck, I kiss his forehead and hold him as tight as I'm holding our girl. "I was so worried."

He slings one arm over Hunter's shoulder. "It wasn't all fun and games," he hedges. "But we did it. It's over. We don't have to worry about either of our moms for a while now."

"Duke didn't take any shit from either of them." Hunter's green eyes glimmer with pride. "He was polite, of course, but I don't think Magnolia or Patricia will be eager to get together again anytime soon." She cups the back of his head and gently brings it to mine, then nuzzles into his chest.

"Today was tough, but this girl's tougher." Leev plants a kiss on the top of her head. "She was brilliant. Everything went as smoothly as it possibly could."

Fuck.

The adoration the loves of my life have for one another fills me with tenderness. I'm so damn grateful Levi was there for Hunter today. That they were there for each other. I'm proud of them for facing off with their moms and navigating what had to be a really intense showdown.

"Perhaps if you released them, Garrett, they could be welcomed home by other people also anticipating their arrival?" Spence says.

The three of us share a look, staving off laughter at his expense. Spence may wear armor made up of a prickly attitude and aloof exterior, but deep down, he's just as fucking soft as me.

Levi breaks away from our trio, strides across the room, and yanks Spence to his feet, capturing his mouth in a searing hot kiss. The Brit's iPad clatters to the floor, but he doesn't so much as flinch.

I'm entranced as I watch them, visions of our hot-as-sin night in the hot tub last week flashing in my mind.

Hunter releases a little whimper of approval.

"My thoughts exactly," I mutter.

When they break apart, Spence starts in with a barrage of questions. He wants a detailed account of the luncheon, down to the lines of questioning from each mother.

While Levi does his best to patiently answer each one, Hunter makes her way over to Si, who stands and gives her a tender, coaxing kiss. He loops his arms around her protectively, and she slots into place against his chest like she was made to be there.

I drink in the moment, reveling in the love swelling in my chest. The ache it causes is new, unexpected, and more than welcome.

Nothing feels as good as this. Being together. Embracing the love, lust, and deeply seated trust we've established among ourselves.

I've never felt as seen, loved, and whole as I do in this moment.

I'd give anything for each one of the people in this room.

I'll give *everything* to ensure we get to live the happily ever after of our dreams.

"Since we're all here"—Hunter turns in Sione's arms, casting her gaze to the carpet—"I want to talk about an idea I had. Something that affects all of us."

Nodding, I return to my seat. Levi joins Spence on the oversized lounge chair. Sione returns to his place as well.

Hunter remains standing.

She inhales deeply, taking her time, then exhales at an even slower rate. She rolls her lips and shifts from hip to hip, surveying each of us.

My gut twists itself into a knot. I can't help but feed off the anxiety radiating from her.

Finally, just as I don't think I can stand one more second of waiting, she speaks.

"I think I should get pregnant. For real."

Chapter 26

Sione

The Brit's posture stiffens and his entire aura flickers like a candle being snuffed out in a windstorm. He jumps to his feet with startling speed and strides forward, getting right up in Hunter's personal space.

"Absolutely not," he snarls, hands wrenching through his perfectly styled hair.

He looks feral. Unhinged in a completely uncharacteristic way. It immediately puts my instincts to protect on high alert.

Rising, I hold out one hand to Garrett and Levi, silently signaling that I've got it.

"Spence." Hunter's voice is soft, one hand resting against her heart. "Hear me out—"

"Pregnant," he seethes, the word a poison on his lips. "That's not a fucking option. That was *never* part of the plan."

I sidle up between them, careful not to make contact but casting out a sense of calm to support them each individually. In my mind's eye, I encircle them both with healing, glimmering light.

It does little good.

"Magnolia already suspects that I'm not," Hunter argues, her lips turned down. "You should have seen her today. The way she looked at me... the way she kept trying to trip me up." A shudder racks through her, but it comes to an abrupt stop when she fists her hands on her hips and widens her stance. "Your plan is null and void if she doesn't truly believe I'm pregnant."

Spence sneers. "Null and void, my arse. She would appear *unhinged* if she implied that you aren't pregnant. She won't embarrass herself like that with her husband. He's seen the paperwork. They both have." He cracks his neck, tension still radiating off him in dark, angry waves.

Hunter takes a tiny step forward and lifts her chin. "And what happens when I don't show? What do we do when she asks to see ultrasound pictures or presses me about the due date?"

"She won't live long enough to ask questions."

Hunter's eyes go wide, then quickly narrow, her brows scrunched together in frustration. "What if she does? What then?"

Spence shrugs, regaining his composure with each passing second. He eyes me, then Levi and Greedy. The three of us haven't uttered a word. Out of shock or respect for their right to hash this out on their own, I'm unsure.

Spence sets his sights on Hunter again. "You aren't making a decision like this out of desperation. It's ludicrous to even suggest such a thing."

She rears back as if he's slapped her, and a tear crests her lashes. "You don't get to decide that for me." She scrubs at her damp cheek, then lifts her gaze to me.

"Breathe, Mahina," I remind her. "Just breathe." I stand still, holding space for her feelings without interfering.

When her bottom lip quivers and her next few breaths grow even shakier, I feel her pain in my soul. It's as if my insides want to escape my physical container.

"Come here," I urge, holding my arms open to her.

With a whimper, she crumples into me.

Spence huffs, the sound indignant.

Greedy and Levi make their way over, bringing with them a modicum of relief from the tension.

"What do you think?" Hunter, clearly not ready to let this go, peers up at me.

I waver between comforting her only and sharing my true thoughts. In the end, the highest good is found in the weight of the truth, even if it feels too heavy for this moment.

"I agree with the Brit."

With a small gasp, she stumbles back. She pulls herself together quickly though, her expression going calm and calculated. "Why?"

Sighing, I scrape my hair back and knot it on the top of my head to buy myself a few extra seconds. "A decision made from a place of fear will not serve any of us, least of all our future children. Creating life to spite someone is not fair to the soul of that child."

A strangled sound escapes Levi. "Whoa."

I side-eye him, silently conveying that I do not appreciate his commentary.

Thankfully, Garrett is gripping his shoulder and murmuring in his ear, no doubt reading the situation with a bit more care.

Hunter sniffles, then sucks in a slow, cleansing breath. Her eyes dance with unspoken words. I watch intently as she settles, her reactive urge to fight simmering as she comes back to herself.

That's my girl.

"What's on your mind, Mahina?"

She stands tall, takes one more deep breath, then looks to each of us before fixing her gaze on the Brit. "I truly want this."

"Help us understand." I ask the question before anyone else can speak or escalate the situation further. She deserves the opportunity to make her case. "What do you mean?"

"I... I want a baby."

The room is silent, although the reactive emotions of the group hum at the highest frequencies. There's excitement. Hope. Despair. Regret. The last one confuses me—it's raw and real, but I can't place its origin. Nevertheless, all feelings are valid. I respect what each person brings to the dynamic.

"I'm not doing anything out of desperation." She takes Kabir's hand. "I just got worked up before I could really explain."

He hums noncommittally. Irritation bubbles on low inside me. She didn't get worked up on her own. If not for his intense reaction, her thoughts may not have become so clouded. Accusing him of such won't serve any of us now.

"Tem…" Garrett slots in by her side, a hand at her lower back.

With a shake of her head, she holds up one hand. "Let me try and get this out."

He nods and stays put. The tension in the atmosphere rises again as, collectively, we hold our breaths.

"I've dealt with enough pain and joy and sorrow over the last few years to know who I am and who I want"—she looks at each of us, her eyes imploring—"I know what I want, too. I want this so badly. To grow our family. To have a little one to take care of and love on. Now. This isn't desperation talking. It's desire. In my heart of hearts, I want to have a baby."

"I'm in," Levi declares.

Kabir chortles, the sound dripping with disgust.

"You're always in," Garrett gripes, his jaw ticking and his eyes roving over the room, as if he's sorting through his thoughts.

None of us expected this. It's a lot, and we each have to handle it the best way we can.

Levi play-punches Garrett's arm. "Hell yeah, I am. You guys have awesome grandparents"—he nods at me—"a supportive dad"—he elbows Garrett—"and a shit ton of family money"—this directed at Kabir. "But when you're raised by shitty parents…" he says, zeroing in on Hunter, his eyes softening, "and you're given the chance to do better, you take it. Let's fucking take it."

For the first time since she said that word, *pregnant*, Hunter smiles.

Focused solely on Levi, she straightens. "You're in?"

His grin is so wide I fear his jaw will be sore as a result. "So fucking in."

Hunter releases a relieved, joyful sigh, but then her expression quickly turns sheepish as she looks to the rest of us. "The timing isn't great, I know that. We're all still figuring things out. Hell… we don't even have a place to live." She snaps her mouth shut, wrings her hands.

Garrett leans in, catching her attention, and gives her a subtle nod. "We're listening, Tem." His focus shifts to Kabir, and his expression goes stony, a clear warning.

When no one interjects, she takes another deep breath. Her aura settles, and sincerity flows through her. "I want to try to get pregnant. All this pretending and talk of what-if got me thinking, and now that the idea has formed, I know with absolute certainty: I want to try."

The authenticity of her statement is palpable. Judging by the way the others stare at her in awe, they feel it, too.

"If you get pregnant and your menses pauses, your condition may worsen." I'm not trying to warn her against it. I just want her to truly think this through before committing.

Lips pressed together, she nods. "I thought of that. But my PMDD may also improve while I'm pregnant."

Fair point. I've long wondered how the hormonal changes of pregnancy might affect her monthly moods. PMDD is a debilitating endocrine disease first and foremost, but it's considered a mood disorder as well.

All is well with my soul as I soak in her enthusiasm.

If she wants this—which I truly believe she does—I want this, too.

Two in. Two still out. There's another heavy pause amongst us. We're teetering on a precipice, so close and yet so far from consensus, it seems.

After a few more moments, the energy shifts again. It's sharp. Urgent. It's loaded and weighted and *sure*.

Garrett surges forward, his face alight. "You really want this?" He cups her face and grins.

She smiles right back. Tears leak from the corners of her eyes, but they're no longer tears of anguish. "I really, really do."

He smashes his mouth against hers, and she kisses him back with just as much intensity.

When they break apart, he runs his nose along her jawline. "Playing pretend is fun, but putting a baby inside you for real?" He groans, the sound deep and primal. "I want it. I want to fill you up and put a baby in you, Hunter."

"Wait. This would be a group effort, right?" Levi asks.

With a smirk, Hunter loops her arms around Greedy's neck. "Yes. As long as everyone wants this, too, I fully intend for it to be a group effort."

I don't allow myself the luxury of sorting through my own emotions. Not yet. The energy inside this room is too charged. It's impossible to distinguish where my life force ends and another's begins. I'll process my personal reactions later. For now, there are logistics to discuss.

"The full moon is in three nights' time."

"What does that mean?" Levi frowns, brows pulled low, clearly certain I've just taken the entire conversation off track.

"It means Hunter will ovulate in three days. If we want to try to get pregnant this month, it needs to be decided now."

Hunter's aura erupts with hope, her optimism and desire so intense, they breach my own energy shields.

Levi worries his bottom lip, but his mouth is tipped up, as if he can't stop smiling.

Greedy shifts his gaze from Hunter to Levi, then back to Hunter again.

Spence stands stock-still, his walls erected to full height, an impenetrable mass of projected indifference.

He shakes his head once. "We're not making this decision tonight."

"Why not?" Hunter releases Garrett and turns to Spence.

Before she can make it to him, his reserves combust into fuel, his repressed emotions bursting into flames.

"Because I *can't*." Fists balled and chest heaving, he storms out of the room, leaving us all shocked and jolted in his wake.

Chapter 27

Kabir

Full access to Decker's home office has been a godsend this week. I've made camp here for the last forty-eight hours, only vacating the space to use the bathroom and eat a few quick meals.

There's work to be done. There's always more to do.

That's what I'm telling myself.

My desire to hide away has nothing to do with Hunter's declaration or my deplorable reaction to her proposal.

I am ashamed of myself for losing my cool not once, but twice within the context of the conversation. Nevertheless, my feelings remain unchanged.

We are at an impasse; I am on one side, while my entire cohort is on the other. I don't trust myself to not lash out again should we revisit the topic anytime soon.

Three curt knocks on the partially open door pull my attention from the memo I'm drafting for the South Carolina Cougars front office. The merchandising ideas for the upcoming season are cheap and tacky. They have another think coming if they want me to sign off on these concepts.

After waiting the socially acceptable amount of time, Kylian enters. He closes the door behind him, then steps forward without preamble, hovering in front of the executive desk.

When I lift my gaze, he wastes no time.

"The armadillo idea is DOA. Jo is too fond of the creature. I can't risk it."

I stifle a laugh. I assumed it would be more of a hassle than it was worth to attempt to inflict leprosy on Magnolia. The diagnosis and antidote would likely come too quickly for it to be truly debilitating.

"Very well," I say, turning back to my computer. "Back to plan B."

Rather than take his leave, Kylian remains planted in front of the desk.

I take a cleansing breath, tamping down on my agitation, and remind myself that he is not privy to the issues I'm facing and therefore does not deserve the misplaced anger I'd very much like to unleash.

"Is there something else?"

He pulls up a chair and takes a seat.

Bloody hell.

I don't have the time or bandwidth for small talk.

But then I remember who I'm dealing with. In true Kylian fashion, he doesn't rely on the social modality, instead barreling forward with his agenda.

"You aren't with your cohort." Eyes narrowed, he scrutinizes me from behind the lenses of his glasses. "Haven't been for the last two days."

"And?" I press. I'm not interested in his general observations. If he has a question, he needs to come out with it already.

"Do you want to talk about it?"

My instinct is to shout no. To shut down and send him away. But I force myself to exhale, lean back in my chair, and, fingers steepled, consider his question.

Finally, I settle on sharing. Perhaps an external opinion will help me navigate the possibilities of what to do next.

"My cohort and I, we are in disagreement about how to proceed with a sensitive matter."

"You against them?"

Nodding, I shove down the frustration and betrayal that flare when I consider just how alone I am in this situation.

"Before we continue conversing, I need to know: would you prefer I listen without comment or ask questions as I see fit?"

I smirk. I very much value Kylian's genius-level hacking abilities and general intensity. His candor, though, never ceases to surprise and impress me. The world would operate in a much more efficient, productive way if everyone communicated the way he does. More Kylian Walshes in the world would be a very good thing, indeed.

"Please feel free to ask questions. The challenge may be of benefit to me."

When he nods and settles in, I launch into my story.

I tell him about how Hunter and I met and how we fell in lust. Though the way she fell apart is crucial to my explanation, I gloss over the most intimate details of her breakdown—those will only ever stay with me. I'm the keeper of her darkness, the holder of her lowest lows. I do share about how we fell in love as she found herself once more and admit that there isn't a version of her I don't love with every ounce of who I am. Once he has all that information, I breach the heart of the issue.

"Three years ago, I underwent a voluntary vasectomy so she would never have to stress about unintended outcomes of any of our encounters. Now, she wants to get pregnant."

Kylian's eyebrows raise above the frames of his glasses. He still hasn't commented, despite my desire for him to do so.

Eager for his input and frustrated to have not received it, I continue. "This request is not because she seeks a temporary solution to our problem. I see the yearning. I know her heart. Getting pregnant now would give her the opportunity to rewrite her story. The chance to carry a child to term. To chart a new path in her subconscious, to redefine what it means to be a mother. I get it. I understand where she's coming from. And yet... I just can't bring myself to get on board, given my personal situation."

He tilts his head from side to side, considering me. "Did she ask you to get a vasectomy?"

"No."

Deadpan, he asks, "Do you make it a habit of making life-altering decisions on your own?"

With a grunt, I push back and stand. Yes, I did this to myself. My past decisions have come back to haunt me. I have no one to blame but myself.

I pace the length of my desk, then pivot and backtrack. "Vasectomies are reversible." I pop the top button of my Oxford, and when I still feel like I can't breathe, I work the next one free. "I knew that if and when we wanted to try for a child, I could have a vasovasostomy and restore my ability to procreate."

"Noted." Kylian watches me pace, silent once more.

Anger bubbles in my veins. "Don't you see, mate? There's no time. She sprung this on me—on all of us—but there's no bloody time to undergo a reversal before the next full moon, let alone recover and confirm the surgery was a success."

Kylian continues to watch me pace, his intense scrutiny unnerving. Minutes pass before I finally break, desperate for him to give me something.

"Well?" I snap, my temper getting the best of me.

He holds up one finger. "Still processing." With those two simple words, he proceeds to sit in silence once again.

Over the next few minutes, my traitorous mood settles. I almost never lose my cool, but agitation and anger have been my default settings since the moment Hunter made her declaration.

Finally, once I've eased back into my chair and my temper has flatlined, Kylian leans forward in his seat. With a tip of his chin, he asks, "What would happen if you were in control?"

I gape. "What sort of question is that?"

"The sort that Jo asks me when I'm spiraling. Decker, too."

Fine. I'll play.

Closing my eyes, I hold tight to the modicum of peace I just mustered. "If I was in control, I'd tell her to be patient. That her mother won't be a threat much longer. That once Magnolia is eliminated, if she still wants to get pregnant, we can try." Then, though it takes all the strength I have to utter the words, to allow myself to be this vulnerable, I add, "I'd ask her to wait for me."

Kylian dips his chin in one succinct nod. "What I'm hearing is that you're concerned she's making a desperate choice and that, from a personal stance, unexpected emotions about not participating in the group procreation sessions have risen."

I scoff. "I would be participating fully in all group procreation sessions, despite my contributions' inability to garner the desired result. As for the desperation..." I rough a hand over my jaw. "I'm not sure. I believe her desire is genuine. She's smart, and she's self-assured and confident in her choices. But she makes hasty decisions, and they're typically grandiose and definitive."

"Was that how this was presented? That she had decided, and that was that?"

With a sigh, I shake my head. "No. She brought the idea to all of us. Her intended timeline is informed by her upcoming fertility window and by the intensity and depth of her longing."

"So it's not a hasty decision, but rather a situation that requires haste."

I scrub one hand down my face. "If I never hear the word 'hasty' again, I'll die a happy man."

Brows knitted, Kylian cocks his head. "What an odd thing to say." He shrugs, then continues. "So the only outstanding issue now is that you can't contribute fertilizer the way the others in your cohort can."

I drop back into my chair with a huff. This isn't helping. Nothing he's said has brought any semblance of calmness or given me any control over the situation.

"Are you going to be with her forever?" Kylian asks.

I scoff. If that isn't the most ridiculous question. "Yes."

"Do you expect the others to be with her forever as well?"

"Yes," I repeat without hesitation. "The five of us... we're endgame."

"Do you all want to sire children?"

Based on the enthusiasm expressed by the others when Hunter brought this up, yes. That does not soothe my defensiveness, though.

"Why does that matter?" I demand.

"Statistically speaking, the sequence of deposit, followed by motility and morphology of the specimen, are the greatest factors that will determine the paternity of a child."

"Meaning?" I press my fingers into my closed eyes.

"Even if you were fertile, there are four of you. Assuming everyone wants a shot—no pun intended; I don't do puns—the order in which deposits are made will likely determine the paternity of the baby."

I let this new information percolate. He's right. Regardless of whether we all want our "shot," only one man's sperm will be responsible for fertilizing the egg.

"Additionally, camera footage shows you've used the lower-level hot tub liberally since taking up residence here. That greatly impacts fertility, although the effects are short term."

My heart lurches. "You've got surveillance cameras on the hot tub?" I hadn't noticed them. Hadn't even considered it when Greedy and I played with Levi a few days ago.

Bollocks.

Although... Perhaps he can provide me with a copy of it to share with the boys. With their consent, we could allow Hunter to view it as well—

"There are cameras everywhere. Except in the bathrooms and bedrooms." His confirmation snaps me out of the fantasy forming in my head.

Bloody hell.

I already know the answer, because I saw it mounted in the corner with my own eyes, but I ask anyway. "In the gym?"

He nods, unabashedly maintaining eye contact. Bold choice now that I know he's seen Levi make a sloppy fucking meal out of my cock.

"Butler's pantry?"

That one elicits a grimace. "Yes, but I've taken that one offline for the foreseeable future."

"Meaning?"

He shrugs. "The threats to our safety via the pantry are minimal. It has no external entrance or exit. It does, however, make an excellent hideaway, as many have discovered. I could cope when it was members of my cohort or yours. But when Mrs. Lansbury and Gerald started making use of the space—"

"I knew it!" I laugh, allowing myself to revel in the much-needed moment of levity.

Kylian glowers and shakes his head, clearly not sharing in the amusement.

"It's a fair assumption that being able to contribute would not increase your odds of impregnating Hunter in a statistically significant way if you're not the first or second man to shoot his shot. Still no pun intended."

Steepling my fingers once more, I let his words fully take root in my mind.

"What is the benefit of her being pregnant with your child first?" he asks.

I consider it. The benefit? There is no benefit. There's longing, of course, but it's informed by my possessive nature and instinctive dominance. I may like the idea, but that does not mean it's in the highest service of our cohort.

"There's no real benefit, I suppose."

He hums. "Would there be a benefit if she carried Garrett Reed Ferguson the Third's child first? Levi's or Sione's?"

Emotion snags me by the shirt collar and squeezes like a vise. They would all benefit in some way.

For Garrett, there would be healing. He and Hunter suffered a joint loss. Although he wasn't privy to it for far too long, that does not invalidate his grief.

Levi could experience the sort of bonding and gentleness all humans deserve. During his formative years, he did not have loving parents or unconditional support. We all strive to give him that now. The presence of a child he fathered would only add to his sense of security and stability.

For Sione, there would be a deeper sense of belonging. His connection to our cohort is the most fragile, both because of his late arrival and his sexuality. I never want him to feel as though his role in our family unit isn't as significant simply because he does not desire physical intimacy with anyone other than Hunter. A child made in his mold could close the loop for him.

For each of them—for any of them—the outcome would be nothing short of beautiful.

I can picture it. Envision their happiness. If I close my eyes and let my mind wander, I swear I can even feel the joy and happiness we'll all share when each of them fathers a child.

Hunter will be pregnant with my child someday. For now, it must be one of them.

"Thank you," I say, sincerity dripping from the two simple words as my mind swirls with all the tasks I need to complete and words I need to say to my counterparts.

With a renewed sense of urgency, I rise to my feet. "I'll be busy for the next twenty-four to forty-eight hours. If you need me, please text." With that, I stride out of the office and pull out my phone.

I open the text thread the guys and I use and shoot off a message.

> **Spence**: I owe each of you apologies, and I owe the group my repentance for my behavior over the last few days. But time is of the essence.
>
> I'm in.
>
> Let's make it special. Meet me on the upper deck in an hour so we can discuss and make preparations for tomorrow night.

With a smirk, I hit Send.

We're doing this. We're really fucking doing this.

I travel only a few steps toward the primary bedroom before I nearly smack into Garrett.

Startled, I jolt back, noting that he's holding his phone in his hand as well.

With a cautious up and down, he tips his chin and smirks. "Got your text."

Right. I was fully prepared to start scheming about how to impregnate our girl. I didn't expect to be presented with the opportunity to make good on my promised apology. No matter. He deserves it. This has been a long time coming for the both of us.

"I want to wait for the others to fully discuss our strategy," I explain. "But first..."

I lean forward incrementally, making my intention clear. When he does not flinch or pull back, I wrap my arms around him and pull his chest against mine.

"I'm sorry," I whisper gruffly into his ear.

His body stiffens, but I hold on, desperate for him to hear me out and understand the gravitas of my sincerity. "Out of all that I must atone for and everyone I need to apologize to, you, Garrett Reed, are my top priority."

Pulling back, I hold on to his shoulders.

He doesn't turn his head or shy away.

"From the moment I arrived here in the States, I've viewed you as an adversary. I knew the power you held over our girl; I understood the connection you shared, the mutual loss you endured, and the significance of your relationship as one another's first. Those were all points I could never compete with."

"Spence, I—"

"Please let me get this out," I insist. Sighing, I drop my arms.

"When I arrived in the US, I never imagined we'd end up here. Loving the same people. Committed to a life that will always be intertwined. My love for Hunter, and now for Levi, is stronger than all the misplaced, envy-inspired animosity I harbored toward you. I'm sorry it's taken me so long to come around and to attempt to explain my heart. It's only recently that I've come to accept that this can and will work. That you and I are not in competition with one another. We are, quite literally, playing on the same team. I know your affections are tailored specifically to Hunter and Levi. But I need you to know this—through loving them, I've grown to love you, too. You complete this family, Garrett.

You are essential to our cohort's longevity and happiness. As such, I'll do everything in my power to support you, cherish you, and champion you, for all the rest of our days."

Garrett stares at me, wide-eyed. "Damn," he eventually says. "That was—"

"Surprisingly insightful and intimate?" I suggest.

He laughs, clapping me on the back playfully. "I was going to say pompous and overdramatic, but sure. Your way works, too."

I can't fight the grin daring to emerge from his jibe. I hope to gods we never lose this—the playfulness and verbal sparring. There's no one else who gives quite as good as Garrett when it comes to retorts and banter.

His face smooths out, and he nods. "Thank you for saying all that."

"Please don't thank me. This conversation is long overdue. Forgive me," I beseech, searching his face and hoping like hell he sees the sincerity in my eyes.

"Consider yourself absolved."

I snicker. He's mocking me, I know. But his reassurance is appreciated all the same.

"Thank you." I wrap him in another hug.

I don't bother warning him that I won't always get this right. We'll both fumble along the way. Sharing partners is bound to have its ups and downs. But I'm fully committed to doing this with them, and with him. Today. Tomorrow. Forever, if they'll have me.

"Thank you," I whisper once more, before cuffing the back of his neck and squeezing. "Now, let's find the others and figure out exactly how we're going to impregnate our girl, shall we?"

Chapter 28

Hunter

As I emerge from the bathroom, I tighten my robe around my waist. I figured I'd be nervous, but the butterflies are fluttering far more violently than I anticipated.

I want this. It's a reminder and a mantra. I want this with everything I am.

Once Spence was on board, plans formed quickly. Joey did me a solid and ensured her cohort would be at Decker's cabin for the next few days. It's Valentine's Day weekend, so it made sense that we all have our own space anyway.

We have the whole house to ourselves, and tonight, there's just one thing on our agenda.

Sex.

Sex, but also so much more. This isn't just our first five-way as a polycule.

This is all of us, coming together—literally—with the intention of creating a new life.

As I step into the room and the scene in front of me registers, I gasp.

Warm, golden light flickers from battery-operated candles of different shapes and sizes covering every surface. Long shadows paint the walls, outlining my men as they lounge around the room and on the bed, already in various stages of undress.

Sione is sitting in a chair to the side, shirtless. Levi and Greedy are both leaning against the footboard in nothing but boxer briefs, pressed shoulder to shoulder with their arms crossed over their naked chests. Spence is standing in the middle of the room, wearing trousers and a half-unbuttoned Oxford.

I approach slowly, quietly, not sure whether I should announce my presence or wait until one of them notices me.

"We could blindfold you," Spence suggests, stopping me in my tracks.

What?

"Blindfold who?" I'm not missing out on one second of this sex-fest. I'll be lucky if I remember to blink.

Suddenly, four sets of hungry, intense eyes turn to me.

"Mahina."

Sione is on his feet and stalking toward me before I can zero in on him. With his arms around me, he lifts me in a little half spin.

"You look beautiful. Glowing. Absolutely radiant."

"*Si*." I laugh as he puts me back on my feet. "It's a little early to be using words like 'glowing,' don'tcha think?"

"Never."

He bows low, his dark hair curtaining us, creating a temporary privacy shield.

"You're sure?"

Like it always does when he's near, a serene, soothing calmness washes over me. I smile, peck his lips, and look him in the eye, baring my truth and letting him see straight into my soul.

"I've never been so sure of anything in my life."

I want this with every ounce of my heart and every part of my soul.

Sione responds by nuzzling into my neck and inhaling deeply. It grounds us both while simultaneously stoking the fire that's been growing low in my belly all evening.

"What's this about a blindfold?" I ask, stepping back so I can survey the others.

Levi and Greedy each meet my gaze, their eyes hooded and lust-filled, like they want to devour me individually and together. A shiver racks through me. Then, suddenly, Spence is at my back, his proximity causing goose bumps to erupt all over my skin.

"It's for Levi, love," he murmurs. "Our boy's still worried about his ability to perform in this room." His breath tickles my neck. He caresses my collarbone with the back of his knuckles, then one finger hooks the hem of my silk robe. A swift tug has the fabric cascading down my body.

A collective intake of breath inspires more goose bumps, along with a wave of heat to rise up my neck and into my cheeks.

I thought about wearing lingerie. Something strappy and sexy. Even buying a new set for the occasion.

Ultimately, I decided against all that.

So now I'm standing completely bare before them. Stripped down. Wanting. Eager to be filled up.

"Fuck." Levi pushes off the end of the bed and strides toward the three of us, his bright blue eyes feral and hungry. "Forget everything I said. I'm fucking ready to go."

Grinning, I reach for him.

Before I can make contact, Spence captures my hand and turns me to face him instead.

His blue-gray eyes pierce through me, seeing every layer of who I am and accepting every low moment and shadowed thought I've ever endured. When he looks at me like this, I know I'll never succumb to my lowest lows. He won't allow it. He's never shied away from my darkness. He knows the darkness himself, yet he remains unashamed.

"We have a plan," he advises. With his hand in mine and three steps back, he guides me farther into the room.

Sione follows, his fingertips grazing down the curve of my spine. His touch is tender and loving, as is his presence.

"If you'll have us." Spence glances beyond me to each of the guys before his hooded eyes settle back on me.

His face dances in shadow; the soft light cast from the candles around the room only makes the dark stubble on his face and the angular lines of his jaw appear sharper.

"We intend to thoroughly worship every inch of you, Firecracker. Then we'll take turns, one by one, filling you up until you're bursting with fertile, life-giving seed."

He drops to his knees before me.

My heart catches in my throat.

"Sione will go first." He tips his chin to the man at my back before placing a kiss low on my abdomen.

Over my womb. Right where a baby would be.

As if on cue, Si loops one arm around my waist and pulls me back until I'm leaning against his chest.

"Then Garrett. Then Levi. Then, finally, me."

He looks up through his long, dark lashes, his expression somber. "We both know I won't be the one to give you what you want, Firecracker. Not this time." He presses another kiss to my pelvis, this one so low the scrape of his stubbled chin tickles my mound. "But I'll do everything in my power to ensure we succeed tonight. I'm sorry for how I reacted before. Your happiness is my happiness, love. I can't wait to see you ripe and round with our child."

Our child.

It doesn't matter who impregnates me. Regardless of paternity, the five of us are forging a commitment that will change us forever. We are a unit. We'll forever be connected by the actions of this night and the creation of what comes next.

My throat clogs with emotion as I consider Spence's words. He's so invested. So sincere. Everyone is committed to this plan, but his willingness to participate is a sacred gift I'll cherish forever.

"Are you with us, love?"

Snapping out of my revery, I reach back for Sione with one hand and scrape my nails along Spence's scalp with the other. "Always."

I want to be with them always.

I want to feel this loved and secure always.

I want to live without fear or secrets or any of the heartbreak we survived to get to this moment.

I want to savor this night and honor the sanctity of the act we're about to commit.

I want them, all of them, always.

"Very well." Spence smirks. "Garrett? Levi?"

There's a rustling behind me, but I don't move.

Spence, hands resting on my thighs, homes in on one guy, then another.

"All right, boys. It's time to make sure our girl is fully prepared to take everything we intend to give her tonight."

Sione's hold on me tightens, and on either side of me, Greedy and Levi sink to their knees.

My breath catches and my heart takes off, but a moment later, Si distracts me, kissing along my neck while one giant tatted hand snakes around the front of my body. He cups one breast and captures the nipple between his fingers. I can't help but lower my head and watch him rub and pull until my usually pink nipple is red and taut.

He finds my other breast, repeating the motion before tweaking and tugging on both tight buds in sync. Electricity travels from my tits to my clit, tingly warmth collecting in my core and creating a pulse between my thighs.

I'm lost to his ministrations, mind, soul, and body, my hips rolling of their own accord until my pelvis connects with something warm.

Something warm and soft. Something hot and hungry.

The tip of a tongue traces around my clit. Teeth nip at the apex of my thighs. Lips glide over my pussy, the caress agonizingly slow and unexpectedly tender. But the amount of connection, the intensity of pleasure...

There's not just one man feasting on me right now.

"Shit." I shudder. "Are you—"

Greedy pulls back, lips glistening. "Yeah, Tem. We're all going to make you feel good at the same time."

Without preamble, he dives back in.

I sink back into Sione's embrace, seeking his mouth in a desperate attempt to feel them all everywhere. He feeds me his tongue, moving it in and out of my mouth in slow strokes, licking along my lips and rubbing the tip against mine as the others pick up the pace between my thighs.

I grip two heads of hair, mindless, and pull them impossibly closer. Seeking more. Desperate for everything they're willing to give.

When I finally break away from Si's kiss, I drop my head and let out a long, low groan.

Spence is in the middle, crouching lower than the other two so he's squarely centered between my thighs. He places sensual kisses around my opening, his hot, talented mouth making my legs quake. Then, with his head tipped all the way back and his chin pressing into my taint, he fucks his tongue into my hole.

"Spence," I cry, shaking against the pleasure warming all my limbs.

Panting, I look down again. Greedy is gripping the hair at the back of Levi's neck, the two of them kissing. When they break apart, they both zero in on me.

"Hold her open like this." Levi uses one thumb to spread my pussy lips wider, exposing my clit in the process.

Greedy follows the direction, murmuring "so fucking pretty," before placing a kiss on the already aching bud.

Once I'm fully exposed, Levi and Greedy lap at me, their tongues fighting for dominance as they lick and press into my bundle of nerves. They inspire a blur of sensation, making it impossible to discern where one ends and the other begins.

They alternate kissing, sucking, and flicking, all while Spence dips into my pussy as far as he can reach.

It's the sharp pinch of both nipples—the reminder that Sione is here, too, and they're all working together for my pleasure—that grips my insides and causes the first swirl of tightness.

"Boys," I mewl, running my hands through both Greedy's and Levi's hair.

Their mouths work faster. Their sucks and flicks grow more intense.

My internal walls quiver around the tip of Spence's tongue, desperate and greedy to be filled to the hilt. I want them all. I want them *now*.

"I'm going to come," I pant, the tension in my core winding tighter.

Head lolled back against Sione's shoulder, I give in.

I give in and give up and hold on and let go, all in one glorious moment of surrender.

Sione kneads and squeezes. Spence licks and fucks. Greedy and Levi lap at me as one, their tongues dancing and caressing in the most erotic blend of ecstasy.

The orgasm starts in my chest. It winds tighter, tighter, and tighter still, until the tension radiates through my arms, legs, and torso in the most agonizingly exquisite swell of bliss.

A mouth clamps down and sucks hard on my clit, and the world bursts into technicolor. I careen through the stratosphere at sunset, pinks and oranges and golds blinding me with their brilliance as the air grows thin and I gasp from exertion.

All the tension that has ever existed in my physical container seeps out of me. Wave after glorious wave of pleasure carries me toward the horizon, my screams of ecstasy only audible once my ears stop ringing and I regain a sense of time and place on this planet. Only then do the ardent ripples bring me back to myself.

I'm a panting, balmy mess by the time I come down.

I've barely begun to catch my breath when Spence rises to his knees, grips my chin, and moves my head so I'm focused on his face.

"That's one," he declares, eyes flashing wickedly. "Take a leg and hoist it onto your shoulder, boys. Si, switch with me. She's got at least two more in her before she's thoroughly sated and ready to take our cocks."

Chapter 29

Sione

I love her like this.

I love her every way, always, but like this—pliable, hazy-eyed, and lost in this moment—is when my beautiful girl shines as bright as a perigee syzygy.

"Look at us."

She lifts her head and gazes down to where our bodies connect.

The black ink adorning my dick disappears each time I'm sheathed inside her. When I pull out, her pussy clings and stretches around me as if it can't bear to be without the connection for a single moment. I'm mesmerized by the sight of our joining, so full of emotion I worry I'll choke on it, just as I'm honored by the sanctity of what this encounter means.

The others asked me to go first.

They wanted me to have this—to fully participate in a way that most aligns with who I am and how my sexuality presents—so that we could all contribute to this experience.

It's not lost on me what going first signifies.

I was the last to meet Hunter. The last to arrive in her life, and the last to join the cohort. It's unlikely I'll ever fully weave the sexual and romantic parts of myself with the others in this group.

Yet they asked me to go first.

She lies on her back, arms wrapped around my neck as I roll my hips, connecting us over and over again.

"You feel so good, Si," she praises. "You make *me* feel so good."

Tears gather in her eyes as she regards me, biting her lip, watching and waiting and expecting so much. I want to give her everything. Doing so is a privilege I'll cherish forevermore.

I'm first.

It's an honor and a responsibility.

"I'm close, Mahina. I'm going to unload as deep as I can reach. I'm going to offer you my seed, and I want you to take it all. Can you do that for me?"

With a shuddering exhale, she nods.

I hold myself in plank position with one arm braced near her head, then caress her torso with my free hand. My fingertips find her clit with ease; my body knows every inch of who she is and what she desires. Gently, lovingly, I rub.

Little circles that match my thrusts to start.

As I pick up my pace, I increase the intensity and press into her most sensitive pleasure point, clenching my thighs to stave off my own release until she's right there with me.

"I'm ready." She sighs, blinking so her tears fall down her rosy cheeks.

"Come with me," I murmur, rubbing and thrusting and allowing all the primal, carnal urges of my third eye to guide us both to orgasm.

She spasms and whimpers.

I tense, peak, then unload.

Each pulse of my cock is timed perfectly with the clenching of her pussy.

Her body hungrily, greedily, willingly welcomes my seed.

I was first.

She's my forever.

Regardless of the outcome of tonight, I'll never forget this moment and what it signifies for me within this group.

As we come down, I bow my head low, kiss the moisture from each cheek, and seal my lips over hers in a sensual, worshipful kiss.

Chapter 30

Greedy

I'm next.

And I'm an anxious, writhing mess.

Partly because Levi's on his knees before me, sucking on my cock like it's a popsicle he's enjoying between football two-a-days in mid-August.

Partly because this is really fucking happening. Hunter wants this. I want this, too.

I just don't want to let her down.

Levi swirls his tongue under the head of my cock in a way that has tingles erupting at the base of my spine. Shit. I can't get carried away.

"Ease up." I run my fingers through his thick blond curls and tug.

He pops off my dick and smirks up at me. An instant later, though, as if he can sense my trepidation, his expression goes soft. "You've got this, G."

I offer him a half-hearted smile.

He lumbers to his feet, rising slowly to protect his still-healing leg. Once he's standing to full height, he regards me. His usual playfulness has been replaced with steady intensity. He's looking at me with so much concern and care I can't stand to hold his gaze.

"Hey," he murmurs, catching my chin and turning my face back. "You've got this." He moves behind me and loops his arms around my chest so we're both facing the bed.

Spence has relegated himself to the armchair in the corner, every so often darting a lustful look at Levi. It wouldn't surprise me if my boyfriend goes to him next.

"Look at them together." His mouth is at my ear, his breath hot on my neck. With both hands, he grazes my lower abs, then pulls me in tighter and rests his chin on my shoulder. "Look how beautiful they are. Look how happy she is. You're going to make her feel just like that, G. Our girl can't wait for you to be buried deep inside her."

With a playful bite to my shoulder, he sways, forcing my body to move with his.

"Garrett. Are you ready?" Sione's words are shallow and melodic as he struggles to catch his breath.

We planned all this at Spence's insistence. We agreed to wait until each man "tapped out" before attempting to take his place. Sione's still hovering over Hunter, but the goal here is to transition from cock to cock with minimal loss of cum.

We're going to move fast, keep her plugged. We won't waste a single drop.

"You've got this," Levi encourages once more. "I'll be right here for both of you as soon as you're done."

I crane back and smash my mouth against his in a sloppy, grateful kiss. He's right. I'm ready. We want this. I've got this. Let's fucking go.

I'm on my knees, hovering close, squeezing my aching erection, when Sione finally slides out of our girl.

She keeps her pelvis tipped up, holding her thighs open so I can seamlessly slot into place.

Sinking into her this time—in this moment, for this purpose—is unlike anything I've ever experienced.

We both moan as I enter her warm, dripping channel. I slide in effortlessly, all her arousal and Sione's cum creating the perfect oasis for our pleasure.

When our eyes lock, an instant zing of primal need shoots straight to my balls.

All anxiety and trepidation disappear when she shifts beneath me. She was made to take me like this. She was made for all of us, and I fully intend to make the most of my turn.

"Look at you. You're so fucking perfect, taking everything we want to give you."

I bend low and kiss her, ravishing her mouth and jaw and neck before moving on to her breasts.

"Fuck, baby. I can't wait until these perfect tits are filled with milk. Will you let me suck on them then?"

She whimpers, clenching around my length like a vise.

"You love that idea, don't you, Tem? You're going to let me drink from you and savor every fucking drop." I push up, desperate to see her face.

She's slack-jawed and languid, running her fingertips over her nipples, pinching as she loses herself in the fantasy.

"First, though, I need to put a baby in you. I'm going to fuck you hard, Tem. I'm going to breed you. Are you ready for me?"

"Yes. Please. Fuck me, Greedy."

Goddamn. I lift my fist to my mouth and bite down hard. I can't come yet. I won't come yet.

"I fully intend to. Turn over for me, Tem. Don't let me slip out, but get on your hands and knees."

Carefully, she flips herself over, keeping my dick buried deep in her pussy, just like I asked.

"Good girl. Now press your body into the mattress, but keep that ass up." I smooth one hand along her spine, guiding her lower. Then I grab a pillow and stuff it under her hips to better support the position.

So what if I did my research and plan to fuck her in a way that optimizes my goal?

The sight of her perfectly positioned like this leaves me breathless. Naked with her pretty blond hair cascading all around her shoulders and back. Arms stretched out in front of her, one cheek pressed to the mattress. The globes of her ass spread wide just for me. Fuck. I'm not going to last long.

I can't fucking wait to unload.

More importantly, I can't fucking wait to create the life we both want and deserve.

"Hunter?" My tone is far gentler now than it was only a moment ago.

She peeks up, her brows lifted in surprise.

Bending forward so my torso covers her back, I speak directly into her ear. "I love you, baby. This, you, them? It's all I ever wanted. Whatever happens tonight, tomorrow, or years from now, it'll all be okay."

She worries her lip, sparkling green eyes searching my face. "How do you know?" she asks quietly.

Easy.

"Because we'll be together. No matter what happens or doesn't happen, regardless of where life takes us or what it throws our way, we'll be together. I never gave up on us, you know that, right? And I swear I never will."

Her body shudders. Blinking, she nods. "I love you, too. So damn much."

I hold her, ensuring she feels it all: The power of our connection. The promise of what's next. The intensity of my devotion.

Eventually, she settles beneath me. Her breathing levels out first. Then her hips grow restless, and she starts squirming. That's when I know she's ready.

I trail kisses along her spine as I retreat. "Hold on, Tem. I'm going to fuck you hard and fast."

I piston my hips forward, and she thrusts back, trying to match me.

"Easy," I scold, pressing both hands into her low back. "Let me do my job. Let me make you feel good and fill you up."

Once she's settled, I thrust again, rolling my hips and adjusting the pillow every few seconds as I search for what I need.

The second I hit it, I know. Her reaction is immediate and visceral. "There," she moans into the mattress.

I rut into her with abandon, desperately plunging as deep as I can go, hitting that sweet spot over and over again.

She tenses and squirms, but she grips the sheets, doing her best to remain still and take it.

"You're doing so good, baby. You're taking my cock so well. You're gonna take my cum so well, too."

With a moan, she tenses again.

She's right there. Right fucking there.

I'm close, too.

This is it.

I drive as deep as I can go, eyes rolling back when her pussy chokes my cock and holds it in place. Right up against her womb. *Right where it fucking belongs.*

"Fucking take it, Tem," I groan, spilling inside her in long, pleasurable pulses as her pussy milks me for everything I've got. "Take it. Keep it. It was always meant to be yours."

Breathless, I collapse but splay my hands on the mattress on either side of her so I don't crush her.

When my lips find her cheek, it's wet with tears.

Startled, I crane back and search her face.

"Tem. Look at me."

She does.

"Are you—"

With a laugh, she shakes her head. "I'm good," she promises. "I'm perfect." She's still crying, but she's smiling, too. "I just can't believe we're really doing this. Nothing has ever felt so right."

Chapter 31

Hunter

"Goddamn. I could come just from watching you two," Levi admits as he crawls up the mattress to where Greedy and I are spooning.

"Agreed," Spence chimes in. He's lounging toward the top of the bed, having offered the chair to a sated Sione after he emerged from the shower.

Greedy's still nestled inside me, intentionally plugging me up as he softens. He hasn't stopped peppering my bare shoulder with kisses, telling me he loves me, confessing his excitement, regardless of whether what we're doing tonight will take the way we hope it will.

Levi presses against my front, and I close my eyes and sigh contentedly. Being sandwiched between my boys like this is like being in one version of my personal heaven.

He kisses my closed eyelids. "Don't tucker out on us now, Daisy. It's almost my turn."

Feigning a yawn, I wiggle forward, just enough to brush my overly sensitive clit against his massive length. A shiver runs up my spine on contact, sending me arching back against Greedy. The way the guys groan in unison makes my heart take off. I roll my hips forward again, seeking that delicious friction from Levi.

My breathing increases, coming in shallow pants. My inner walls flutter.

I crack my eyes open and home in on Levi's cock. The thick head is leaking precum as it nudges against my clit and occasionally travels lower to brush against Greedy's body.

Flovely.

I just got myself all hot and bothered while teasing Levi.

"Look how pretty you are." He brushes the tip of his dick against my clit again, this time with more intention. "Look how gorgeous you are stretched around G and dripping with our seed."

"Dripping?"

Spence's curt single-word question pulls me out of the moment.

"There should be no dripping. If Garrett is no longer able—"

"Relax." Levi cuts Spence off before he can really get started. "I'm right here. We're not wasting a drop."

As if proving his point, he lines himself up with my entrance.

"Fuck, that feels incredible," Greedy groans from behind me.

"Look at us."

I tuck my chin and drink in the sight. Cum has started to accumulate around the base of Greedy's cock as it softens. My cunt is red and swollen, so thoroughly fucked and yet still so hungry for more. Levi's fat head is pressing right where Greedy and I are joined, the three of us melding together in a union of flesh and desire.

Greedy clears his throat. "Do you think—"

"I don't fucking know," Levi grits out before he can even articulate his question. "But I really want to try."

"What?" I pant, my voice reedy. I need them to switch. To move. To do *something*.

My first love is growing hard again, I swear. My fake boyfriend turned real boyfriend is right there—right fucking there—just one thrust from breeching my hole.

Greedy sits us both up without pulling out. "Baby, do you think you could take us both? At the same time?"

A tidal wave of desire washes over me, heating me from the tips of my ears to my toes, making my core spasm around him. *Fuck.*

Yes?

No. There's no way. Is there?

Yes. I can do this. I will. I want it.

Now.

"Are you considering double vaginal penetration?" Spence's voice is barely audible over the blood whooshing in my ears.

The man would be a real mood killer if he wasn't such an attentive, demanding lover.

"I can do it." I glance back over my shoulder at Greedy, then focus on Levi. "I can take you both."

Levi does the same, looking from me to Greedy and back to me. Then arching up and peering at Spence.

Is he—what? Asking permission? Seeking guidance?

I crane my neck, confused.

"By all means." Spence smirks. He's fisting his cock now, squeezing the tip the way he does when he's trying to keep himself from coming too soon. "If she says she wants it, it's your duty to give it to her." Then, softer, he adds, "This doesn't weaken or undermine the plan, Champ."

Oh.

My heart.

Levi wasn't asking for permission. He was checking in to ensure his idea wouldn't detract from our ultimate goal.

"But if you're going to do it, make it quick. She's relaxed and loose now, but you're far too large to attempt DVP once Garrett is fully hard again."

"You're sure?" Greedy asks into my neck.

Levi and I nod simultaneously, his face as bright as mine feels.

"Fucking get in here, then, man. I can't stop how fast I'm growing."

"Okay. We've got this." I don't know if Levi is pumping himself up or trying to reassure me. Either way, he shakes out his shoulders and says, "G, roll back and turn her to face you. Let her lay against your chest, then spread her legs wide for me."

We move as one until my chest is pressed into Greedy's and I'm positioned in a way that keeps him buried inside but gives Levi total access from behind.

Levi stands and situates himself between my legs, fists his cock, then guides the tip back and forth over my already well-fucked hole. Greedy's growing harder by the second. I need Levi inside me *now* if this is going to work.

"Kiss him, pretty girl," Levi demands. "Don't stop unless you want me to stop. Got it?"

"Yes." Fervently, I smash my mouth into Greedy's.

"Here we go," Levi murmurs.

Greedy feeds me his tongue, distracting me from the hot, tight pinch between my legs. "Fuck." He whimpers and writhes beneath me as Levi works himself into my pussy.

"Fuck, indeed," Levi says, the tremble of his hands apparent when he grips my ass.

Their pleasure galvanizes me. I breathe out and kiss him harder, focusing on my breath, on keeping my muscles relaxed, and on the way Greedy's tongue so perfectly strokes against mine.

"Hang on, G," Levi mutters.

Greedy lets out another choked whimper.

As Levi works himself in farther, the stretch grows more intense, then merciless. It burns, but in a way that makes me crave more.

I'm so full, but I can't fucking stand the lack of movement.

I want this.

I do.

Only I no longer know whether it's possible.

Levi is *so* big.

Greedy is hard again.

It's too much. I can't. I don't think I can—

"Breathe, Mahina," Sione coaches from out of sight. "They're in. You're already there."

Fuck.

He's right.

They're in.

We've never been connected like this before—the two of them, physically sheathed together because of me.

I open my eyes and break from Greedy's kiss.

When I glance back, I gasp.

Both my boys are burrowed in my cunt—Greedy's all the way in, and Levi's about halfway sheathed. They're consuming every inch of space, stretching me in a way I've never dreamed of experiencing.

We're doing this. We're really fucking doing this.

I give them both a tentative squeeze, and in response, Greedy groans and Levi growls with a ravenous hunger.

"Absolutely exquisite," Spence says from the head of the bed, his gaze heated, feral.

I catch his eye, my body heating from the carnal passion emanating in his stare. He's looking at me as if I'm the most beautiful thing he's ever seen. He's looking at me as if he wants to be right up in here, claiming my body and taking his rightful place deep in my core.

The ferocity is there. The fire behind his eyes burns hotter than the flush of my body. He looks from me to Levi, then down to the place where we're joined.

Fuck. I wish he could be in here with us, too.

Not tonight, though. Tonight, we'll stick to the plan.

"Leev," Greedy croaks. "You feel so fucking good. You both do. But I don't know if I can move without slipping out."

My sweet Duke leans over me, grips his nape, and kisses him. "I've got you."

Then he buries his face in the crook of my neck. "You're okay?"

I'm more than okay. I'm on the precipice of combusting. There are no words to describe the sensation. All I know is that I want more. I want to feel it build. I want to soak them both. I want all of us to peak together, their essence erupting when our orgasms crescendo inside my body.

"Please move," I choke out.

"I concur. Fucking move, Leev," Greedy groans.

"I love you. Both of you," Levi says, hovering close. His tone starts sweet, but in the next second turns fierce. "I'm about to prove how much I love you by fucking you both so hard you forget your own names."

He starts slow, but quickly finds a rhythm.

Greedy barely moves, instead holding me, kissing my mouth and my neck, telling me how well I'm taking our boy and how amazing it feels to be inside me at the same time.

"Leev. Fuck. Every time you thrust all the way, it feels like you're fucking me, too."

"This is the greatest moment of my life," Levi says. "Why haven't we been doing this all along?"

I snort, inadvertently bearing down slightly and making both guys moan.

"Fuck." Greedy pants in my ear. "I'm going to come again. This wasn't the plan. I don't want to—"

Levi freezes. "Hey. You're okay. You can come, G. I want you to come with me."

I nod my assent, too lost in pleasure to respond with words.

"What's happening right now is exactly right." Levi thrusts, his pace picking up further. "This is how it was always meant to be."

"Fuck. It feels so good. So fucking hard. So fucking tight." Greedy drags a hand low, fumbling at first, then wedging it between our bodies to connect with my clit. "I'm close. Together?"

"Yeah, G. We're going to fill her all the way up. Let's come together."

I peak first—I think. The orgasm blossoms through my low belly and washes over me in soft, hazy waves. There's no room for my inner walls to spasm. I'm stretched too wide for my core to pulsate and clench. Nevertheless, pleasure and power wash over me as my boys spill inside me.

They fill me. They complete me. As they soften, they kiss me and kiss each other, the three of us a sated heap of sweat and satisfaction.

I've been emotional all night, but I don't feel compelled to cry right now. If anything, I want to laugh. I want to marvel at what we just accomplished and rejoice in the beautiful, unexpected magic of all that's still to come.

Chapter 32

Kabir

This is it.

The final step in our carefully laid out plan. The last hurrah, so to speak. We've nearly accomplished what we set out to do.

I'm thoroughly satisfied with the proceedings thus far. Despite the slight deviations from the plan, we worked well together, giving everyone an opportunity to participate individually.

Leave it to Garrett to find a loophole that allowed him to make two deposits.

Although I can't fault the man for trying. Watching Hunter take two cocks in her needy little hole was almost enough to send me over the edge.

Now, it's finally my turn.

Naturally, I did my research. Since I cannot contribute a viable specimen to the mission, I am determined to make my impact in other ways.

Garrett and Levi have retreated to one side of the bed. Sione is still sitting in his chair.

My girl is in the center of the mattress, sleepy, spent, and very thoroughly fucked.

Her hips are propped up with two pillows, but based on the dribble of cum leaking from her cunt as I climb up beside her, that's not enough. With a *tsk*, I catch it with my finger and show her.

"Waste not, Firecracker. Your boys worked hard for this. We're not letting a single drop out of this cunt until you're pregnant with our baby."

Propped up on her elbows, Hunter bites her lip and spreads her legs wider.

Gently, I lift my hand to her center, then push the cum back into her hole with my middle finger. I crook against her G-spot as I pull out, testing her level of sensitivity.

As expected, she jolts.

I smile wickedly. If she's hyper-sensitive and extra responsive like this, then that'll only make my job tonight all the more fun.

"Kabir. Please wait."

Startled, I rear back and turn to Sione, who is approaching.

"I know it's now your turn. But before you begin..."

He lowers his head, and I follow his line of sight to his cupped hand.

"One more deposit," he explains.

As he extends his intricately tattooed arm, it dawns on me. He came again.

He meets my eyes, then looks to Hunter and the boys. "Witnessing you take her that way—together..."

He shakes his head and exhales audibly, as if he's unable to find the words to describe how watching our girl take two sizable cocks in the same hole has affected him.

"My body reacted viscerally. As if my soul wanted to contribute more, too. I hope it does not make you uncomfortable or like I used your experience to—"

"Si. No." Garrett leans over, offering calm reassurance. "That wasn't just between us. Everything that's happened tonight—it's for all of us."

Hunter holds an arm out, beckoning Sione closer. When he's within reach, she cuffs his neck and pulls him down. "Is that for me?" She kisses him on the mouth, running her hand through his hair. "You're so good to me, Si. I love you so much."

They kiss again, Sione still cupping his cum as Hunter tries to pull him onto the bed.

"I want to put it in you," he murmurs. "If that's okay with the others."

"Go on, then," I encourage. "Push it in. Fill her up."

Pausing, Sione regards all of us again.

"Together," he states. As if it's the only way.

Eyebrows raised, I regard him for a moment, but quickly concede. "Together," I repeat, shifting to make room for Garrett and Levi as well.

I allow Sione to do the honors, pressing his curled fingers against Hunter's cunt as she rolls her hips, seeking his touch.

"Are you ready for this, baby?" Greedy asks.

We take turns touching her, caressing her pussy lips and collecting pearls of cum to press inside her.

We fill her the best we can.

It doesn't take long to determine that it's too much. She's full. There's so much cum she can't possibly hold it all in.

We take turns sweeping it up and reinserting it. Over and over. Filling her. Spreading our cream. Working as a team to make sure every drop she can take is pressed deep into her cunt.

Sione uses two fingers. Then Levi and Greedy work together, each using one.

We're nudging and pushing it back in, over and over again, until eventually Hunter is writhing and whining once more.

"Spence," she pants, begging me to give her what only I can.

"Patience," I scold. "Wait until your boys are done."

Taking the hint, the others complete their final ministrations, then settle back. Levi and Garrett spoon beside her. Surprisingly, Sione doesn't retreat to his chair, but instead sits up against the headboard with his legs spread wide so Hunter can lie back against his chest.

"Spence," she whines again.

My needy little cum slut.

I know what she wants. I know what she needs. Tonight, though, isn't just about the two of us. I'm not comfortable degrading her in front of the others, nor am I comfortable slipping into our dynamic when she's this far gone.

I am, however, prepared to exhaust her with a final orgasm, using my release to plug her up and seal the deal.

"You need to come again, Firecracker?"

"Yes," she pants. "Please, Sir."

"Be careful what you wish for, love. I still need to make my deposit, and based on my research, the contractions from orgasm help drive the sperm higher to your womb. I've been waiting all night to have you. It's my turn now."

She whimpers, writhes, pants.

"Sione, hold her for us, yes?"

He nods.

"Garrett, suck on her tits the way she loves."

He gets into position.

"Champ."

Levi snaps his head over to me, his expression eager.

"Come over here and work this vibrator while I fuck our girl."

We all set to work, taking our positions.

I prepare myself, lining up my cock with her puffy, glistening cunt. The moment I push in, I'm met with resistance.

"Bloody hell. She's so fucking tight."

"Hang on." Levi turns on the vibrator and presses it above her clit just like we discussed.

Hunter moans. It's a deep, guttural sound, confirming he's found the perfect spot above her clitoral hood to drive pleasure deeper and higher into her core. The crura of the clitoris is a few inches long and extends deep beyond the exposed glands of the female form. By focusing there, we'll ensure Hunter experiences a deep, full-body orgasm without abusing her overly sensitive clit and G-spot.

"Just like that, Champ," I encourage. "Watch how she blooms for us."

Hunter digs her heels into the mattress, and her pretty pink nails disappear into the flesh of Sione's thighs.

Externally, her body tenses. But internally, she relaxes, and I easily slide home.

I watch, enraptured, as Garrett sucks her nipples into taut peaks and Levi works the vibrator right where she needs it. Sione holds her steady, smoothing one hand over her hair and offering low whispers of praise and encouragement.

She's exquisite.

They're sensational.

The sight of their reverence and love for her inspires my balls to tighten and my body to tense in anticipation.

"This is it," I tell them all. "I'm going to come inside her, fill her to the brim, and seal in everything you've given her tonight. She's so full, all because of you. She's going to be pregnant, all because of you."

Hunter's eyes fly open.

There she fucking is.

The connection between us is powerful. Neither of us needs to speak. I don't issue a single command. She's right there. This moment is what we've hoped for. This experience has been *everything*.

Her mouth falls open in a silent scream as her body ignites in a firestorm of pleasure.

My thighs clench and my core hardens as her needy, desperate, cum-filled cunt tugs on my aching cock. She milks me—she squeezes the life right out of me—greedily pulling my essence into her core and combining it with the others.

By going last, I ensured the least viable sperm would likely leak out first. It also allowed me to witness the evening unfold and to hover above it all until this moment.

We all played our parts, and we played them exceptionally well.

Now it's up to fate to decide what happens next.

Chapter 33

Hunter

I'm buzzing with adrenaline and leftover surges of pleasure. I can't lie still, let alone sleep.

Spence, Greedy, and Levi are all zonked out, their legs a tangled mess on one side of the mattress.

I'm not cold, but when Sione wraps his arms around me and pulls me back into his orbit, I realize I'm shaking.

I always have trouble sleeping when I ovulate. I also struggle to fall asleep after an orgasm. It's extremely unlikely I'll get much rest tonight considering I just had—shit, I lost track of how many, though Spence could tell me when he wakes.

With a sigh, I reposition myself. Nothing helps.

Always so in tune with my state of mind, Sione smooths a hand down my hair. He repeats the motion, petting me and coaxing me closer until I'm snuggled tightly against his frame.

"That feels good."

"We timed this perfectly, Mahina. You're doing so well. Such a beautiful vessel for the life we're going to create."

Tears spring to my eyes, but they have nothing to do with the sweetness of his words.

"What if it doesn't work? I don't want to disappoint them." It takes all I have to fight back the sob that wants to break free from my chest.

My emotions are all over the place—another clear sign I'll ovulate within the next twenty-four hours. I hate feeling like this. I know I'm being unreasonable, but this is PMDD, plain and simple.

Some women feel fine up until ovulation, then experience intensifying side effects as menstruation nears. I'm the opposite: my anxiety and mood shoot off like a solar flare when I ovulate, calm down for a week or so afterward, and then steadily increase the closer I get to my period. Knowing there's a medical reason for what I experience should help, but it rarely does.

This isn't how I'm prone to think, I know that, but when my hormones rage and the phase of my cycle hits this intensely, I have no choice but to buckle up and hang on for the ride.

"If it doesn't work *this time*," Si emphasizes the last two words, "then we pivot and try again. We follow the tides, see this cycle through, and wait for what next month brings. Nothing you do could disappoint us. We're in this together."

He says it so casually. As if all our hopes and dreams aren't hanging on my ability to get pregnant.

Get it together, Hunter. This shouldn't be that big of a deal. No one's hopes and dreams are on the line. This isn't our only shot.

Sione buries his face in my hair. "Your aura just thinned significantly. What are you thinking?"

That I'm useless.

That this is the stupidest idea I've ever had.

That I can't even handle my own mood swings. How the hell am I ever going to be a good mother?

"Mahina."

His voice snaps me out of my head. "Let me in. Let us all in. Let us be here for you now. You've endured the flames on your own for far too long. It's time to try softer, not harder. Let us love and support you through what happens next, whatever that may be."

Tears seep out of me as my body deflates. With a cleansing breath, I do what Si suggested and try to be gentler with myself.

You're doing your best.

Whatever happens will be okay.

You are your own person, and you have so much love to give. You're going to be a great mom someday.

"Thank you," I whisper into the dark as my anxiety ebbs.

"It may take months to get pregnant, Mahina. That's common. Or maybe it won't happen for years. Regardless, the love in this room—the way we all so willing and lovingly filled you up tonight—can't be diminished. The lowest lows won't affect it. The toughest times can't weaken it. You are safe. You are loved. You never have to face the dark nights alone. Not ever again."

Chapter 34

Greedy

The light, perfumy fragrance of the first dogwood blooms of the season waft through the cracked windows of the car. It's not really warm enough to be driving with the windows down, but the sun is shining bright, and the fresh air is unmatched.

"You two warm enough back there?" I turn the heat up one notch to fight the chill we're willingly letting into the car.

"Hmm?"

I meet Hunter's gaze in the rearview mirror. "The air, Tem. Are you warm enough?"

She waves a hand. "I'm fine. Levi gave me this."

Levi snickers.

The *this* she's referring to is his well-loved South Chapel Football hoodie from high school. Last time I checked, it was in my drawer back at the Crusade Mansion, but clearly, he reclaimed and reassigned it.

Joke's on him. I have full access to all his clothing now that we live together. Which is one of the main reasons we're making this trip today: none of us have enough to wear, and we really need to refresh our wardrobes now that spring has officially arrived in North Carolina.

I peer at them once more, needing a look to soothe my own nerves. Levi has his arm around Hunter's shoulders, and he's whispering in her ear. When he pulls back and kisses the top of her head, one side of her mouth twitches in an attempted half smile. Ultimately, it falls flat. She looks just as preoccupied now as she has all morning.

Despite the fresh spring air and the warmth of the sun on my face, I feel the same way.

We're heading to my father's house, the three of us, to grab fresh clothes and other items we want to reclaim. This visit is long overdue, but we decided to wait until things cooled down. Spence thought it best we wait until Magnolia was as weak as possible before being in the same space. The rest of us wholeheartedly agreed.

According to my dad, her health is rapidly declining. He told me last week that she doesn't even get out of bed sometimes.

She's no threat to the three of us now, just a nuisance.

She's texted Hunter every day since the luncheon a month ago. Since Kabir tracks all of the woman's correspondence, he knows when she contacts Hunter, what she says, and all about her manipulation tactics. She has used them all in her effort to convince her daughter to visit her, move back home, and invite her to a doctor's appointment.

It weighs heavily on Hunter. It's why I insisted we get this over with today.

Our saving grace in all of this is that Magnolia has no idea we've been staying at the Crusade Mansion. Her attempts to find us have grown desperate in the last week or two, which confirms just how clueless she really is. According to Hunter, her mother has never even met Joze, and because of how uninvolved she was with her daughter's life when she was young, it's highly unlikely she'd recognize Decker or the other guys from their high school days.

Today's trip will be in and out. We'll grab what we need and a few things we want, then get out of there once and for all.

Gripping the steering wheel, I turn onto the familiar street. This is where I grew up. It's heartbreaking, how unwelcome I now feel in my childhood home. I glance back at Hunter and Levi again. Her head is resting on his shoulder and her arms are wrapped around his bicep.

She's worth it. He's worth it. We're worth it.

Soon, this'll all be over. That knowledge is what galvanizes me when negativity tries to take over.

Now is not forever. The situation is awful, but temporary.

Over the last few weeks, we've started making tentative summer plans. We've got a few months yet, but Spence has some business in London he'd like to personally tend to and doesn't want to be away from the group. Sione jumped on the idea of an extended summer trip to Europe, insisting we visit his grandparents' villa. Levi has an appointment at the post office to apply for passports next week.

Summer in Italy.

Visiting Lake Como.

Eating and drinking delicious food and wine all day. Skinny dipping at night.

It's the visual of Hunter and Levi basking in the glow of the moon while they swim, naked, that I'm focused on when I pull into my dad's driveway.

Which is why I do a double take when I see his car in its usual bay.

It's a Friday afternoon. Why isn't he at the hospital?

I park the car and unbuckle. Briefly, I entertain the idea of talking to my dad while I'm here. We had dinner together last week at the hospital. I went there with every intention of telling him about Hunter and me, but as he droned on about the clinical trial he's looking into for Magnolia, I lost my appetite and my desire to get through to him.

I'll always regret not telling him about the two of us when I found out he was with Magnolia, but I can't go back and change that now. After so much time, the best I can do is ride this out, wait for Magnolia to perish, and hope like hell that afterward, there's enough of him left to reclaim some semblance of a relationship.

Before I open the door, I shift in my seat. "All right. Grab what you need from your bedrooms. We'll make a big pile by the staircase, then bring it down together."

"Got it." Levi throws the truck door open and climbs out, then extends his hand for Hunter.

He's right.

We've got this.
In and out. Easy peasy.
We have nothing to worry about. I hope.

Chapter 35

Hunter

In and out. That was the plan.

Yet I can barely maneuver in and out of my old bedroom without Magnolia trying to wedge between me and the doorframe and disrupt my flow.

She's everywhere. Flitting about and pretending. She talks nonstop, even though I don't engage with most of what she says.

She looks *awful*. Her face is gray with a yellow undertone. Her make-up no longer matches, and the caked-on layers of cover-up make her look even more unwell.

"What names are you considering?" She's leaning against the wall in the hallway opposite my bedroom door now.

Rather than answer her, I turn on my heel and drag a full hamper behind me.

All I want are my lighter spring clothes and some mementos from London and Italy. I didn't bring a lot with me when I moved into Dr. Ferguson's house in August, so it shouldn't take long.

I slip through my balcony door and head straight to Levi's room, where I jiggle the handle. When the door doesn't open, I knock quietly.

He appears quickly and waves me in, brows furrowed in concern. "You okay?"

"Fine." I roll my eyes dramatically. "She's standing in the hallway and won't stop asking questions. I figured it'd be easier to bring things out through your room than mine."

Understanding registers on his face. "Good idea. Drag everything you want to the balcony door. I'll haul it over here and get it into the hallway for you."

Lightness washes over me. Like sunshine after an unexpected downpour.

"Thank you." I push up onto my toes to kiss him. "Love you."

Before I can pull away, Greedy appears at the open balcony door.

"Hey. Less kissing. More packing." His tone is all tease, but the words are a good reminder that none of us want to be here any longer than we need to be.

"Magnolia keeps coming in and out of my room, like she's purposely trying to get in my way."

Frowning, he tugs his phone out of his pocket and checks the time. "How much longer do you think you need?"

I puff out my cheeks and release a slow breath.

I'd love to spend an hour packing up all my toiletries and carefully selecting what items I want from my closet, but given the time constraints we're facing—and Magnolia's meddling presence—I can get it done in half the time.

"Is half an hour too long?" I hedge.

Greedy's face softens. He steps forward and pulls me in for a one-armed hug, planting a kiss to the top of my head. "Take all the time you need, Tem. I don't want to rush you. I just want to get out of here as soon as reasonably possible."

"I'm done, so I can help. We'll work fast," Levi assures him.

Greedy cocks a brow. "I saw your level of commitment to the tasks at hand just now."

Levi snickers. "Jealous, G?"

"The clock is ticking," I remind them both, before they can really get into it. "How about I hand you things and you pack them for me?" I ask

Levi. We brought a few boxes, but those are already full. Thankfully, I can fill the luggage still tucked away in my closet.

Levi shuffles out the door and holds out an arm. "Lead the way."

"Wait," Greedy hedges. "If it's okay with you guys, I want to try to talk to my dad. I wasn't planning to, but I think he's down in his office. I feel like I have to try. I promise it won't be more than a few minutes."

"We're good," Levi assures him. "Do what you need to do."

We part ways, Greedy back through his room, with Levi tailing me into mine with a hand on my hip.

I flash him a half-hearted smile over my shoulder, then lead him over to my closet.

"Almost done," he reminds me with an affectionate squeeze. "Put me to work so I can take you home."

Home.

This place was never home.

The four walls of the house I grew up in may have been once, but I disassociated from that version of my life long ago.

I've traveled across the world to escape things I could not face. From London to Lake Como, then back here to the house where Greedy grew up. In each place, I've only ever been a tourist. A visitor in my own life.

Not anymore.

I have a home. A place where my heart is full and my soul can rest.

Even without the security of a physical dwelling for my family, the four men who love me—and each other—come together and complement one another in the most fortifying ways.

Home.

It's not a place.

It's a feeling, a shared look, a delicious snuggle session, a sultry rendezvous in a pantry. Home is wherever they are. Wherever we can all exist, out loud, without apology or preamble. Home is the only place I want to be.

"Let's get this done." I haul out my suitcases and pass them over to Levi, then spring into action.

"Darling. Look what I found."

Avoiding Magnolia is impossible now that we're packed up and almost ready to go. I'm rolling my smaller bag into the hallway when she tries to stop me *again*.

Barely there fingertips brush against my forearm.

I jolt as if I've been electrocuted and stumble back.

She pretends not to notice my reaction. Or maybe she's not pretending. She always was exceptionally talented at blocking out anything that wasn't about her.

"Look." She thrusts a silver photo frame at me. It's simple in design but sturdy in weight.

"You were so cute," she coos, peering over my shoulder. "I don't have many memories from your early years—motherhood is exhausting, as you soon will learn—but at least we have photos to look back on."

She's standing eerily close. I take a step to the side to put a bit of space between us, but she simply follows.

"I've got more things from when you were little stashed around here somewhere."

I press my lips together to hold back my commentary. I'm almost certain she threw out all my baby things when she moved in with Dr. Ferguson. I have distinct memories of stuffed black garbage bags and a dumpster that occupied our driveway for weeks. It's highly unlikely she kept any items for sentimental reasons. In fact, I'm surprised she even has this picture.

"When was this taken?" I squint down at the tiny baby wearing a white christening gown. I didn't even know I was baptized.

"Hmm?" Magnolia hums noncommittally.

I study the picture more thoroughly. Obviously, I wouldn't remember the moment, but it's weird to not even recognize the image.

Niggling unease tickles up my spine. I shouldn't care, yet I have to know.

I flip the frame over and carefully pry up one of the metal closures securing the back in place. I move on to the next, being sure not to damage the frame. I'm working on the third prong when she clutches my wrist.

Two of her nails are chipped. That's the first thing I notice.

The tightness of her grip—as if she's trying to crush my bones and turn me to dust—is what registers next.

"What are you doing?" she hisses.

What *am* I doing?

In and out. Easy peasy.

Having a full-blown confrontation with Magnolia was not part of the plan.

Boldly, I yank out of her grasp, then look her square in the eye. "I don't think this picture is me."

Her face screws up in disgust. But instead of an indignant gasp like I expect, she snarls.

"Ungrateful brat." She reaches for the frame, but I hold on to it tighter, refusing to let go.

If my hunch is right, and I'm *not* the baby in this picture, then I'm holding a picture of sweet baby Greedy. I pull the frame to my chest and cradle it. I'm not letting her take this from me for anything.

With one big step backward, my calves brush a suitcase, but I successfully free the frame from her clutches. I glare at her, daring her to come for me again.

Her face softens.

For a heartbeat, I naïvely hope she's given up.

I should know better. That's not Magnolia's style. Instead, she changes tack.

"You know." Her tone is so soft I'm forced to lean forward to catch the words. "I had the *worst* sciatic nerve pain when I was pregnant with you."

Eyes hardening, she gives me a once-over, her focus lingering on my stomach in a way that makes me nauseas.

She takes another small step toward me, but I stand my ground, clinging to the picture and refusing to cow to her manipulative intimidation tactics.

"My hips burned, and the stretch marks were"—she turns her head, eyes shuttered closed, and clutches at her chest, over the place where her heart would reside if she had one, as if the memory is painful to recall—"they were awful. But it was the sciatic nerve flare-ups, the literal pain in the ass, I hated most."

I'm tempted to roll my eyes. To tell her to leave me alone. For now. Forever.

She takes another bold step forward, gets right up in my face, and slyly reaches around to jab one finger into my lower back, just above my ass cheek.

"Right here. Like a pinch." She prods at me again.

Like this, she has me pinned, with the suitcases at my back, the wall to one side, and the stairs on the other side.

I freeze. My instincts scream.

This isn't safe. It's not just her presence or the maniacal glint in her eye.

This is all wrong.

Magnolia's not well.

I inhale deeply and attempt to cry out, "Le—"

The sound is cut off when Magnolia slaps a hand to my face, silencing me.

"Hush, darling. This is between you and me."

The sting of the slap causes tears to well in my eyes. I fight against them, willing them to reabsorb. The last thing I need is for her to sense my weakness.

I ease one hand down my hip, desperate to fish out my phone.

She catches the movement, her eyes flickering, and I freeze.

Suddenly, it feels critical to distract her.

"Did—did it ever get better?" I need her to stay focused on my face. Ignore my hands. I need to get her talking again.

"Better?" She barks out a humorless laugh. "No. It only got worse," she sneers. With the pure hatred oozing from her, one would think she's talking about a trial much more severe than a nerve issue. "The pain would come out of nowhere. It was debilitating. Once, I tripped over absolutely nothing and landed straight on my ass. I sprained my tailbone, but of course, since I was *pregnant*, they wouldn't give me anything for the pain."

Her breathing has picked up, the rise and fall of her chest noticeable as her stale breath warms my face.

"The ER doctor told me it was fortunate I was standing on carpet when I fell."

I slip my phone out of my pocket and cradle it in my palm.

An eerie calm settles over us. Magnolia takes a micro-step forward. I have nowhere to retreat to, so I shift ever so slightly in response, trying to get her out of my face.

"They told me that I could have been in real trouble had I been on a hard surface. Or worse. Had I been near stairs." She darts a look at the staircase only an arm's reach away.

It all clicks, and panic lances through me, sharp and hot. Fumbling, I lift the phone, but in my panic, I fumble, and it slips between my fingers.

It hits the hardwood floor before soaring down the stairs, banging on half a dozen steps on its descent.

Magnolia watches the phone.

I watch Magnolia.

At the same time, we both move, and I try to scream once more. Nothing comes out. I can't utter a sound. I'm struck silent with fear as she lurches forward.

She grips my shoulders tightly, and as I work to shrug her off, her nails dig into the tender spots between my neck and shoulders. I bend and twist and take a step back, desperate to get out of her grasp.

"Levi!" I try to call out. His name is no louder than a choked whisper.

"*Shut up.*" Magnolia squeezes harder. Her hands aren't around my neck, but she's clutching my shoulders like her life depends on it.

Oh. Shit.

She wouldn't.

Would she?

"That boy only cares about you because you're pregnant with his child," she sneers, her grip never loosening.

Dread swirls violently in my belly. Dark spots dance in my periphery. Either she's found a pressure point, or my body's shutting down in panic.

I clutch the framed picture of baby Greedy to my chest, and with my free hand, I grope for something to hold on to.

I find the banister and grip it tightly, but a moment later, Magnolia homes in on my white knuckles and breaks into the evilest of smiles.

"You think he'll still be attracted to you when your tits sag and your stomach pooches out? Don't be delusional. I've seen the way the boy looks at your stepbrother. You may have tricked him into knocking you up, but he's in love with someone else entirely."

Someone else. *Someone else*. My heart leaps. Greedy's here, too.

I open my mouth to scream for him, but before I can utter a sound, she slaps me again.

On instinct, I rear back. One heel slips off the top step and lands hard on the next stair, sending a jolt of pain shooting up the back of my leg.

"Darling. Our genes just aren't meant for pregnancy."

The sweetness in her tone startles me more than the slap. I search her face, desperate to read her. To figure out what she's thinking. To piece together what just changed.

When I home in on her face, she smiles and lifts one hand. The other is still firmly digging into the side of my neck. She cups my face, then brushes her thumb along my cheekbone.

"You and I," she whispers, "we aren't cutout for motherhood."

Understatement of the century.

"I gave up everything for you." Her green eyes, so much like mine, darken, and the gentle hold she has on my cheek morphs into a burning grasp. Her voice drops, and she inches closer still.

I step back, steadying myself on the top stair.

"Yet here you stand. As bratty and defiant as ever. *Refusing* to help your own flesh and blood."

There it is. She hasn't mentioned surgery or the transplant all day, but it's always there. The undertone will exist during every interaction we have for the rest of our lives.

"And to think," she muses, a playful smirk tugging up one side of her mouth. "All that's preventing me from having the life-saving surgery I need is that boy's baby growing inside you."

Her smile falls, and her eyes go hollow, the sea-glass green turning to the color of a bottomless swamp. All her features contort.

"Don't," I beg.

My heart thunders in my ears, and panic races through me, making my knees quake.

"Mom. Please. Stop. Don't do this."

Her expression remains flat, placid. Determined and unyielding.

She inhales.

The action reminds me to take a breath, too.

As she exhales, she releases her hold on me, takes a few steps back, picks up my largest suitcase, and charges toward me, using the luggage like it's a battering ram to crash against my unsteady form.

When I exhale, I finally release the scream I've been desperate to make, clinging to the photo of the baby boy who grew into the man I love. I cradle it close, unwilling to let him go, knowing damn well I'm about to break his heart again.

Time slows as I fall, but there's no stopping the events that are already in motion. The impact of the heavy suitcase, the way I careen back. It's all inevitable. I close my eyes and block out the sensation of falling.

It feels too much like running. And that's the saddest realization of all.

I promised them I was done.

I promised them I wanted to stay.

My back makes contact with the stairs, and a *clunk* resonates down the hallway.

Blinding pain lights up my insides. From my head to my toes, fiery agony burns through me.

It won't last long. Soon, I won't feel anything. I'll feel nothing and be nothing, once and for all.

My fate is set. My future snuffed out.

I just hope they don't regret me.

Greedy. Levi. Kabir. Sione.

I hope that when the loss grows stale and the pain of heartbreak dulls, they forgive me. For as many times as I left them, I hope they know that, this time, I was desperate to stay.

I hope they remember me. That they keep on loving one another. That they miss me when I'm gone. That they'll think I was worth it, despite it all.

Because they were worth everything to me.

Another scream.

Another clunk.

It's then I realize I'm not the only one falling.

The suitcase.

Magnolia.

We all go tumbling down toward the darkness. In sync. In harmony. As if this was always how it was meant to be.

Chapter 36

Kabir

"Ease off the throttle," Sione encourages.

I do as he instructs, and when I reduce our forward momentum and bring the vessel to a steady deceleration, he nods approvingly.

We're in the middle of the lake, just the two of us. He's teaching me to operate a water vehicle in preparation for my upcoming boating license exam.

Kylian offered to issue a license to me—apparently that's something he's able to do—but I insisted on learning for myself.

I'm the only individual within my cohort who doesn't know how to operate a boat, and I'm tired of relying on the others when I want to leave the isle.

It's imperative since we intend to stay at the Crusade Mansion for the remainder of the spring and plan to visit Lake Como this summer as well.

Plus, Captain has a nice ring to it. It's a touch American, but still honorific and esteemed. I quite like the idea of having Hunter call me Captain on occasion. As long as we steer clear of the colloquial and seemingly facetious "Cap," as Decker Crusade is often called.

"Shall we practice dropping anchor once more before heading back?" Sione asks.

I nod but am quickly distracted by a notification on my phone.

There's the usual ping, but the set of vibrations that follow has me puzzled and eager to check the screen.

The blaring alarm that's sounding off by the time I pull the device from my trousers, though, turns my blood cold and sends my blood pressure soaring to life-threatening metrics.

"It can't be."

I stare, bewildered, at the alert flashing harshly on the screen.

"What's happened?" Sione steps up beside me, hovering over my shoulder as if proximity will provide enlightenment.

I don't answer. I can't.

All I can do is stare at the red light pulsing on the screen.

The internal tracker embedded in Hunter's neck does more than provide geo-location. The rice-size device is equipped with a full bio-feedback panel and a fall alert function.

It wasn't that I was concerned that she had an increased risk of falling. I chose the additional feature so I could be informed of other sudden drops or jumps, should the intrusive thoughts take hold of her and motivate her actions once more.

They never did, thank gods. I haven't worried about her in that way for years.

In fact, I had all but forgotten the sudden fall feature existed.

Fumbling, I silence the alarm, intent on calling her. Or them. But I'm clumsy in my pursuit. I can't act fast enough. Can't get my hands to follow the orders my brain is giving. I scroll, curse, press the wrong icon, then curse again.

"Here." Sione lifts the phone from my hand. "Who am I calling?"

My brain short-circuits. She was with Garrett and Levi. Which one is most likely with her now?

"Levi. Call Levi."

Swiftly, he finds his number, clicks on his name, then turns on speakerphone.

It rings and rings. We hover and wait.

When his voicemail picks up, I'm struck with the urge to snatch the phone away from Sione and chuck it into the godforsaken lake.

I settle for taking a cleansing breath and calmly asking him to try again. The call goes to voicemail once more.

"Call Hunter," I demand.

Her voice fills the silence, asking us to leave a message.

"Try Garrett." I look from the mansion on one side of the lake to the marina on the other. We're precisely midrange, equidistant from both shores.

It isn't until the fifth ring, when I'm certain it's going to voicemail, that he picks up.

We're met with no greeting.

Instead, there's commotion.

Yelling.

Muffled voices and clambering footsteps.

Garrett is screaming at his father, his voice far away. "Dad, make sure they send two ambulances. We need two units."

Sione freezes, his eyes shooting up to meet mine.

A pit opens up in my abdomen while we stand side by side, unable to do anything but wait until Garrett gets onto the line.

All we know is that pandemonium has erupted at his father's house, and the resulting turmoil sounds to be of catastrophic consequences.

Finally, after literal minutes pass by with nothing more than screams, sobs, and soft murmurs punctuating the line, Garrett says, "I'm here." Before we get a word in, he adds, "Wait. Hang on." Then a muffled "I'm going in the ambulance."

I fight back every impulse to demand his attention and hammer him with questions.

"Garrett. We're here," Sione reminds him. Where his tone is calm, a tumult of emotions rages inside me.

"Hunter fell down a flight of stairs. Or, more likely, Magnolia pushed her. She's covered in lacerations and likely has several broken bones. She's currently unconscious. She might have—she—fuck."

A sob escapes him, interrupting his report.

"Where are you headed?" Sione presses.

"Lake Chapel General. Through the ER. Meet us there." With that, the call drops.

Sione shifts his focus to me and searches my face. His expression is even, subdued. How the fuck can he be so serene?

I sink to my knees, agony and utter disdain crashing over me in undulating waves. The scream that escapes me can likely be heard for miles. Everyone. Everywhere.

Good. Let them hear me. Let them fucking know. I'm coming, and I have no more restraint, resolve, or sensibility left to temper the vengeful beast inside me. Someone will pay. I'll make sure of it.

I scream until my vocal cords fray and my larynx collapses.

Only then do I rise, reclaim my phone, and ask Sione to take me back to the Crusade Mansion. I'm fully prepared to enact the plan I've been plotting for weeks.

Chapter 37

Levi

I can't see. I can't fucking see.

Every time I blink, new tears form. The world is distorted and blurry and bleak, as if I'm trapped in an alternate reality. Nothing makes sense, and I can't even get G to talk to me.

That's the worst of it. He's shut down, totally unreachable. Every time I look at him, a fresh shroud of guilt washes over me.

I was the one upstairs with Hunter. Whatever happened between her and Magnolia, it happened on my watch.

They took her back—somewhere. Fuck. I don't even know where they took her. Is she okay? Does she need surgery?

Greedy swore she had a pulse. That means she'll be okay, right?

"G," I try for the tenth time.

"Don't," he snaps back. He's refusing to let me get a word in. To apologize. To explain.

Fucking hell.

Hands clenched into fists, I kick the row of plastic chairs lining the far wall, sending three of them clattering into an upside-down heap.

I'm still panting and staring at the mess a few moments later when a man wearing light blue scrubs with a hospital badge clipped to the pocket peeks around the corner to the alcove we're standing in.

"Everything okay in here?" He looks from me to Greedy, then to the cluster of scattered chairs off to the side.

"He's fine. We're fine." Greedy's voice is suddenly even, his tone brooking no argument. To the outside world, including this stranger, we're *fine*.

My guilt turns into anger at how easily he can shut me out and carry on. He rode in the ambulance with Hunter. I had to drive the truck. We're supposed to be a team—why the hell is he refusing to engage now?

Panic floods my system.

What if he's acting this way to protect me? What if she's more hurt than I realize and he's just waiting for the others to get here so he only has to explain it once?

Does he know more than I do? Why isn't he filling me in?

I take two long steps forward, ready to demand he talk to me, but before I can, his dad rushes into the room, and the sight of him sucks all the air right out of my lungs.

Dr. F freezes when he's sees Greedy standing stock-still with his arms crossed over his chest, his face blanching.

They stand off, neither speaking as the seconds tick by.

Finally, in the lowest, most grave voice I've ever heard escape G, he says, "Magnolia pushed her down the stairs."

A shocked, exasperated gasp fills the silence. "Garrett," Dr. Ferguson scolds. "I understand you're upset, but to throw around unwarranted accusations—"

"*Enough.*" G charges toward his dad, fuming.

Instinctively, I follow, ready to have his back, support him, whatever he needs.

"She pushed her. She fucking *pushed* her. If you'd open your goddamn eyes and pay a single modicum of attention to anything besides work and your flighty, deranged wife, you wouldn't be so fucking surprised."

All the calmness. All the inferred control.

It's gone. Vanished.

G wasn't blocking me out. He was barely holding his shit together and harboring it close so he'd unleash on the person who actually deserves his ire.

"Garrett, please—"

"No, Dad. This isn't a discussion. This isn't a debate. I heard Hunter's fucking scream from your office. She was pushed. Magnolia fucking *pushed* her."

Dr. F hangs his head. He looks so small. Frail and older, somehow.

With a subtle shake of his head, he lifts his gaze and focuses on his son. "We don't know that. Not for sure."

Greedy stiffens, his posture embodying the dismay and disappointment engulfing me in this moment. I used to admire Dr. Ferguson. Hell, I used to be jealous of G because he had such a great dad. But what sort of parent ignores all the ugly they'd rather not see, picking and choosing when to show up for their kid, when to stand at their side?

The jealousy that's long lingered in the back of my mind evaporates. No longer do I wish Dr. F was my dad the way I did growing up.

No. As I take in the meek man before me, I'm disgusted more than anything.

"I have nothing left to say to you, then," Greedy replies, whisper-soft.

With a sigh, Dr. Ferguson looks over G's shoulder at me, his eyes searching and desperate. Whatever he sees in my expression shuts him down once again.

"I'll be in my office." With that, he turns on his heel, leaving the waiting area without another word.

I step forward and place one hand on G's shoulder. He needs to know I'm here. That I'm not going anywhere. When he's ready, if he needs me, I'm right fucking here.

Without warning, he slumps back, giving me all his weight. With an *oomph*, I hold him up, steadying him. I thread my arms beneath his and around his torso and rest my chin on his shoulder.

It's not enough—it's impossible to dull the edges and soothe the ache of this moment—but it's all I can give him right now.

"I love you." This is the least romantic setting. We're under the most dire of circumstances. Even so, I need him to know. In the face of the most harrowing day of our lives, I just need him to fucking know.

"I love you, too," he sniffles, smoothing his hands down my forearms. A silent sob rolls through him.

I hold him tighter, determined to absorb as much of his pain as I can. His breathing is shaky for a few inhales. Then, suddenly, it's not.

G scrubs at his face, turns in my arms, and looks me square in the eyes. "Let's go find our girl."

Chapter 38

Greedy

The only light in the room comes from the medical equipment. The red, blue, green, and blinding white. Some flashing, some glowing steadily.

Hunter is hooked up to two or three monitors and receiving an IV drip to keep her hydrated. The staff swore she woke up in triage but was too confused and disoriented to give them any information, including her name.

Only when I introduced myself—and painfully used the term *stepbrother* to get permission to stay past visiting hours—did anyone give much consideration to Hunter's situation.

All we know is that she fell, that her face, neck, and arms are covered in small lacerations, and that they suspect a concussion, but won't know for sure until she wakes up and they can evaluate her cognition and recall.

There's been no mention of broken bones or internal bleeding. Although I can't imagine she doesn't have at least a few cracked ribs after a tumble down that many stairs.

The lacerations don't make sense. How did she get so cut up? They're sprinkled all over, and the one on her jaw was severe enough to require stitches.

We know little about the events that led to the fall. She's only been settled on this floor for a couple of hours. By morning rounds, we should have more information about the severity of her injuries.

Likewise, by morning, our girl will hopefully be awake and able to tell us herself what happened.

For what feels like a lifetime, Levi and I sit in silence on the vinyl couch shoved against one side of the hospital room with our legs press together. Every now and then, he'll rest his head on my shoulder or I'll have the urge to squeeze his knee, thankful to have him by my side. He's like a tether, tugging at me, reminding me I'm not alone when my thoughts turn too dark or when hopelessness surrounding my dad and Magnolia sets in.

The beeps of the monitor and the occasional alarm across the hall at the nurse's station are melodic background noise, almost inaudible over the loud, intrusive thoughts vying for dominance in my brain. I don't know how much time has passed—minutes, hours, half the night—when I'm jolted awake by a sharp knock on the closed door.

Before I can rise, it swings open. Kabir and Sione stand in the doorframe, illuminated from behind by the harsh fluorescent lights in the hall.

My heart pangs at the sight of them. *Finally*.

It's been hours since we arrived. Why the hell has it taken so long for them to get here?

I lean forward, ready to stand and greet them, but before I can, Kabir whispers "don't" through the darkness.

Breath held, I search his face. What the fuck? Why wouldn't he want me to come out into the hall and get them up to speed?

I blink at him, wondering if I misheard him, but then he holds up his hand and shakes his head again.

Angling back against the couch cushion, I side-eye Levi. He's fast asleep, his head bobbing at an awkward angle as he snoozes with his arms over his chest.

I turn back to the others, annoyed, honestly, that they haven't even attempted to enter the room. They need to see this. To see the state of our girl. To see exactly what Magnolia did. I open my mouth to tell them as much, but the vibrating of my phone snags my attention before I can make a sound.

> **Spence:** I won't make it to the hospital tonight, I'm afraid. I have an appointment with my accountant I can't reschedule. Si and I will be by tomorrow, bright and early.

By the time I've finished reading the text, the door is being pulled closed and the room is cast in nothing but the glow of medical equipment once more.

Chapter 39

Kabir

It was never a question of if, only when.

Though the how was still undecided. Now the scenario we're preparing to deploy lends itself to the easiest of executions with the simplest of clean-ups required. Despite the vengeance still alight inside me, or maybe because of it, I was positively chuffed when the pieces fell into place with such precision.

Dark men's scrubs, size medium.

A nondescript gray Toyota idling at the loading dock.

A perfectly timed distraction on her hospital floor.

It's all set, ready for me to put the plan into motion.

We debated between insulin and acetaminophen for weeks. Now that intravenous access is an option, I've decided I don't want to choose. I'll use both.

If I can't physically maim or leave any evidence on the outside of Magnolia St. Clair-Ferguson, I want her insides to twist in anguish as she races toward a swift and immediate end.

"Please don't come inside with me."

Sione is a good man. Sensitive in ways I can't begin to fathom. I fear what I'm about to do will change how he views me. I'm certain he knows my intentions. That, I can live with. For him to bear witness to my actions? To have that visual burned in his mind's eye for all the rest of our days? I can't bear it.

"I won't. But I will be waiting out here, ready to support you however I can when this is done."

His words touch me. Though I do not anticipate needing any support, the relief coursing through me is one of the highest exhilarations I've ever experienced.

Almost time.

Almost done.

Almost handled, once and for all.

Kylian enters the hospital room, right on cue, an oversized laundry bin rolling behind him.

"Dr. Walsh," I remark blandly, poking fun at the black scrubs Kylian has donned for the occasion.

"Sir Spencer," he retorts as he approaches.

I don't continue the tête-à-tête. Instead, I snap my mouth closed, allowing the sight before us to speak for itself.

"Well done, you," he murmurs. "One down. Six to go."

Right. As part of our pact, I have agreed to help Kylian dispose of the six wankers who dared to assault Josephine when she was in high school.

Although I suspect we've got quite a bit of time before Kylian will be ready to take definitive action. Despite being very black and white in regard to most things in life, he apparently wants to toy with his prey a while longer.

I've studied the Gannt chart he created. The six insufferable bastards have years of suffering ahead of them before they'll pay the ultimate price.

No matter. Murder isn't for the faint of heart. Thankfully, I've never felt faint a day in my life.

Calmness washed over me as it was happening.

Magnolia seized in quite a dramatic fashion. It was exquisite, really. I stayed close, overseeing the entire ordeal so that I can tell Hunter with full confidence that the threat has been eliminated for good.

It has.

I witnessed it.

I made it so.

"She's been wiped from the system," Kylian confirms. "Between the shift change and my perfectly timed data scramble, it'll take hours for the staff to realize they're short a patient. By the time the administrative level can be coaxed into caring, all physical traces will cease to exist. Anyone's best guess will be that she walked out of her own volition without informing anyone."

"Very good. Very good, indeed."

Chapter 40

Sione

Kylian exits the room, brow furrowed and focus fixed on the device in his hands. He's seemingly startled to see me when he pulls the door closed behind him and looks around the hall.

"Why are you still here?"

Unable to articulate the sensation—the certainty that I can and will be of service, just not yet—I turn the question on him. "Why are *you* still here?"

"Clean-up," he deadpans.

Fair enough. I tip my head in respect. "I, too, am standing by for clean-up. But of the energetic variety."

Kylian nods, as if he's not surprised. "Kendrick told me you are into new-age, alternative medicine. He said he felt the best he ever has after you performed some sort of spell on him."

I can't help the grin that takes over my face. That "spell" was a simple reiki healing session as part of his recovery on day two of the Combine. Though I get the impression Kylian is not in the headspace to listen to me explain chakras and ancient healing modalities.

If he's still helping Spence, he needs to stay focused.

"Thank you," I murmur sincerely. "You are the sun of your cohort, Kylian Walsh, but you've also proven to be an essential star in ours."

Light blue eyes search my face through square-rimmed glasses. "If that was a metaphor intended to imply significance, then Jo is the sun," he corrects. "Always my sun."

The frequency of his life force shines brighter now that he's thinking of her. His dedication is admirable.

"Very well, then. You are the gravitational pull of your group. You are one they rely on to keep the planets aligned and the universe in harmony."

His lips turn down slightly. "Do you always speak like that?"

"I do. Is that a problem?"

Levi has teased me for my flowery prose in the past. By the way Kylian's words land, though, I worry there's more than just unfamiliarity underlying his question.

He blinks at me before looking away. "No. It's not. I just needed the assurance that the way you're speaking is the norm. That you aren't mocking me."

"Never."

Kylian's frequency settles, my answer clearly satisfactory.

"Okay."

"Okay."

We stand quietly in the hall, sentinels hovering on either side of a portal, until Spence finally emerges.

"All yours," he tells Kylian. I chance a glance into the room. It's pristine, with no traces of life physically or energetically. A large laundry cart sits idly, filled almost to the brim with sheets and towels.

The irony is not lost on me. The unceremonious exit is valid in my mind's eye.

Magnolia is gone.

Magnolia can never hurt Hunter again.

Spence turns to me, eyebrows raised. "There's an empty ward two floors below us. It's part of an upcoming remodel. I thought perhaps we could retire there until the timing aligns for us to join the others."

With a nod, I extend one arm, signaling for him to lead the way.

We walk in silence, no words exchanged, but with each and every step, the leaded weight of what he's just done bears down on his soul more heavily.

By the time we travel down an empty stairwell, find the deserted hall, and select a vacant room, Spence's subtle body is weeping from exertion. His mind and spirit are so bleak they're no more than a dim flicker.

Instinctively, I rest my palm on his back, guiding him to the single bed in the middle of the sterile environment.

"Lie down," I implore.

Once he's supported by the mattress, I close the door, block it with a chair, and quickly grid the space.

"For the collective good of all beings." I trace the reiki symbol in front and above me before repeating the universal activation phrase three times.

"What are you—"

"Shh," I soothe. "How do you feel?"

He swallows hard, the sharp angle of his throat bobbing. He's fighting it. Resisting the despair he needs to process before it takes root in his soul.

"Tired," he finally admits.

He's chosen the most palatable description. Defeated, thin, wrecked, or raw are all equally fitting.

"Lie back, brother. Rest. I can help, if you're willing to accept it."

His back meets the mattress once more, but he keeps his head propped up, his exhausted eyes watching me with hopeless vacancy. "How?"

"May I enter your energetic field?" I ask.

He murmurs a "yes," then tips his head back and closes his eyes.

The moment I insert myself into his aura, I'm engulfed in pain. He tries to fight it, to bury it deep, but it's there. It's all-encompassing.

Power. Control. Dominance. Pain.

Influence. Clout. Charisma. More pain.

All parts of his being have been stained. All aspects of his brilliant mind are warring against the experience he just endured.

His soul is sobbing. The chakras from his third eye to his solar plexus are congested.

"May I put my hands on you?"

He agrees easily, his subconscious speaking now. His physical body is finally resting, his eyes dancing behind closed lids as his consciousness fights to catalog and protect him from the horrors he committed.

I start at the top, channeling energy through my being with the intention of empowering him to feel and heal. I follow my typical flow, moving my hand placements down his body when I feel called to do so.

When my palms connect with his rib cage, there's clear conflict.

A searing hot resistance burning deep in his solar plexus.

"You're blocked." Eyes closed, I channel more energy into the space where his rib cage ends.

"I know." He sighs. "It's stuck."

Affection warms me. He's not the powerful CEO, the dominant lover, or the aloof alpha male I've grown to know and tolerate.

In this moment, he's simply human.

"Keep breathing," I encourage.

He does. I do, too.

Several minutes pass. Sweat gathers on my brow. A single drop rolls down my neck. Then, finally, the energy I'm channeling through him unblocks the release.

Spence sucks in a sharp breath. He responds beautifully to the dislodgement. The emptiness in his chest fills with light, love, oxygen, and hope. Positive and neutral energy illuminate him from the inside out. Every time the healing light touches the darkness that remains, it flows around it like a gentle caress. I've never witnessed anything like it. The lightness doesn't absolve the dark. Instead, it accepts it and accommodates it.

It makes sense. The darkest parts of him are still worthy of light and love, because his murkiest morals and darkest deeds only exist in the interest of the highest good.

He gasps, his chest shudders, and then his body goes still.

I observe him for a few more minutes, ensuring his spirit is sated and that I haven't missed any tears in his aura. Once I'm satisfied that I've done all I can for now, I tell him, "I'm exiting your field," and do just that.

His breathing deepens, but he makes no attempts to sit up.

When his eyes blink open, solidarity and understanding pass between us unlike never before.

I've witnessed the darkness inside him. It's there, and there it shall remain. Its presence is intentional. Purposeful. Beautiful, even.

"Do you want to talk about it?" I let the question linger. It's vague, the *it*, by design. What he did and how he did it. What he felt and what he's feeling now. My goal in this moment is to support him in any way I can.

"There was—there was this light. But it didn't glow. It was murky green, like the dying light of a neglected antique. It was right here." He presses his hand to his sternum.

Humming, I nod once. "I felt it, too."

"I think it left," he muses, clearly still out of it.

"It did," I assure him. "It left, and it'll never return. We're safe, Spence. We're safe because of you."

His eyes well with tears as he receives my message and accepts it for what it is: immense gratitude and pointed assurance that although what he did was wrong, he did the right thing for his family.

Eventually, he collects himself and dons his usual armor.

"We have to wait here until morning." His tone is authoritative, his chin lifted and his eyes piercing.

I take his hand in mine. "Sleep. I will sit guard. Nothing physical, spiritual, or otherwise will harm you while you rest."

With one last flash of vulnerability, he whispers, "Thank you."

His eyes are already closed when I reply.

"Rest easy, brother. The worst is over now."

Chapter 41

Greedy

"Son, wake up."

My brain is pulled from its drowsy state with such intensity I can't pinpoint the source of the voice. Heart lurching, I jackknife to sitting, my eyes flying open. Did something happen? Did Hunter wake up?

"What's happening? Is she okay?"

"No. She's gone."

I scramble to my feet, nausea roiling in my gut, and scrub the sleep from my eyes. My heart rate has tripled, but quickly, thank fuck, I spot Hunter, and relief washes over me so violently I stumble.

She's not gone; she's right there.

Bruised. Cut up. Swollen.

My beautiful angel girl, her blond hair fanned out around her like a halo against the thin pillow under her head.

"She's right there," I whisper, intent on keeping our voices down so she can get the rest she needs.

"What? No." The volume of his words makes me wince. "Not Hunter. *Magnolia*. Magnolia's gone."

I exhale the most steadying breath I can manage. Of course this is about fucking Magnolia.

With bated, hopeful breath, I ask, "What do you mean, gone?"

"She's *gone*. She left. She's not in her room, not in the computer system, and everyone in this goddamn hospital is acting like she never existed! She's not at home or answering her cell. Her injuries were too severe for her to just get up and leave."

His agitation and desperation are like living entities in the room, causing the air to charge. What he's saying makes no sense at all. And yet... Spence was here. But he didn't want me to know. Magnolia is gone, and apparently, there's no trace of her at all.

"Let's go out in the hall. I don't want to disturb Hunter." I shake Levi awake, and when he cracks his eyes open, I say, "Everything's okay, but I'm going down the hall to talk to my dad. Spence and Sione should be here soon."

"Got it. I'm up." Sleepily, he stands and stretches his arms overhead.

Satisfied Levi won't let our girl out of his sight, I put a hand on my dad's shoulder and guide him out of the room. As I turn back to close the door, I catch Levi gingerly climbing into the hospital bed. I can't fight my smile or the tenderness that makes my chest constrict. I love them both so much. I'll do anything—fight anyone, including my own father—to ensure their safety and well-being.

My mind drifts to Spence and Sione as I follow my dad down the hall. I don't know where they are. More importantly, I don't know what they did. All Spence's secretive planning makes sense now. I'm about to look my dad in the eye and swear I have no idea what happened to Magnolia, and it'll be the truth.

His office is several floors above where we currently stand, but there, we'll have complete privacy. We walk the hall and take the elevator up in silence.

He's barely closed his office door when his panic flares once more. Eyes wide, he takes a step closer to me. "You have to help me. We have to find her."

His office is large and well-appointed. It's the place he spent most of my childhood. Rather than at home with me.

Resolutely, I shake my head. "Magnolia pushed Hunter down the stairs, Dad."

His body stiffens. "You don't know that."

"I do. I heard Hunter cry out. I think you heard her, too."

Hands in his pockets, he stalks around his executive desk. Rather than sit, though, he paces. Three strides to the right, then three strides to the left, like a caged animal with no way out.

"Magnolia fell, too. Don't you understand?"

Frustration ripples through me. He's the one who isn't comprehending. "Magnolia—" I inhale a calming breath and choose my tense with the utmost care. Although my gut tells me she's no longer a problem, I have no interest in breaking that news to my dad. "She's not a good person. She's been manipulating Hunter for years."

"That's not true."

His blind determination to defend her frays my final thread of patience.

"It *is* true," I holler, arms flung out wide. "Magnolia mistreated Hunter for *years*. In high school, she'd leave her alone for days at a time. She wouldn't pick up groceries or check up on her daughter. Sometimes Hunter wouldn't eat for an entire day because she didn't feel safe leaving her room. Magnolia wouldn't even meet up with her in Europe when Hunter tried to make contact. She's not a good mother. She's not a good *person*."

I'm breathless by the time I end my tirade.

His shoulders lower. "How...how do you know all that?"

There it is. I tip my head back and close my eyes, digging deep for the nerve to confess what I should have told him years ago. With my gaze still fixed on the ceiling, I speak.

"Because Hunter and I were together before you and Magnolia were a thing."

The room is silent. Too silent.

I drop my chin and look at him, worried he didn't hear me.

His face is screwed up in devastated bewilderment. Oh, he definitely heard me.

"What?" The word is more of a croak.

"We met at the end of our senior year. We fell in love the summer before college. We were together for the couple of months before you and Magnolia 'introduced' us at your engagement dinner."

Swaying, he grips the edge of his desk. "Why didn't you say something?"

Rage rushes through me at his question. *Why didn't I say something?* I was a kid. He was the adult. "Because you don't *listen*."

Fuck. It felt incredible to let that out. Though it isn't the full truth, nor is it fair to my dad. That night at the country club was a literal nightmare for my girl. She was experiencing so much more pain and loss than I could have even fathomed. She asked me not to tell them about us, and I naïvely agreed, thinking we'd figure out a plan together once the dust had settled.

That's not all on my dad.

"I'm sorry." I swallow past the lump in my throat. "That's not fair. Originally, I didn't say anything because it was awkward. We were young and had no idea how to handle the situation. But soon after that night—" A wave of regret and sadness washes over me. "Something changed. You changed. You only heard what you wanted to hear and saw what you want to see. I always assumed that was because of Magnolia."

He shakes his head, his mouth opening and closing, but he doesn't speak.

"You were happy, I get that. You were busy, too. But you missed a lot. Remember my freshman year? I was struggling. I lost weight. My grades were so bad I had to drop two classes in order to save my GPA. That didn't occur out of nowhere. I was heartbroken. Devastated. A shell of a human. And you didn't even notice."

"I—" Eyes wide, he huffs out a breath. "I don't really remember any of that. I don't know what to say."

I stare back at him from across the desk, showing him my truth. I won't argue with him or beg him to believe me. My experience is valid. It's real, whether he believes me or not. Given his devotion to Magnolia, there's a good chance he won't accept my version of events. That's okay. At least I tried.

"You and Hunter?" he asks, disbelief etched into the wrinkles and worry lines on his face.

"Yes." I nod resolutely. He needs to know. "Since the summer before college."

"And now?"

"I've loved her all this time. I still love her." The *still*, though, doesn't feel like a strong enough word for my devotion. "I love her more than ever," I amend.

He only gapes at me, his lips turned down in a confused frown.

"I didn't want you to find out like this, but you deserve to know the truth. The *whole* truth. Hunter and I are together. Levi and I are together, too. The other two guys we've been spending time with... they're... involved as well. It's complicated, but we're making it work. And Dad?"

He holds my gaze.

"I'm happy. *Really* happy. I love Hunter. And I loathe anything that negatively impacts her, including her mother."

His eyes widen, but I press on before he can argue.

"Magnolia makes her miserable. She dims her light on a good day. She kidnaps her or shoves her down the stairs on a bad day."

His harsh inhale tells me the joke didn't land. With a shake of his head, he looks over my shoulder to the door, lost in thought. After a few breaths, he focuses back on me.

"Do you think Magnolia left on her own?" he asks pathetically. "I don't know what to do. Should I file a missing person's report?"

Disappointment washes over me. Despite everything—baring my soul, sharing my truth, and trying like hell to reason with him—he's intent on living in his own world. It's like he's been brainwashed. Like it's impossible for him to even consider anything beyond what he's believed to be true for all these years. He's not stupid. But in this moment, there's no getting through to him.

Still, I need to try. I want to try. I don't want to lose my dad, but I'll walk away if I have to.

"Dad. If Magnolia left..." I swallow thickly, working through how to phrase what I have to say. I'm almost certain she didn't *leave*, at least not of her own volition. But if that's what he needs to believe, I won't argue. "If Magnolia left, it would be the best thing for Hunter if she never came back."

With a startled choke, he clings to the edge of his executive desk with both hands and wordlessly drops down into his chair.

"Don't look for her. Please. Don't go after her. If she left, let her go. Don't choose to chase her. Choose Hunter. Choose *me*."

He hangs his head and shakes it back and forth, then lifts his palms to his eyes.

"Please, Dad. Please choose us."

Eventually he straightens, and when he meets my gaze, I swear a flicker of confliction burns behind his irises. But then he blinks, and the hope is snuffed out once more.

"I have work to do," he says calmly. Dismissively. "Please let me know if anything changes with your sis—with Hunter."

I bite my tongue so hard my eyes water. With a single nod, I back out of the office.

Chapter 42

Kabir

My eyes fly open. I feel reborn.

Slowly, I sit up and find my bearings. Sione is awake, sitting cross-legged on a worn vinyl couch, watching me.

"Let's go see our girl."

We leave the room exactly as we found it, then travel down to the main lobby to use the bathroom and freshen up.

When we emerge, we stop by the visitor desk, ask for information, and receive official visitor name tags.

As the elevator door opens, I nearly trip over my own damn feet out of eagerness, and Sione snickers beside me.

"Right, then." I straighten my jacket and run one hand through my hair.

In unison, we stride straight for the room, not even pausing at the door.

Inside, I make a beeline for the bedside.

Hunter lies flat on starched white sheets, positively ravaged with bruises and cuts and swollen patches all over her skin. Her chest rises and falls in a reassuring, steady rhythm, bringing a modicum of relief with each inhalation.

Levi is curled awkwardly on his side next to her, his large frame twisted in a way that can't be comfortable.

Though sometimes comfort isn't about physical ease, I suppose.

Hovering closer, I tuck a lock of blond hair behind her ear and press my lips to an unmarred patch of skin near her temple.

My beautiful, resilient Firecracker.

For a moment, I pause there, recalling the meticulous planning that occurred over the last twenty-four hours, as well as the precise execution. With the memories comes a strange solace.

It was for her. For them. For us.

And it was all worth it.

Levi brushes his hand over mine, pulling me from my thoughts. Silently, I meet his gaze and desperately try to communicate that we're safe, but that he can't ask questions or know anything about what happened last night.

When he nods slowly in response to my unspoken plea, I capture his hand. Fingers laced with his, I hold tight and gingerly move around the hospital bed.

When I reach his side, I bend low once more and kiss his forehead. "Are you well, Champ?"

The door cracks open, drawing the attention of the three of us awake in the room. Garrett walks through, then promptly closes it behind him.

Levi smiles that bright, brilliant, all-American smile that makes my insides riot with appreciation. I want more. More moments with him, with her, with all of us. More smiles, more laughter, more life without having to live in fear.

He takes Garrett in, then turns back to look at me. "I am now," he finally answers. "Help me up."

Still holding his hand, I cup his elbow and pull him off the bed.

Sione is right there, prepared to slot in and fill the empty space Levi left beside Hunter.

Together, Levi and I shuffle to the couch and sit. Garrett snags a plastic chair and spins it, then spreads his legs wide and straddles it.

"My dad knows about Hunter and me. Me and you, too." He nods at Levi, his expression uncertain. "About all of us, to an extent."

Levi's response is a sharp hiss.

Garrett cups his knee and gives it a reassuring squeeze. "Don't stress, Leev. He won't judge us. Hell, I don't think he even processed half of what I said, considering his one and only concern is Magnolia."

"Magnolia will no longer be a problem," I decree.

Both men go quiet, their attention shifting to me.

Levi's body tenses beside me. "Did you—"

I hold up one hand to silence him.

"So she's really—"

A curt glare shuts up Garrett as well.

"Magnolia will no longer be a problem," I repeat. "Magnolia will never be a problem for us again."

As my words sink in, the worry ebbs from each man. Though, unsurprisingly, a hint of pensiveness remains. There's concern there, but not fear.

"She's free," Garrett whispers, his gaze set on the woman we all love, who's still sleeping soundly with Sione by her side.

She is.

If I end up serving a lifetime of karmic repentance or burning in hell for all eternity because of what I did, it will be worth it.

Chapter 43

Greedy

A soothing blanket of calm covers us now that we're all together and on the same page. The four of us lounge around the room, content to take turns lying next to Hunter as we wait for her to wake up.

Okay, content may be a generous description. Spence and Levi are louder than they've ever been, as if they can't help but try to speed the process along. Sione and I share a different opinion. If her body needs rest, she should have it. If her brain needs a break, she should take that, too. The monitors tracking her vitals adequately assure me she's okay. When she's ready, she'll wake up. Until then, we're not going anywhere.

A few nurses have come in to check on her, but none have jostled her enough to wake her.

A soft knock on the door around midmorning has us all on alert, and when it swings open and four doctors sweep in for rounds, Kabir and I are on our feet.

More than one brow furrows when they catch sight of us.

"Hi. I'm Garrett, Dr. Ferguson's son."

Without suggesting we step out of the room, they introduce themselves. One of the doctors sidles up to the charting computer, logs in, asks me to confirm Hunter's name and birthdate, then presents.

"Patient presents with multiple lacerations and bruises following a fall down a full flight of stairs. Collarbone and rib fractures are suspected but unconfirmed. The initial brain scan was clear, showing no signs of bleeding or swelling. Mild concussion expected, to be confirmed once the patient wakes up.

"There were no alcohol, drugs, or other foreign substances in her system in the initial blood work. She's receiving six hundred milligrams of acetaminophen every six hours for pain."

My chest tightens, stealing the air from my lungs. "That's all you're giving her?"

She fell down an entire set of stairs, she's absolutely covered in injuries, and they're giving her an over-the-counter pain reliever and nothing more?

"We can put orders in for more, but only once she wakes up and remains that way so we can complete the full assessment."

Fuck this. What if she's in so much pain she can't wake up?

"Anyone with eyes can see she's severely injured," I snap.

Sione steps up behind me, placing a gentle hand on my shoulder.

"I agree. We can wake her now if—"

"*No*," I bark.

Despite how badly I want to know the extent of her injuries, she needs to rest. To heal. Even if it prolongs our emotional suffering.

"Very well. We have questions for the patient about how she fell, as well. If she passed out or experienced a bout of low blood pressure—"

"We believe she tripped and fell down the stairs." It's a bald-faced lie, but it's the best option to protect Hunter from any level of suspicion, should my dad actually file a missing person's report for Magnolia.

"Right. Okay. There's not much more we can do until she wakes up, then. She'll be here for at least a few days so we can monitor her blood pressure and sugar levels. You lot can make sure she's eating small meals throughout the day. An ultrasound tech should be in later, but the nurses haven't reported any bleeding, so there's minimal concern there."

Sione's grip on my shoulder squeezes like a vise.

"Ultrasound?" I ask. "For what?"

The presenting doctor stumbles, clearly concerned she shared something she shouldn't have.

No one else attempts to intervene, so I repeat my question. "What's the ultrasound for?"

I've never been more grateful to be the child of the chief physician at Lake Chapel General.

With a defeated sigh, she says, "According to her chart, the patient is pregnant."

Breath catching, I whip around and focus on Spence.

His brow is furrowed, and he looks just as bewildered as I feel.

He clears his throat and straightens his cuffs. "Was that information previously entered into the patient's chart?" His tone is cool and uncaring, his inflection at odds with the desperation plaguing me.

The doctor clicks around the screen, then shakes her head. "No. Blood work at admission shows the patient's hCG was seventy-eight thousand milli-international units per milliliter. The test results are dated yesterday." Her eyes widen with understanding, and she looks up from the computer. "This makes more sense now. That's why they haven't confirmed the broken ribs or collarbone. The MRI was strictly to check for brain swelling and injuries to her head. No X-rays were ordered because of the baby."

Because of the baby.

Because of the baby.

The room spins and blood rushes in my ears. The doctors may continue to talk, I don't know. I can't hear a thing. As they exit, I force myself to breathe and turn to glance at each of the guys. Their expressions are just as shocked, dazed, and ecstatic as mine.

Hunter's pregnant.

Chapter 44

Hunter

Above me, all around me, the sky is a rosy expanse dotted with the puffiest pink clouds. The air smells like strawberries. A scent so sweet I can almost taste it each time I inhale.

I can't help but giggle at the absurdity. Clouds aren't supposed to be pink. There's no way this is real. Yet I'm more than happy to play along, delighting in wisps of wonderment as they gently brush past me like the aurora borealis painting the sky.

Warmth spreads through me.

It's like taking off wet clothes, putting on dry pajamas, and wrapping in a fuzzy blanket. It's that first bite of dessert: rich, sweet, and deliciously indulgent. It's the giddiness of starting a new book when there's nothing but time, quiet, and solitude lending themselves to hours of reading.

I'm warm from the inside out.

I'm safe from the crown of my head to the tips of my toes.

There isn't a dark cloud in sight. Not in front of me or on the horizon. I'm surrounded by beauty and hope. Awash with contentment and peace.

Limitless joy illuminates me.

No more running.
This is it.
This is my life.
This is my life.
Is it really possible for this to be my life?
A burst of color catches my eye. Then another. It's different but just as vibrant.

Reds and purples. Blues and oranges. Bold hues juxtaposed against a cotton candy sky. Some whiz by. Others glide without rush. A few more pass before I realize what they are.

Paper airplanes.

Each one is jetting off in the same direction, determined to make their one and only flight worthy of the journey.

A niggling sensation in my gut tells me to turn around. Without hesitation, I obey and find an enormous arch. Color, light, and radiance shine down, creating a perfect rainbow. The glow emitting from it is the warmest, most welcoming invitation.

As I study it, I realize the warmth isn't coming from the rainbow. If anything, the colors of the rainbow are unremarkable compared to the rest of the sight in front of me. The real magic, an ethereal glow, comes from the love and goodness shining below the massive colorful arch.

Beneath it, four figures stand.

My heart. My lightness. My joy. My hope.

I would recognize them anywhere. What I don't recognize is the bundle in the arms of one of the forms. Or the way they fuss and coo at it, forming a massive man puddle of emotion. Whatever it is, it—and they—belong to me. This is true. For the first time ever, I know in my heart of hearts that we're safe.

We'll be okay.

We'll be more than okay.

There's only lightness now; there's nothing left to run from.

Tears of relief, joy, and sheer exhaustion prick behind my eyes. The pressure rises, uncontrollable, the tears demanding to escape.

The first drops fall, rolling down my temples and into my hair.

Calloused fingers quickly brush them away.

A shiver travels up my spine.

Never before has there been a person waiting, ready to catch my tears. To even realize I'm crying. Now, with my guys, I can't shed a single tear without being comforted.

With a labored, painful breath—shit, that hurts—I force more oxygen into my lungs. The air clears away the edges of my pink-infused dream. After a few more arduous inhales, I'm fully awake. And in almost agonizing pain.

I crack one eye open, then the other.

Steady green orbs stare back at me, searching my face.

Greedy.

"Hi," I croak.

"You're awake," he whispers, the two words a grateful prayer. He pulls back a few inches and, louder and much more enthusiastically, he declares to the room, "She's awake!"

I wince. My dry throat burns when I attempt to swallow, and pain is starting to register in the oddest places. On my cheekbone. Between my neck and shoulder. In my low back. Behind my right knee.

But it's the throbbing headache that surprises me the most.

"Water?"

Greedy backs away quickly, and only a moment later, there's an oversized cup with a bendy straw at my lips.

"What's your pain level, Tem? Want me to call the nurse in?"

Right. I'm in the hospital. Thanks to another run-in with Magnolia.

Flovely.

I should ask about her. Discern who knows what about what happened at the top of the stairs. Fresh tears well at the prospect of having to rehash the incident to the guys.

They don't deserve this. I don't either. I may have lost the genetic lottery, but that doesn't mean the people I love should have to endure this kind of—

"Firecracker."

I lift my head quickly, and a sharp pain lances my temples. I wince again, then wince harder when even that hurts. Damn my Pavlovian response to Spence's intensity.

"Oof. Sorry, love," he murmurs. "Can you get the nurse back in here as soon as I'm done?" he gripes. "She clearly needs better pain management."

Greedy shifts back, and Spence sits on the edge of the bed closest to me and clears his throat. "We need to talk to her before calling anyone else into the room."

Levi and Sione have made their way to my other side, each taking a turn to bend low and kiss my head. I try to smile, to express at least a facsimile of a greeting, but everything hurts, so the best I can manage is a slight grimace and a squeeze of their hands.

Spence and Greedy stare at each other, locked in a silent argument. Surprisingly, Spence is the first to defer. With a muttered "right," he takes my hand.

"Before anyone else arrives, I need to tell you something."

Nodding, I press my elbows into the mattress, trying to shift up the bed. Pain sears through me, intense enough that I immediately give up.

Wordlessly, Greedy pushes a button on the bedrail, and the head of the mattress elevates.

"Do you remember what happened at Dr. Ferguson's house?"

Another piercing pain, this one deep in my chest. "Yes."

Spence lifts a finger to my lips before I can fill in the blanks. "No," he corrects. "You don't remember anything."

I frown, which causes a tight burning pain to bloom on my cheekbone. Gingerly, I press two fingers to the spot, finding the scratchy texture of a bandage where I expect to find skin.

"They used the smallest thread size available," Greedy assures me. "The scar will be almost imperceptible."

"Focus, love. You don't remember anything," Spence repeats, garnering my attention again. "There's more."

Stilted silence blankets the room for several heartbeats, but no one speaks.

Eventually, Spence says, "Last night, I put a plan in place to ensure Magnolia can never contact you, touch you, or even look at you again."

Put a plan in place.

The word choice sticks in my brain. The way he said it and the follow up explanation...

"She's gone?"

"In every sense of the word," he confirms.

"No more fear, Mahina," Sione soothes, crouching to eye level. "I was there. Kabir was so very brave, never faltering, as he eliminated all future threats."

"Did you—"

Spence's finger meets my lips once more. If I wasn't in so much pain, I'd bite him. I have questions, dammit.

"Many, many pieces must still fall into place before we are free and clear. Even so, I can say with certainty that you are safe, love. You are safe in a way you haven't been throughout your entire life. You don't have to worry, or run, or think of her ever again."

Understanding prickles in my subconscious.

Magnolia is gone.

Magnolia can't get to me, not now or ever again.

Eyes closed, I search for an ounce of the guilt or grief I should feel if what I think Spence is hinting at is true.

I come up empty.

But as the seconds tick by, the emptiness doesn't keep.

It's washed away by waves of relief crashing into me. Entire swells of liberation pour into my soul. A feeling akin to joy lights up my insides, and I'm instantly transported back to the sweetest pink-infused dream.

No more running.

This really is my life.

"Thank you," I choke out on a sob.

I'm not sad. Not in the least. I'm so grateful I could burst. Even so, I can't quell the tears.

"Tem." Greedy takes my free hand. "There's something else you need to know."

My lungs seize up at the gravity in his tone. It's a very rough spot to be in, I realize quickly, because my chest fucking burns as if I've been stabbed.

"What's wrong, Mahina?" Sione coaxes.

"My chest hurts." White-hot pain sizzles along one side of my rib cage as each word leaves.

"They suspect at least a few broken ribs." This is the first time Levi has spoken. In a move that looks like it could have been choreographed, Sione rises, and Duke takes his place squatting near the bed.

"When will we know for sure?"

Sione's hands are now resting on my upper thighs, his body bowed over me. His touch doesn't take away the pain, but whatever he's doing does feel good enough to distract me. I reach down instinctively and run my fingers through his silky strands.

"We won't," Greedy replies. "Because they just came in and told us you're pregnant."

My body seizes once more: Lungs, face. Hands and fingers.

I'm frozen, suddenly sure I hit my head much harder than anyone suspected.

Finally, when I can breathe again and the pain subsides, I turn my head to Levi.

He's grinning. Actually grinning.

My heart sinks. He shouldn't be. This isn't real.

Maybe I'm dreaming again. Maybe I never woke up.

Could this be a flashback? Levi and I have been here before. In this hospital. Learning about my pregnancy.

Instantly, sorrow streaks through me.

Levi wasn't smiling that day. Greedy never knew. I hadn't even met Spence or Sione yet. Now, though, they're all here, surrounding me, smiling, grinning, downright jovial.

Fresh tears well in my eyes. I hate that I have to disappoint them. This isn't then, despite how desperately I wish I could turn back time.

"I'm not pregnant," I rasp. I had a period just a few weeks ago. It was a little early, and it only lasted a few days, but after going off birth control the month before, I expected it to be a little wonky.

"Baby." Greedy crouches on the other side of the hospital bed, taking my hand and tracing lines in my palm. "I think you might be."

The words are reverent, hopeful. It guts me to have to crush him. This man has never-ending faith.

Could it be that the doctored labs Spence presented us with earlier in the year made their way into my medical chart? Is that what's got the guys' hopes up?

As if reading my mind, Spence uses two fingers to tip my chin back so I'm looking at him. "The results from Crusade Labs wouldn't be in the system here, love. Apparently, the labs they drew last night showed positive hCG. That's why they couldn't do X-rays or confirm your breaks." The warmth in his expression radiates like the heat of the sun, the hopefulness sinking into me, all the way to my bones.

Pregnant.

For real?

"I don't even understand how..." I reclaim my hand from Levi and instinctively lower it to my stomach.

"Uh, we were all there, Daisy. You included."

I roll my eyes and swat at his backward hat. Instead of knocking it from his head, I cause a fresh wave of pain to sweep over my shoulder blade.

"Garrett, I swear to gods, if you don't call for the nurse this instant—"

Greedy pushes the call button before Spence can finish the threat.

Lifting his head, Sione places a chaste, tender kiss on the hand I'm resting low on my stomach. Then he rises. "The timing makes sense if your last period was not actually a shedding."

We're all silent for a beat. Then another. Looking at each other, marveling over the possibility that this could be real.

Greedy bends low and brings his lips to my ear. "Take another test, Tem. For me."

Chapter 45

Hunter

When Joey arrives, she swings the door open, plants one hand on her hip, and looks me up and down.

"See? She's fine," she says over her shoulder to a person, maybe people, we can't see. "Wait here." She strides into the room, closes the door behind her, and hits each and every one of my men with the surliest, nastiest stare.

"You all have some serious explaining to do."

"Good to see you too, Joze," Greedy teases from the vinyl couch. He's been pacing since we texted Joey two hours ago.

She sent a message not too long ago, saying she had to stop at the drugstore on her way because she swore she had a pregnancy test at home, but couldn't find it anywhere.

Whoops...

"Don't start with me, Garrett Reed," she singsongs, sashaying over to my bedside. "There are two very agitated men outside those doors who are, A, livid our afternoon in an empty house for the first time in *months* was interrupted, and B, even more perturbed I wouldn't let them come into the drugstore with me."

"Perturbed?" Levi mouths, face scrunched up in bewilderment.

"Sorry." The word, like every other I've uttered, makes me wince.

Joey's attitude evaporates in an instant. She's by my side a second later.

"No one's mad at you, babe. I swear. Though I do have some questions." She raises both eyebrows, all sorts of mischief painted on her face.

"Help me to the bathroom?"

The nurse came by and removed the catheter an hour ago and helped me use the toilet on my own, but with all the fluids they've been pumping into me, I could burst again already.

With slow, deliberate movements, aided by Sione on one side and Joey on the other—although all the guys are squirming and anxious to jump in and help—I make it to the small bathroom.

At the door, I look back, wildly nervous and nowhere near as hopeful as they look. I worry my lip as I take in each guy. Should I invite them in here? They won't all fit, and if they can't all be here, I don't know how I'm supposed to—

"Go on, Mahina," Sione encourages. "We're okay to wait here."

Like always, his soothing tone calms me.

"Shouldn't they have these available here?" Joey quips once we're in the bathroom with the door shut behind us. She thrusts the plastic drugstore bag out, the sound loud in the small, tiled space.

Wincing, I hold out a hand.

With a squeak, she yanks it back and pulls the box out for me. "Do you want to pee on the stick or into the cup?"

My eyes go blurry. God, she's so kind and beautiful and helpful. I wish I could stop the waterworks. It hurts when the salty tears streak down my face and sear the little cuts from the broken glass of the picture frame I clung to as I fell down the stairs.

Flovely. Now I'm crying and in even more pain.

"Cup, please," I sniffle.

"Hunter." Her bright blue eyes go wide as she takes me in, then they start to fill with tears. "Shit on a crumbly cracker." She drops the open box and still sealed contents on the counter and wraps me in a gentle hug.

I squeeze her back, despite the aches and pains. I'm just so damn grateful to have her in my life.

She's the very best friend a girl could ask for. I don't know what I would do or who I would be if she hadn't swept into my life last August.

"I didn't realize you were genuinely upset," she says into my hair. "I was just teasing the boys. But you're really worried, aren't you?"

She pulls back and holds me at arm's length.

Oh. The air rushes out of me in a painful breath. "*No*. I'm not worried at all about this." I sweep a hand through the air, gesturing to the half-opened pregnancy test supplies scattered around the sink. "I'm just really glad you're here. That you dropped everything. That you came—"

Fresh tears wash over me and steal the words out of my mouth. Head lowered, I sniffle and wipe at the corners of my eyes.

"Babe," Joey deadpans.

When I peek up at her, she's back to her usual sassy self: both hands on her hips, one brow arched.

"There isn't anything I wouldn't do for you. There isn't a person in this world I'd let stand in my way of getting to you when you need me, our cohorts included."

I scrunch my nose. "Cohort is really the word we've settled on?"

Joey snorts. "Kylian and Spence use it regularly. I don't think the rest of us have a say when those two put their heads together."

A sense of knowing nudges at my subconscious. Spence. Kylian. I turn to Joey, contemplating how much to say, or if I should say anything at all.

On a whisper, I confess, "I think Spence..." I search for the words but come up short.

"Unalived Magnolia?" she asks, deadpan. "Shmurdered the momster? Deleted your egg donor?"

"Joey!"

"What?" She throws her head back and cackles. "You're the one who always sends me those videos where people recommend books without using the words 'kill' or 'murder.' You have no one to blame but yourself."

The last statement hits hard. She's right. Magnolia is... gone, based on what I've surmised. And there's no one to blame but me.

"Hey, Hunt?"

"Hmm?"

"How'd you get all those cuts and bruises?" She traces a perfectly polished red nail along a particularly nasty purple patch above my elbow.

I don't answer. I don't have to. She knows. Just like she knows this is the reminder I need to pull me out of my darkening thoughts.

"She wasn't giving up, babe. I laid awake so many nights worrying, knowing damn well you weren't safe while she was still breathing. Kylian assured me Spence had it under control."

I gasp at that confession.

"It was her or you, Hunter. And I'm really, really glad it wasn't you."

She pulls me into another hug, this one tight and desperate, but comforting all the same.

A knock on the other side of the door startles us apart.

"Josephine?"

Eyes wide, Joey slams her palm against the solid wood separating us from her husband. "Decker Crusade, I told you to give us a minute—"

"It's been ten minutes, Siren."

"Shit." She grabs a disposable cup from a stack by the sink and hands it to me. "Fill 'er up," she tells me. Then she whips around, faces the door, and yells, "We need three more minutes."

The "pee in a cup" method is far less messy than the "try to aim your urethra and temper your flow enough to pee on a stick" method. Lesson fucking learned.

I cap the test and turn it over right away, ignoring the questioning look my best friend gives me.

While we wait, she helps me wash up, spraying a bit of dry shampoo she pulled from the drugstore bag on my scalp and handing me a fresh toothbrush and mini toothpaste.

"You're a lifesaver," I praise. I'm desperate to feel some semblance of clean.

"Better than a life-ender," she quips.

A mix of horror and delirious giddiness courses through me. "*Joey*," I shriek, my new toothbrush hanging from my mouth.

"I'm kidding."

"Girl." I lower my voice. "Seriously. If Spence hears us joking about—"

She holds out her little finger. "I pinky promise not to make any comments, jokes, or other remarks about what your man may or may not have done to the woman formerly known as Magnolia."

I link my little finger with hers, then release her, rinse, and spit.

"Are you upset by any of it?" She casts her focus down, fiddling with her phone as the timer counts down on the screen.

"Not even a little," I confess. I'm hit with a zap of guilt about that, though it's not nearly as intense as it maybe should be. "Does that make me a bad daughter? A horrible person?"

She lifts her chin and looks me in the eye. "Not even a little."

The alarm on her phone rings. Time is officially up.

I snag the stick off the counter, keeping it turned down so I can't see the results. Before Joey can question me, I throw the bathroom door open and find myself under the scrutiny of six very curious men.

All my guys—plus Decker and Locke—stand around the room, on edge.

"I'll get them out of here," Joey murmurs, hand held out. "But first, may I?"

Grinning, I hand her the plastic stick. I can't resist watching her face as she reads the result. She gives nothing away. I should have known. She has the best damn poker face I've ever seen. She hands the test back to me, collects her men, and heads for the door.

Once it's just the five of us—my *cohort*, apparently—I shuffle over to Greedy and hand the test directly to him.

He flips it over with so much urgency, he nearly drops it. Then he lifts his head, smiles so wide I can see his molars, and lets out a resounding whoop.

"You're pregnant!"

Chaos ensues. All my guys clammer for a peek at the test, each of them surveying the thin white stick with the kind of admiration one would expect they'd have for the actual baby.

"You're pregnant." Greedy loops his arms around me with the gentlest of touches and brings his lips millimeters from mine. "It worked, Tem. It worked. We're having a baby."

He blinks, the motion sending tears streaming down his cheeks. Tears that match my own.

We're having a baby.

When I look back on this day, I won't think of it as the day I woke up in the hospital riddled with injuries. Nor will I remember it as the day I found out my lover killed off my mother. No, when I think back, this will be the day I found out I'm having a baby. For real. With the men I love by my side.

Sione and Spence clap each other on the back, then in a unified front, they peel Greedy off me so they can wrap me up in a hug.

Just when I think my heart can't handle another shred of emotion, Greedy tackles Levi on the squeaky vinyl couch, and chants, "We're having a baby! We're having a baby!"

Chapter 46

Greedy

I can't stop smiling. My face hurts, and it may be frozen like this forever, but I don't fucking care.

The expression slips, though, when I get a text from my dad, asking me to come down to his office at the first opportunity.

Only half a day has passed since our last face-off. Despite that—or maybe in spite of it—plus everything that's happened since, I'm a changed man.

What Spence did for Hunter stirred up a lot of questions inside me. Like: Where's the moral line? More importantly: Where am I not willing to compromise?

The lengths I'll go to protect Hunter and our family have no discernible bounds. My dedication is limitless, our love an infinite loop.

By the time I reach my dad's office, I've settled on what I'm not willing to accept any longer. If he can't prioritize Hunter or me and do right by his kids, then I'm no longer interested in salvaging my relationship with him.

As I approach his desk, he looks up to acknowledge me, but quickly lowers his attention to the piece of paper in his hand.

"Have a seat," he says softly.

I do, dropping to the edge of one of his visitor chairs, anxiously waiting for him to take the lead and give me a hint about which direction this is going.

Clearing his throat, he sits up and passes over the paper he was looking at. Though it's not a paper. It's a picture.

It's in rough shape, aged and slightly yellow around the edges, with a few distinct bends and creases across the face of the baby who's offering a gummy smile to the camera.

"The paramedics handed it to me before they left the house. That's you, kid. That's you."

I study the old photo. It doesn't take long to realize that I recognize it. It used to sit on my mother's vanity in the primary bathroom. Gingerly, I lift it and flip it over. In the lower right-hand corner, in her recognizable loopy scrawl, reads: *Garrett Reed, 8 months old.*

Emotion clogs my throat. God, I miss her so much. She would have loved Hunter. She would have loved Levi, too. What I wouldn't give to have one more day with her. To listen to her sing. To introduce her to the loves of my life. To tell her the best news ever: that she's going to be a grandma.

My father clears his throat once more, the sound jerking me out of my pensive thoughts. "I loved this boy so much. I loved being a dad." His words are sincere, and from my own experience, I know it to be true. So how the hell did we end up here?

"I loved going to your games, spending time with you here, at the hospital. Listening to your mother sing to you for hours on end. I'd come home from second shift and find you curled up under her piano, fast asleep, with the sweetest, most content smile on your face."

I smile now, and warmth spreads through me. I remember those nights, too. The cool parquet flooring, the pillow forts I'd create. The way the music vibrated through my body as she practiced for hours on end. I didn't mind that she was lost in the music; I just wanted to be near her.

"I don't know what happened." He sobs, his chest heaving with sorrow.

I swallow hard, then peel the picture off the desk once more. Warmth and happiness thread through me as I look at the downy-haired baby, with his toothless grin and bright green eyes. An extra pang strikes my heart as I picture another downy-haired baby. The one Hunter once carried and lost. Quickly, though, my thoughts turn to the one she's carrying now.

There's nothing I wouldn't do for that baby. Regardless of paternity or timing, the child is mine, just like I am theirs. I haven't even met them, yet I know without a shadow of a doubt there's nothing I wouldn't give them.

I'm still studying the photo when my dad continues.

"After your mother died, we were okay, you and me. Surviving her loss..." He trails off.

The death of a beloved partner or a parent isn't something anyone just gets over. Grief lingers, and it grows. Sometimes it attacks out of nowhere.

"You and I were closer than ever after your mom died. I made sure of it, because I promised her I'd be there for you. But then... you kept growing. You got busier. You had school. Sports. Friends and football. I wanted you to have those things," he quickly adds. "I encouraged you to be involved, to always try your hardest. I put in more hours at the hospital and chased every promotion to fill my time. I thought we were both happy.

"You may not believe me, but I didn't *want* to date," he states. "But I felt like I needed to. Especially as you got older, and you started looking at colleges."

Oh, the irony. I stayed close to home, attending South Chapel University, but not just because of him. Also because of her.

"I felt like I needed to put myself out there and show you I would be okay once you moved out. I wasn't any good at it, though. Most women I took out didn't like that I worked so much. That if I wasn't working, I was with you. There wasn't much of me left for anyone else. Magnolia..." He heaves out a breath. "Magnolia was a breath of fresh air."

I shudder internally at the mention of her but remain stoic on the exterior.

"She didn't care that I worked too much, that I didn't have a lot of time or attention to give her. Hell, sometimes I think she preferred it that way.

"Our relationship was convenient. The timing is what sealed the deal for me. I was just grateful to have someone, knowing life would only get busier for you once you went to college. Garrett..."

He's quiet for a long time. So long that I'm certain he'll leave it at that. Instead, his breathing stutters, and he roughs a hand down his face. "I messed up. I never imagined..."

This time, he does leave me hanging.

How much does he know? Does he believe that Magnolia has been gunning for Hunter since she came back to town?

Hope flares inside me.

"I don't even know where to start, but I know I owe you an apology. You, and your—Hunter."

Blowing out a breath, I set the baby picture on the desk between us. "You're *really* going to need to stop almost calling her my sister."

He lets out a dry chuckle. "You're telling me, buddy."

Face falling, he sits up straight and rolls his chair all the way forward. I instinctively sit up straighter in my own seat, matching his posture and waiting with bated breath for what he'll say next.

Somberly, he tells me, "What happened at the house last night was an accident."

All the hope I'd just let fill up inside me bursts like a balloon meeting a popcorn ceiling.

"Dad, I know you don't want to hear this, but you need to understand—"

He holds up both hands, and out of habit and respect, despite my desperation to reason with him, I fall silent once more.

"It was an accident," he continues, each word spoken with care, "because anything besides an accident would require a police report. Which would then lead to the question of where Magnolia is, which could, in turn, lead to a missing person's investigation."

Understanding dawns, and all the air escapes from my lungs. Is he saying what I think he's saying?

"We can go a different route, of course. If Hunter feels it's necessary to press charges, or if she wants to file a missing person's report. But if we all agree that what happened yesterday was an *accident*..."

Tears well in my eyes. He's not being dismissive. He listened. He's accepting my plea, aligning himself with us. He's truly letting her go.

I can't sit in my seat for another second. I'm on the other side of the desk with my arms around him in the space of three heartbeats. "Thank you, Dad. I love you."

He sinks a little deeper into my hold. It really hits me then. He's my dad, but he's a person, too. A hopeless romantic at heart, who does his best to give everyone the benefit of the doubt, to see the very best in others.

He was a victim of Magnolia's manipulations just like we were.

He was betrayed and lied to, and he deserves answers for all the bullshit she pulled. Answers he'll never get, I realize. I squeeze him a little tighter. It isn't until he releases me and pulls back that I break away.

"I'm so sorry for what happened," I tell him. It's the truth. I feel for him, and he needs to know he's still worthy of love. That he has a family who loves him.

He rises to his feet, dusts off the front of his pants, his chin lifted, and my worries ease.

"It's okay," he says. "Magnolia left. She has a history of running. This time, though, I won't be chasing her."

Chapter 47

Kabir

I stay close, sheltering Hunter's back, as we make our way down the dock. They kept her in the hospital for three more nights, which Garrett insisted was typical, given the injuries she experienced and the amount of time she was unconscious. I'm quite glad for the care she received, but I'm ready to get her home.

There was never a question about whether we'd head back to the Crusade Mansion. Though the threat has been eliminated, after Hunter's ordeal, we need the safety of the familiar place, where we're surrounded by the people we know we can trust.

The others know what I'm planning to do. They all agreed, albeit some more begrudgingly than others.

As our crew shuffles onto a pontoon ahead of us, I place a hand on Hunter's shoulder to stop her from following.

"Wait here, love. We'll get the next one."

A look of puzzlement overtakes her face, but she doesn't push back or question me.

Using my newly acquired skills, I prepare the second pontoon. I'm not comfortable enough on the water to commandeer a speed boat just yet.

Besides, we're not in any rush. It'll take a while to get through what I must explain.

Once we're on our way, I beckon, and Hunter joins me behind the helm.

She slips into my lap, and I gingerly circle one arm around her from behind, cognizant of her injuries.

"I need to tell you something."

Sighing, she leans back against me. "Okay."

Without preamble, I announce, "I killed Magnolia."

Her posture doesn't change. Her breath doesn't catch. All the reactions I expected and have been mentally preparing myself for have amounted to nothing.

Instead, she turns her head slightly and rests her cheek against mine.

"I figured," she eventually admits. She laces her fingers with the hand I have splayed gently across her lower abdomen and brings the other to my jaw, holding my face steady as she nuzzles deeper into me.

She's pouring love into me. It's palpable. I can practically taste the gratitude she wants to express when she presses her lips chastely to mine.

Her reaction is so eerily calm I worry perhaps the implications haven't clicked with her.

She stills, pulling back and searching my face.

"I just confessed to an egregious act against humanity—to an outright crime in most developed nations. Talk to me, love. How does that make you feel?"

Hunter erupts into a fit of giggles, clutching her middle. They stop abruptly, and she winces, but gods, it feels good to hear her laugh. Even if it happens to be at my expense. "You're not my therapist, Spence."

I grip her chin and force her to look at me. "Did you really just laugh at me, Firecracker?"

She grins, biting her bottom lip, clearly holding back another outburst.

"Don't think just because you're injured—"

"And pregnant!" Another giggle.

"—that I won't put you on your knees and fuck your mouth slow and steady until there's so much drool on your face and arousal dripping down your thighs, you're a sopping, needy mess."

Her bright green eyes take on that hazy, lust-filled dream state I know and love. Though it is not possible at this point, given her myriad of injuries, my girl wants to *play*.

We can, however, engage in a little light petting. Before I can lean in and feed her my tongue, she pulls back. Her lips press into a thin line and her eyes darken with worry.

"What?" I demand, tension pulling at my shoulders. "What is it, love?"

With a visible swallow, she whispers, "Everything's going to change." A slow inhale, then exhale. "My body. My... limits. What we can do..."

Ah. There's the rub.

"Not everything has to change." I gently grasp the hair at her nape. "I'll do my due diligence and research what's safe. As long as you are amiable and it won't harm you or the child you're carrying, our dynamic can remain intact."

Her eyes light up. "Promise?"

My brilliant, beautiful girl. There's nothing I wouldn't give her. No version of life I want to live without her by my side.

I tuck her hair behind her ear, then bend low so I can whisper her my vow.

"Have faith, love. You can be the mother of their children and still be my needy, cum-guzzling whore. You have three holes, after all."

She squirms in my lap—that's my fucking girl—then turns her head, giving me access to her mouth so I can kiss her thoroughly. When we break apart, panting, she grips the back of my neck like she's desperate to never let me go. "I love you," she professes, the three words a song brought in on the cooling night air.

"I love you, too, Hunter."

Though we've had a moment's reprieve, I can't let the other half of my reason for bringing her across the lake alone drift away. "There's one more thing I need to share with you."

She rests contentedly against my chest, peeking up. "What's that?"

What do Americans often say? "Here goes nothing"? This certainly feels like more than nothing.

"There's a tracker inside you," I confess, chest tight, as if my body isn't quite up to speed with my mind. As if it isn't ready for the potential fallout.

Hunter shoots up, turns, and hits me with a searing scowl. *There she is.*

"A *what*? Where?" She runs both hands up and down her arms, searching for the device she's unwittingly carried with her for a few years now.

"Right here." I smooth my thumb over the base of her skull. "It's tiny. Smaller than a grain of rice. It was implanted in London, after your... episode."

Her mouth drops open, then snaps shut. She repeats the gaping motion twice before finally finding her words. "Thank you for telling me."

That's it. That's fucking all she says.

I'd keel over from shock if I wasn't already sitting.

"You're not upset?" I press, blinking rapidly. "I implanted a tracking device inside your body without your consent, Firecracker. I kept it from you for *years*."

Brows raised, she scrutinizes me. "When you put it like that..." Quickly, her face splits into a smile. "No," she says with a shake of her head. "I'm not upset. I won't sit in judgment of anything any of us has done while trying to survive. The tracker... it's how you found me here, yes?"

I nod.

"And when Magnolia took me to New York?"

Another nod. I'm beginning to see her point. I was so worried about her reaction, I had completely disregarded how practical and self-aware she can be.

"Would you like to have it removed?" I trace the invisible lifeline with the pad of my thumb.

"No," she replies, her eyes brightening. "But I want to put one in you."

I scoff. "Me? Why?"

A giggle escapes her, and she clutches at her midsection again with a wince. "The guys told me about your little speech at the med spa, you know." She sits up straighter, clears her throat, and in with the most gods-awful accent I've ever heard in my life, says, "I'm Kabir Spencer. I'm from everywhere. I own everything."

She's mocking me. The little minx.

Her eyes grow hooded then, and she leans in close. Licking her lips, she says, "That all may be true. But at the end of the day, you belong to me."

Bloody hell.

"Will you ask the others if they'd like trackers too?" My question is teasing and light, but there's a gravitas in the air as I await her answer.

Shaking her head, Hunter meets my gaze. "No. Only you, Sir. I want to share this with only you."

I smash my lips to hers, using enough fervor to tell her exactly what I think of this idea without being too rough.

Yet I can't help the self-doubt-fueled question that comes out of my mouth when I eventually pull away.

"Why just me?"

For a moment, she pants, catching her breath. I savor the sight of her, wanton in my lap, alone on this boat, in the middle of the lake, finally safe and sound.

"I may be getting ahead of myself, but some day, if it makes sense for practical or legal reasons, I may end up marrying one of the guys."

I still, a dark dread curling like smoke through me. "You wouldn't choose me?"

If looks could kill, she could toss my body out of the boat this instant. "I will not be *choosing* anyone. Full stop."

I can't help but smile. Full stop is a British term, and one I'm quite certain I taught her.

Softer, with both hands stroking my hair, she says, "You're not likely to need insurance or citizenship. And I know this"—she eyes her stomach, which I immediately cover with my hand protectively—"did not happen the way you wanted it to go."

"No," I bite out. "Don't think of that again, Firecracker. I love you. I love this baby." I splay my hand wide, savoring the connection that warms my insides when I think of the life growing inside her. "I'm sorry for my previous behavior. It was selfish and shortsighted for me to be so reactive. This is exactly what I want—with you, with them. I've already scheduled an appointment to have my vasectomy reversed this summer. My time will come soon enough."

Hunter sinks against my chest, and we sit in idle silence, allowing the movement of the lake to sway us to and fro.

Eventually, she peeks up through thick lashes, her face puzzled.

"What is it?" I ask.

"Were you there when they put it in?"

"Pfft. They? I'm the one who placed it, love. I wasn't about to trust anyone else with my most precious possession."

Her eyes spark with a myriad of emotions: Desire. Appreciation. Possessiveness. Arousal.

"That settles it. I'm placing yours. Staking my claim. I'm putting a tracker inside you, Kabir Spencer. You're mine, and you'll never escape me."

Bloody hell.

"You're sure you don't want yours out?" I ask again.

She shakes her head resolutely. "I'm sure. I want to share something with just you."

"And you want that something to be matching subdermal tracking devices?"

Her lips twitch. "What can I say? I read a lot of dark romance."

Chuckling, I kiss her hair, savoring her scent. Then I situate her so I can reach the throttle and navigate toward home. She'll be my undoing, this one. I am beyond prepared to spend a lifetime catering to her every whim, caring for her every need, and loving her with all that I am.

"Endgame," I whisper as the motor whirrs.

"Endgame," she replies, settling back against my chest with a contended sigh.

Just as it was always meant to be.

Chapter 48

Sione

Brightness radiates from the rocky beach, despite the way the sun sinks below the horizon across the shore. Glimmers of hope and joy crackle amongst us, the energy of this night alive and sparkling. The warmth coursing through me has nothing to do with the roaring flames. It does, however, have everything to do with the jubilant spirits of the nine other people laughing, talking, and mingling around the bonfire.

Hunter is home. After a few nights in the hospital, and a few additional labs and scans to confirm all was well with the pregnancy, she's returned to the Crusade Mansion. She spent a week in bed, per Greedy and Spence's insistence. Now that she's better healed, we've gathered on the beach for a celebration of sorts. All of us reunited once more.

We aren't just celebrating Hunter's homecoming and improved health tonight.

Josephine's cohort is aware that Hunter is with child. It would be hard to keep it from them, considering we all live together and intend to do so until the end of summer. That, and Hunter has acquired an intense aversion to the scent of roasted nuts.

She couldn't even walk past the pantry without feeling queasy. From there, it didn't take long for Josephine's cohort to figure it out. Much to Decker Crusade's chagrin, entire shelves had to be cleared out and relocated to the garage.

Near the fire, Kendrick barks out a loud, boisterous laugh. Levi delivers a punch line, inspiring more laughter, while Greedy stands beside him and subtly scowls. His frown doesn't keep. Within seconds, he's laughing, too. When Josephine joins them, Levi dives into a humorous explanation.

I'm growing fond of this place. Lake Chapel. The Crusade Isle.

The juxtaposition between the constant company of a full house and the seclusion of the private residence creates a syncretic harmony within my soul. There's always something going on or someone to talk to here. Just like there are always moments of solitude to be found.

Delicate hands ghost over my obliques and around my torso, followed by a familiar warmth.

"No new water." Hunter shuffles up beside me to stand at the lake's edge.

The smile that overtakes me is so wide it causes my cheeks to burn. Every time I'm reminded of the baby, I'm filled with so much effervescent joy I fear I may float away.

Right now, water is accumulating in her uterus, providing a cushy, blessed sanctuary for our child. Right now, the water is home to the new life we created. Together.

I'm fascinated by the process. Absolutely feral for information and knowledge on the subject. I'm intent on learning all I can about pregnancy, especially as it relates to caring for Hunter and keeping her as comfortable as possible.

I've always known I wanted to help people, but only recently did I realize the pointedness of my life's ambition. I want to provide chiropractic care to support individuals' fertility journeys. I want to provide as much ease as I can to the physical containers responsible for creating and growing life.

"What are you thinking about?" she asks, leaning a little more into my side.

Wrapping one arm around her, I kiss the crown of her head. "I'm thinking about what you asked me a few months ago. About this place. About our situation."

She peers up at me, searching my face.

"Remember when you asked me if I'm happy here? If it's all right with you, I'd like to amend my answer."

She sinks her teeth into her bottom lip, but quickly nods.

"We're home. You, me, the guys, our child? We have created a sanctuary that's as impenetrable as it is beautiful. I love it here, Mahina. I never want to be anywhere but right here, by your side."

"I love you." She kisses my ribs, pulling me from my thoughts.

Before I can return the sentiment, the rambunctious group by the fire snags our attention.

"How many last names is the baby going to have?"

Locke, Kendrick, and Levi are engaged in a heated discussion—again—centered around the fact that we do not intend to find out the paternity of the child.

Our cohort has already discussed it. We have a plan. We know what we want and we're committed to the promises we made to one another.

We won't be seeking any sort of paternity test for this baby or for any of our children unless there's a medically necessary reason to do so.

There may be obvious outward traits, of course. And I'm sure it will be possible to sense the way the soul of the baby mirrors the fabric of each of us individually. But we're all in agreement. This baby is ours. Hers, mine, theirs. *Ours.*

"I have six names total, not including my honorific," Spence remarks. He's sipping from a flask, because he refuses to use one of the vibrant red cups the others seem to be so fond of.

"Your honor-*what*?" Locke asks.

"My honorific title. I'm knighted. My full name is Sir Kabir Kareem Alexander Louis Cornelia Spencer."

Josephine chortles, then doubles over laughing, the contents of her red cup sloshing over the side. "Stop. Stop it *right now*."

She's the one who ought to consider stopping. I'm afraid she'll pass out at the rate she's gasping for air.

When she finally stands, she points at Spence. "I thought she only called you Sir in the bedroom." She bursts into another fit of giggles.

Decker appears at her side, taking the cup from her hand. Then he wraps his arm around her shoulders. "She's had a few Tom Collinses," he informs us. As if it wasn't abundantly clear.

"Hey." Josephine snatches her red cup out of his hand and downs the rest of her beverage in a huge gulp. "My bestie is pregnant, so technically, I'm drinking for two."

With a grin, Hunter squeezes me. Then she makes her way to Josephine's side and engulfs her in a hug.

After a moment, Josephine pulls away and holds her at arm's length, her eyes wide and her expression mischievous. "I have an idea."

Hunter presses her lips together, clearly trying to keep from laughing. We all gravitate closer but give the girls space, watching their exchange.

"All this talk of names and titles... The answer's been right in front of us all along. You should name the baby after *me*."

Hunter's face screws up, but she takes the bait and plays along. "And why's that?"

Josephine huffs, clearly offended. "Because I'm a motherfucking prize, Hunter. You said so yourself. And because my first child has to be named after you. It's only fair."

Hunter laughs, her joyful exuberance filling the warm night air. "Two fair points, Joey Crusade. There may be a law career in your future, after all."

Decker guffaws, bringing his hand to his chest. "Hold up. We have to name our first child after Hunter? Why is this the first I'm hearing about it?"

Josephine's eyes practically bug out of her head. Quickly, though, she schools her expression, spins on her heel, and turns on the charm.

"Funny story, really. You're going to love this, Cap. Remember that time I wore the wrong jersey to Shore Week?"

The others break off into small groups, continuing their previous conversations and enjoying the jovial mood that true happiness and contentment bring with such ease.

Across the flickering flames of the bonfire, Garrett appears behind Hunter. Levi steps up, kisses her cheek, and rests his head on Garrett's shoulder. Spence strides over and throws his arm around the three of them, holding them tight.

Hunter's face tightens, her gaze searching the beach until she spots me. When our eyes connect, she offers me the most effortless, dazzling smile.

She's glowing. Luminous.

She's never looked more beautiful than in this moment.

She reaches out one hand, calling to me.

I traverse the rocky beach, giving the flames a wide berth, then rightfully join the group.

We're here. We made it. The bonds we've developed were created by the kind of magic poets write about and romantics dream of.

No wrong moves.

No more running.

This is it.

Nothing has ever felt so right.

Epilogue 1: Kabir

Six Months Later

"That's it, Champ. Fill her to the hilt. Look how desperate she is for your massive American cock."

"Fucking hell," Levi groans, his head tipping back.

He's sandwiched between us, taking me like a good boy while Hunter writhes on her side and attempts to fuck herself up and down on his shaft.

Attempt being the key word here, because Hunter's stomach is magnificently round and growing fuller by the day, making it hard for her to get traction in any position.

Thankfully, I'm feral enough for all of us. Each time I forcefully thrust into Levi, I drive him forward, allowing him to penetrate her more deeply.

These moments between the three of us are rare, but they're deliciously carnal. Primal. Hot and hungry.

"That's it. Fucking take it, Champ. I swear to gods I'm going to come so hard my dirty little slut will feel it, too."

"Shit," Levi curses, eyes squeezed shut like he's holding himself back from the edge.

Then, with the flip of a switch, he stiffens.

"Shoot. I meant shoot." His body locks up. He's frozen, his ass clenching around me.

I'd quite like the sensation of being held in his viselike grip if I wasn't also concerned about his sudden change in demeanor.

His bright blue eyes search my face, a panic-stricken look marring his expression. When I just stare back, deadpan, he turns to our girl. Finally, he chokes out, "You're sure the baby can't hear us?"

Hunter rolls her lips, fighting back a laugh.

We all have our hang-ups surrounding her pregnancy, and the closer we get to her due date, the more pronounced they seem to become. Sione is our go-to baby expert. He hasn't stopped researching since the day we found out Hunter was really, truly pregnant. The man is an endless chasm of wisdom. Wisdom he doesn't know how to filter, apparently. This is his fault. He's the one who mentioned months ago how babies can hear and even distinguish between voices from within the womb.

Hunter reaches out and rakes her fingers through Levi's curls, soothing him the best she can. In an effort to help calm him, I kiss his nape, savoring the salty notes on his skin and the way it harmonizes with the familiar musky scent of his body wash.

"I promise the baby's okay. He can't understand any of Spence's dirty talk. And we're going to slip up sometimes. It's okay. Don't beat yourself up." Hunter's eyes heat, and she grips Levi's hair, pulling tight. "But Duke?"

"Yeah, Daisy?" he murmurs into her neck.

"I'm close. I can't get there on my own. *Please* help me finish."

Without another moment of hesitation, he rolls his hips forward, filling Hunter while I thrust into his ass. We're moving more slowly now. I ease in and out of his tight hole while he makes love to our woman. But once he finds his rhythm, our shared passion quickly restores to its full intensity.

I close my eyes, reveling in this moment and fighting like hell to stave off the orgasm that's desperate to rip through me and fill Levi's perfect arse.

Fuck. Envisioning it is too much. Eyes open again, I search for a distraction, but the sight of them together, the sight of all three of us united, is just as arousing as any image my mind can conjure on its own.

The feeling of the two of them here with me is exquisite.

The feeling of the three of us together? Extraordinary.

The feeling of belonging—of being loved and protected within a core family structure, after having been on my own for so long—is as disorienting as it is liberating.

I'm not alone. I'll never be alone again.

I'm wanted, not for my brains, my money, my businesses or my power, but simply because of who I am.

That knowledge and the sense of belonging that comes with it make the world glow brighter and our future that much more exciting.

Hunter whimpers, bringing me back to the moment, her breathing fast and hard as pleasure builds inside her.

Levi groans, his ass clenching and his thrusts increasing in intensity, making it a challenge to keep up, let alone stay mounted on top of him.

No matter.

The vibrancy and strength of our connection are more potent than ever. Nothing could detract from our mutual pleasure now.

We are inevitable.

"Right there. Right now." Hunter lifts her hand, reaches around Levi, and searches for me.

Knowing exactly what she needs, I curl myself over Levi, giving her access. She cuffs the back of my neck, her delicate fingers brushing against my nape where the internal tracking device she put inside me resides.

She cries out. Levi does too. Angling lower, I capture both her mouth and his in a sloppy, hungry kiss, and I spill all that I am inside the man I love most.

"Right here. Right now," I murmur against their lips.

There's nowhere else in the universe I'd rather be.

Epilogue 2: Greedy

A Few Weeks Later

"It's a boy!"

It's a boy. It's a boy. It's a boy.

I have a *son*.

The birthing suite is abuzz with energy. If energy is even the correct term to describe the chaos happening all around me. The room is loud and crowded. It's overstimulating and incredible. Between the hospital staff, Sione's doula trainer, and our entire cohort, there's hardly any room to move.

Hunter was exquisite and the baby is here. *I have a son*. I'm so overwhelmed with joy I don't know what to do with myself.

Hunter's birthing plan called for minimal support staff in the room while she labored. That request was honored, and only when it was time to push did a slew of new faces join us.

It's crowded in here now, but that tends to happen in any room we find ourselves in.

Our cohort continues to grow. Because today, we've added an entire human being to our unconventional, remarkable family.

Our son.

SO RIGHT

As much as I want to see him, study him, count his fingers and toes, he's across the room, on the other side of this sea of people, being cleaned up and checked over. Spence and Levi are hovering over one of the nurses as she weighs him and completes the required newborn screenings. They've got him. He's safe.

Hunter, the beautiful mother of my child, is lying back with her eyes closed, a dreamy look painted on her face as Sione strokes her hair and whispers in her ear.

I want to go to her. I want to meet my son. I want to be in two places at once. Instead, my feet are cemented to the floor, keeping me frozen in the middle of the room as I take it all in.

We did it. We made it. This is real. This is right.

With a shuddering breath, my temporary suspension eases, and I force my feet to move. I stride over to Hunter and gently take her face in my hands.

"You did so well, Tem."

Her eyelids flutter open, her gaze slightly unfocused as she takes in the noise and chaos behind me. "He's okay?" she whispers.

There's no tempering my face-splitting smile. "He's perfect. You're perfect." I kiss her forehead, then look over to the weighing station, where the nurse is swaddling the baby and Spence and Levi are watching intently. "They're almost done checking him out. The others haven't left his side."

Though she nods in response, her bottom lip trembles and her bright green eyes fill with tears. "Greedy. I want to hold our baby."

Her request guts me. Urgently, I nod and straighten to full height. This moment is years in the making. The feral need to give her exactly what she wants seizes me, tightening around every organ in my body.

After all this time—after what we lost, and the way she suffered—I refuse to allow another minute to pass in which she doesn't have him in her arms.

"Mom is asking for her baby," I call out, my gaze still sent intently on Hunter. He was placed on her chest immediately after birth, but now it's been close to five minutes since they took him away. That's too long. They need to be skin-to-skin so they can bond.

"Uh-oh. Garrett used his dad voice on us already," Spence strides over to the opposite side of the bed. He's beaming, wearing a grin bigger than I've ever seen from him before.

The terse look I give him wipes the proud smirk right off his face.

"Come along, Champ," he tells Levi, making room for our boyfriend at the bedside.

Levi doesn't look up. He doesn't reply to Spence, acknowledge me, or even look at Hunter or Si as he carefully makes his way over to the bed. He's singularly focused on the tiny swaddled bundle he's cradling in his arms.

He's transfixed. *He's in love.*

"He's perfect," he chokes out. When he finally lifts his head and meets my gaze, his bright blue eyes are brimming with tears. "Greedy. Our son is perfect."

My heart triples in size at the immediate, natural, loving reaction he has to our child. It's life-altering, watching the bond developing between the two of them. But a stronger urge rallies inside me, reminding me of what's most important in this moment.

"Hunter needs to hold him. Right now," I explain, choosing my words carefully to ensure the urgency of the matter isn't lost while preserving the feelings of the man experiencing the pure love between parent and child for the first time in his life.

Levi's focus shifts to our girl, and the look on his face turns to one of understanding. He gets the weight of this moment. He knows what it means for her, to hold a baby in her arms after all this time. What it means for all of us, to bear witness to this experience and allow it to imprint on our hearts.

Sione helps her sit up, supporting her back when she winces and shifts her weight. He places a pillow behind her, then another one under her left side.

Bending low, Levi uses the gentlest, most deliberate movements to shift the baby into Hunter's waiting arms. "There ya go, Mama. Say hello to your son."

Tears stream down her face as she studies the gift in her arms. "Hi, baby."

I wipe away the moisture from my own eyes as I watch her holding him for the first time.

This is it. This is everything we yearned for. All we dreamed of when we agreed to grow our family.

She kisses the top of his head, and when she straightens, I catch the dark hair peeking out from the pink and blue knit hat. He was blood-covered and pink from screaming when the doctor laid him on her chest, but now that he's calmer, there's a distinct golden-brown hue to his skin.

He's clearly Sione's child by blood.

All along, we said it didn't matter.

Even so, I wondered, worried even, that, deep down, I might feel differently if the baby looked distinctly like one of the other guys once he was born.

He's here. He does look like someone else.

Without a shadow of a doubt, I know now that his paternity truly doesn't matter.

He's mine, as I am his.

They're all mine, just as I am theirs.

Seeing him in the flesh, knowing he is our first earthside baby, and that his little soul joined us at the exact right time, is soul-affirming. It makes this life make more sense.

I haven't even touched him, yet I love him so much it hurts. There's an ache in the center of my chest, more profound and intense than any love I've ever known.

He's here. He's perfect. He's mine.

Easing onto the bed beside Hunter, I wrap one arm around her shoulder and kiss her hair.

Then I focus on our son. I try to speak. Nothing comes out. I try again, this time choking out a single garbled syllable. Finally, I clear my throat and take a cleansing breath.

With a single finger, I stroke his cheek. "Hey, buddy. I'm your dad."

Hunter bursts into tears again.

"Oh, Tem." I try to soothe her, but I can barely take my eyes off the baby in her arms.

"I'm fine. *I'm fine*. It's just the hormones, I swear."

Sione loops an arm around her neck and hugs her to him, holding her steady. "It's not just the hormones. It's this *gift*. Feel it, Mahina. Feel it all. We'll never get this moment back."

Hunter bursts into fresh tears.

Spence shoots him an incredulous look, but thankfully, doesn't sling one of his signature jabs.

Our son lets out a little wail then, as if he's trying to match his mama.

"Hey, you're okay, buddy," I soothe. "Mommy's got you. We've all got you." I kiss his forehead, not bothering to hide the tears streaming down my face.

Sione cups a hand over the one Hunter has supporting the baby's head. "I'm your Tamai," he tells his son.

Levi crouches so he's face-to-face with the baby. "I'm your Pops." He grins up at me, then Hunter and Sione, before finally looking back at Spence, a mischievous gleam suddenly glinting in his eye. "And that's Daddy Spence."

Kabir sidles up behind Levi and places a hand on his shoulder. "That is *not* the name we agreed upon."

Levi rolls his eyes. "Yeah, because we didn't *agree* on anything. Our kids aren't calling you Sire. Full Stop."

Chuckling, I finally tear my gaze away from the precious bundle in Hunter's arms to see who may still be lingering to overhear this ridiculous discussion. Only then do I realize everyone has cleared out. We're alone now. Just the six of us.

"What about his name?" Hunter asks, still transfixed by the sweet babe in her arms. He cries out again, and she shushes him. "Are you hungry, little man? Should we try to nurse?" She looks from one of us to another, seeking reassurance. "We're still set on his name?"

"His name is perfect," I assure her.

It's classic and strong, but unique in its spelling. Representative of our family, though neither Sione nor Levi felt compelled to include parts of themselves in our son's full name. Spence did—of course he did—and once I thought about it, I decided I wanted to be included, too.

Jole Kabir Ferguson St. Clair.

"I love his name," Levi confirms. "Although I still don't get how 'Jole' is close enough to 'Josephine' to satisfy this little pact you two made in a women's restroom during a football game."

With a grin, Hunter peers up at me. Joze is going to be thrilled—and Jole will grow up knowing he was named after the second strongest, bravest woman I've ever had the pleasure of knowing.

Second, only because his mama holds the top spot.

My first love. My beautiful Artemis. And now, the mother of my child.

"Love you," I mouth to her, too emotional to utter another word out loud.

She presses her lips together, overcome with emotion, too, and nods with a mouthed "I love you, too."

Epilogue 3: Sione

NINE MONTHS LATER

"In here." I tug on Hunter's hand as I guide her into a dark utility closet toward the back of the main house. She tries to stifle her giggles but accidentally sends a broom clattering to the floor in the process. I'm grinning from ear to ear from my own delight.

When I pull on the knob to close the door behind us, I'm met with resistance.

"Hold up." Garrett slinks into the dark space. The small block window on the opposite wall casts just enough light to illuminate the sly grin he's wearing.

"*Greedy*," Hunter squeals in surprise.

"Mind if I join you?"

He's looking at our girl, but his question is aimed at me.

"I do not mind." Looming over Hunter, I dip one finger beneath the plunging neckline of her wrap dress, teasing her ripe, bountiful cleavage.

She's a vision in light lavender, and I've been desperate to get her alone since the moment we arrived in Lake Como this morning.

"But we have to be quiet. And quick. And truth be told, I do have a very specific desire in mind."

I smooth my hand over the expanse of her plump, full breast. When I come into contact with her taut nipple, she gasps. As suspected, she's not wearing a bra, making it even easier to manifest my fantasy into reality.

"I'll follow your lead." Garrett leans in and captures Hunter's mouth in a passionate kiss. He pulls away and ravages her neck before coming up for air. "Put me to work," he says to me. "Tell me what to do. Let me be your extra hands."

"And if I need you to be my extra mouth? An extra tongue or throat, perhaps?"

Hunter whimpers and drops her head back.

Garrett covers her mouth with his hand, eyes sparkling. "I'll do anything, Si. I'm your guy."

Very well, then.

"Get down on your knees before her and feast on her weeping core."

Without hesitation, Garrett gets into position and pulls on the bow holding Hunter's dress in place. "Gladly." Once her full tits and the soft, curved expanse of her stomach are on display, he makes quick work of her panties, leaving her naked and panting before us.

"What are you—"

"Shh." I bracket her face with my hands and kiss her lips. Then, with my mouth, I blaze a trail down her neck and chest. "You know these make me feral, Mahina." I gently squeeze her breasts, rolling her nipples between my forefingers and thumbs. "The way they bounce when you walk. The way they rise and fall when you laugh and press together when you bend down to lift our son." I squeeze again.

She mewls, rolling her hips forward into Garrett's eager mouth. "Every time these tits bounce, I dream about drinking from them. Every time I see your tight, pointed nipples pressing through fabric, I silently pray for them to leak so I can lap up every last drop."

"Fuck," Garrett mutters from between Hunter's thighs. "She's drenched. Your words have her fucking soaking me."

Good. She's going to be leaking all over by the time I'm done with her.

I run my tongue between her breasts, then circle one areola over and over. When she grips my hair and holds me to her chest, I finally take her into my mouth.

I nibble gently to start, easing her into the erotic, needy suckling I'm desperate to unleash. All I've dreamt about for days is having my mouth on her breasts. Her milk flowing freely as her cunt pulses and spasms with pleasure.

The visions have plagued me since we tried it for the first time a few weeks ago. I never would have pegged myself as possessing a lactation kink, but Spence and Garrett have opened my eyes, and now I fantasize about it all the time.

With a growl, I switch sides, desperate to make the milk flow, but wanting to draw this encounter out for as long as I can.

"Do that again," Greedy groans. "She's dripping faster than I can lap her up. I swear there's going to be a puddle on the floor."

"Fuck. Yes," Hunter begs. "Again, Si. Do this side. *Please*." She thrusts her chest forward, pinching her own nipple.

I swat her hand away and take charge, massaging her breast and sucking her deep. When my wanton tugs produce the essence I'm seeking, I groan against her.

Sweetness floods my mouth.

I groan again, then suck harder, only to be rewarded with the most delicious elixir.

"Fuck. Yes. *Yes*," she mewls, her breathing fast and heavy as I pop off and find her mouth.

"You taste so good," I praise, running my tongue along hers so she can taste the sweetness of her own milk.

"Let Greedy try it," she says sweetly.

Grinning, I dive back down and savor a little more of her taste.

"Garrett," I murmur, without breaking contact. Her breast is shoved deep in my mouth when he glances up and meets my gaze. "Open your mouth, brother."

He does what I say without hesitating.

After a firm, demanding pull, I pop off, then aim the stream of milk directly into his eager mouth.

"Fucking delicious," he pants after he swallows, his eyes hazy and lust-filled as he savors the life source of our beloved. "Hottest thing ever,

Tem." With a grunt, he dives back down between her legs to continue eating her pussy.

"Wait," she whines.

Instinctively, we both freeze.

"Make me come by sucking my tits."

"Is that possible?" I muse.

Garrett pops to his feet, wiping the back of his mouth with his hand.

"She's done it before," he says. His face is lit up, but between one heartbeat and the next, the expression falls. "You're okay with this?"

I appreciate his concern. Despite my sexual attraction and desire still firmly focused on Hunter, I've enjoyed a bit more group action lately. Partly out of necessity, because we don't get as many opportunities to give in to our cravings and desires now that we're parents. But also because I have found a deep-seated sense of trust and respect within this group. I'm not afraid to engage in sexual acts near them or alongside them. As long as my pleasure is linked to Hunter, I am satisfied.

"More than okay. Join me, Garrett. What the mother of our child wants, she gets."

I kiss Hunter while he repositions himself. Naturally, he gravitates to the side of her body adorned with the tattoo that matches his own. The constellation Scorpius and a collection of four delicate arrows decorate Hunter's rib cage in invisible ink. She said she drew the line at putting an actual scorpion on her physical container.

While Garrett gets to work, I dip my tongue in and out of her mouth, suckling on her bottom lip as if it's the nipple I desperately crave. "Taste yourself, Mahina. Taste how sweet and juicy and good you truly are."

Once she's breathless and I'm sure Garrett is situated, I bend low again, massaging my designated breast while keenly watching my brother's technique.

"See how the milk blooms with each pull?" I instruct.

Garrett homes in on her breast, causing white essence to leak from her and collect into little droplets.

"She's radiant, isn't she? Such a gorgeous, fertile, sacred vessel. Watch him, Mahina."

"Eyes on me, Tem," he tells her, and when she does, he tips his head back, sticks out his tongue, and lets her fill his mouth, drip by delicious drip.

I dive in and feast on her other side, kneading, pulling, and suckling until a steady stream hits my throat and I have to swallow every few seconds to keep up with the flow.

"Fuck. *Yes*. Suck me. Harder."

I savor every drop that escapes her, lapping at her breast and moaning each time she gives me more. Beside me, Garrett works her over, keeping a steady rhythm. I match it, watching him suckle and pleasure our woman, his eyes closed and his throat bobbing every few moments as he loses himself in his own pleasure.

"I'm close, I'm close," she chants.

Garrett locks eyes with me, and unspoken determination zips between us. We suck harder, tug faster, and ravish her until she's pulling our hair and crying out in ecstasy.

She pulses and spasms and flows; I drink from her and savor every drop of her pleasure.

As her writhing slows, I smooth a palm up her leg. When I find her thigh totally soaked from her release, I grin. Then, with a final suck, I pop off, keeping a small amount of milk in my mouth. Rising, I let it dribble into Hunter's mouth. For a moment, I'm lost in kissing her, my only thoughts involving her lips and the taste of her.

When I finally pull back, her grin brightens the small space, her gaze wild and sated all at once. Garrett rises and kisses her, too, the milky mouthful he saved for her dribbling down both their chins as they lock lips and lose themselves in one another.

With a chuckle, I look down, confirming what I already knew and what I half suspected of Garrett. Hunter isn't the only one who was brought to orgasm by our encounter. My pants are sticky where I released my seed without contact, and Garrett's are darker where he came, too.

"Fuck," Garrett groans, eventually pulling away from our girl. "We made a mess."

Giggling, Hunter reaches past him and grabs several heavy-duty paper towels off a stack. "Good thing we're in the supply closet."

Epilogue 4: Hunter

Two Years Later

It's girls' day at the Crusade Mansion. Joey made official signs and everything.

We've been staying with Joey and her guys all week. Just like the good old days. Except now Mrs. Lansbury works for us (thanks to her "special friendship" with Gerald) and the primary bedroom sees a lot less action when we visit, since we have two Pack-'n-Plays set up in the room.

Classes are over for the semester, but we're sticking around for graduation weekend. Joey, Locke, and Levi will all walk across the stage and receive their master's degrees on Sunday.

I'm so proud of them, even if I am a teensy bit jealous that I'm not graduating along with them.

My guys and I are heading to Europe for the summer again this year. First, to London for a few weeks, then to Lake Como to stay at Villa Viola with Kitty and Otmar for the rest of the summer. Dr. Ferguson is joining us for a few weeks, and Sione's mom is flying in to stay for a week, too.

It's going to be a busy, joyful summer, with plenty of time to see family and enjoy all our favorite restaurants, cafes, and pubs around Europe. But traveling with little kids is not for the faint of heart. I'm already dreading the flights—Jole's ears bothered him the entire flight home from London last August—and despite all the list-making and packing we've been doing for weeks, it still doesn't feel like we're anywhere near ready.

The girls' day Joey insisted on couldn't have come at a better time. It's my last chance to spend quality time with her for a while, and I missed her fiercely while we were abroad last summer.

The guys took my bestie's over-the-top declarations about today in stride. Except Spence. He was less than impressed by the *No Boys or Babies Allowed* posters plastered around the kitchen this morning, insisting he was not a boy nor a baby. He had a point, but Joey wasn't interested in arguing over semantics.

Our two cohorts headed out for the day with strict orders not to return until bedtime. Which, considering we have a one-year-old and an almost-three-year-old in our group, means we'll be lucky if they don't return until seven p.m.

Mrs. Lansbury was permitted to stay. As expected, she's done nothing but fuss over us and make way too much food. She even made my favorite lemon chicken pasta for lunch. The carbs are to blame for my sleepy state, I'm certain. The gentle swaying of the pontoon certainly isn't helping matters.

We've been sunbathing on the lake for almost an hour. Although sunbathing is a bit of a stretch. We're both slathered in SPF 50 from our heads to our toes, with oversized hats and big sunglasses in place, spread out on the sunpad at the back of the boat.

The plan was to drink all day, but my heart's not in it. I've been nursing the same Tom Collins for so long I've had to swap out the paper straw three times already.

In my defense, I have plenty of valid reasons for taking it easy. Rowan still nurses to sleep most nights, despite being fiercely independent and wanting little to do with me during the day. For the most part, she looks just like me. Though she has bright blue eyes I'm almost certain she inherited from Levi, she has the audacity of Spence during all her waking hours. At least she did up until a few weeks ago. She's been extra clingy since her first little molars have begun to break through.

Jole never fussed when he was teething. Jole never really fussed, period. He was an angel baby, and he continues to be the most laid back, easygoing preschooler. Before they left the house today, he said, "Have fun and no worries about sissy. I got her, Mama." As if the four dads accompanying them couldn't handle Rowan without him. My sweet boy.

"What are you thinking about?" Joey asks, nudging my thigh with her knee.

Stifling a yawn, I roll to my side and prop my head on my hand. "The kids," I admit.

She arches one brow, but she doesn't give me a hard time. She would never. She's been with me through it all: Both pregnancies. My debilitating anxiety in the early weeks of my pregnancy with Rowan. The newborn haze. All the sleepless nights. Snotty noses and serious illnesses and all the mind-numbingly dull days in between.

Making, growing, and raising babies consumes a lot of my brain power. It's the season of life I'm slogging through, and it's also why I'm now several years behind my best friend in school.

Sighing, I offer her an apologetic smile.

"You're a really, *really* good mom, Hunter."

I open my mouth to insist it's mostly because I have four super-involved partners by my side, but she lifts one finger and silences me.

"I mean it. You're fucking incredible. Those babies are so damn lucky to have you. But that's not all you are," she reminds me as she grasps my hand. "I'm going to keep reminding you of that, from now until you decide you're done popping out tiny humans."

I snort. For as stressful and intense as parenthood can be, I don't see myself wanting to be done *popping out tiny humans* anytime soon. My PMDD simmers down when I'm pregnant and nursing. Not only that, but I love being pregnant, and I love having babies. Even if I am tired ninety-nine percent of the time.

The other facets of my life are still there—my dream to be a lawyer, my love of romance books and reading, my connection to Joey, my attraction and obsession with my four amazing guys—but they're set on simmer for now, waiting on the back burner until I can give them my full attention.

"I'm sorry I can't be as good a friend as I used to be," I tell her through another yawn.

"Hunter." She scowls. "You're paving the way for me. Do you know that?"

Brow furrowed, I study her, confused.

"You're not just my bestie anymore, babe. You're my role model. I never dreamed of being a mom. In fact, before I met the guys, I was adamantly opposed to ever having kids. Partly because I was scared, but mostly because I didn't think I would be any good at it, all things considered."

All things considered meaning her awful excuse for a mom: a woman who neglected Joey most of her life, then didn't even try to step up and help her when she was sexually assaulted and bullied mercilessly for it in high school.

"But watching you love on your babies and seeing the way they look at you? It gives me hope. Hope that maybe I could be a good mom someday, too."

It's my turn to hold up one finger and glare. "You *will* be a good mom," I correct. "If that's what you want."

Her smile softens, and she lies flat on her back, so I do the same. She inches closer and takes my hand.

"I do want it. But I don't think I would have been brave enough to go for it if you weren't here leading by example."

She gives my hand a tight, quick squeeze.

Grinning, I fight back a snort. "Can you imagine Decker as a dad?"

Joey cackles and shakes her head so hard the boat rocks beneath us. "Oh god. He's going to be so overbearing and protective about *everything*. I take it back. I don't want kids. I can't procreate with that man." She bursts out laughing again.

"Locke will balance him out," I offer.

"Yes. You're so right." She sighs. "Ugh. My *heart*. Nicky will be *such* a great dad."

"He really will be. They all will, babe. And you're going to be an amazing mom. If and when you decide that's what you want."

We're both quiet then, with nothing but the sound of the water lapping at the side of the pontoon to fill in the silence.

The sun is warm on my face. My best friend is holding my hand by my side.

Life is good. So good.

Joey's head must be in the same place, because eventually, she whispers, "Do you ever wonder what we did to deserve all this?"

All this, as in the type of happiness people spend their entire lives chasing after.

All this, as in the happily ever after I never dared to dream for myself. Not until four magnificent men changed the very core of who I am: heart, body, mind, and soul.

I prop myself up on my elbows and shield my eyes so I can really look at my bestie. "First, Josephine Crusade, do I have to remind you that you *are* the prize?"

She smirks, her eyes closed behind her sunglasses, but she doesn't respond.

"You deserve good things. You deserve the very best this life has to offer, no qualifiers necessary."

"You're right," she says quietly. "Maybe after surviving the shittiest shit, life presented us with opportunities, and we were brave enough to take them."

I lift my soggy-straw and glass. "Brave enough to take them and smart enough to never let go."

"I'll drink to that." Joey taps her cup to mine. "To the bravest, smartest woman I know."

Grinning, I bypass the nasty mush straw and sip from the side of my cup. "Right back atcha, babe."

Epilogue 5: Hunter

Five Years Later

I've been up for hours when I hear them outside the closed door.

I have two textbooks open on the bed, along with copious amounts of notes fanned out around me as I work. Finals start next week, but it's Saturday morning, which means the boys and the babies made me breakfast in bed.

On the other side of the door, they shush each other, and I can't help but grin. Every weekend they make a big show of "surprising me," and I dutifully play my part, delighted to see them and soak in time with the entire family piled onto one bed.

Notes gathered, I shut down my laptop.

I'm setting my textbooks off to the side when the sharp knock comes.

"Come in," I call out. As my four guys and our four little ones file into the room, I bite back a smile.

Each of my men has fathered one of the kids—we think. Every now and then I question whether Rowan and her sassy attitude really came from Levi (although the guys insist her spitfire spirit comes from *me*, not him, and her bright blue eyes are a perfect match to his). Then sometimes when I look at Grace, I swear I see a bit of Levi in her, despite her mossy green irises and the dark curls that favor Greedy.

We're not done, either. Now that Xander is only nursing once a night, all my guys are chomping at the bit to make baby number five. It's become a hot topic over the last few months. They can't stop debating over who gets priority in fathering the next one. They're so damn competitive, I swear.

Despite feeling my best when I'm pregnant—I'll take morning sickness and swollen ankles over brain fog and intrusive thoughts any day—I plan to take a year or two off from baby making to finally finish my degree. Hence why I had an IUD implanted at my last OB appointment.

After finals next week, I'll be one year away from earning my law degree. Joey and Locke's nonprofit has been expanding faster than they ever expected. They'll be ready to hire full-time legal counsel in the next year or so, and I want to be that person.

Everything's falling into place. Divine timing, as Si likes to say. I'm elated that I'm so close to finishing law school. I can't wait to walk across that stage and earn my degree.

I lie back against the pillows, waiting patiently as the door creaks open.

Jole files in first, his soft smile and toothy grin lighting up my heart just the way his Tamai's does. He stands off to the side, both hands behind his back.

Rowan charges in next, Sione and Levi sticking close as if they're trying to hold her back. I snort quietly. Good luck to them. Our oldest daughter is already a force to be reckoned with.

Next comes Greedy, carrying the tray like usual, with Grace tucked into the crook of one arm. She can walk on her own, not that anyone would know that, with the way her daddies and big brother insist on carrying her around all the time.

Finally, Spence and Xander enter the room. My beautiful, chubby-cheeked, gray-eyed baby, who laughs and smiles so hard his little eyelashes disappear into his face each time he sees me.

I swear he came out of the womb smiling. His entire persona is the opposite of Spence. His giddiness and general merriment are much more aligned with Levi's personality. His darker skin and intense eyes, though, along with the memo Spence sent out that included words like "motility" and "morphology" and his insistence that the others needed to wear condoms the month our youngest was conceived—because he had a business trip the following month and wanted a fair shot—mean Xander is most likely his.

"Oh! Did you make me breakfast?" I ask in mock-surprise once everyone's in the room.

"We did," Rowan pipes up, one hand planted on her little hip. Okay. Yeah. Maybe she does get it from me... "But all the food's still in the kitchen."

Sighing, Sione crouches low. "Pepe, we talked about this," he says quietly.

It's then that I notice the tray Greedy is carrying is empty.

Well, not empty, but devoid of food.

Instead, there's a blue paper airplane resting on the center.

I look to each of my guys, then home in on the kids. They're all looking at me with various levels of mischief painted on their faces.

"What's going on?"

Instead of answering, Greedy steps forward, lifts the paper airplane, and lets Grace "help him" hold it.

"Ready?" he asks.

Jole pulls a purple airplane out from behind his back. Levi offers Rowan a pink one, handing it over while giving her his stern daddy warning scowl I love. Spence is holding a red paper airplane and booping Xander on the nose with the tip as our baby shrieks in delight.

"Here we go. Three, two, one!"

Four planes come flying toward the bed.

Their single flight.

Their one and only chance to get it right.

They land around me, and I grasp at them as memories flood my system. Memories of heartbreak and final goodbyes. Recollections of fresh starts, hard resets, life lessons, and renewed hope.

I scramble to collect them all, my eyes welling with tears.

By the time they're all gathered in my lap, all eight of my people have climbed into bed.

"Open them, Mommy!" Jole says.

"No, wait!" Rowan reaches over, her little pink fingernail pointing to the number on top of the pink plane. "You have to put them in order first."

Four paper airplanes, numbered one to four.

I arrange them in front of me, then, holding my breath, open up number one.

Will.

That's all it says. One single word.

The red plane is next. I find one word inside it as well.

You.

I tear open planes three and four, barely registering the letters on the page until I've laid them out side by side.

Pink. Red. Purple. Blue.

Will. You. Marry. Us.

"Yes!" I squeal, scooping the creased papers up and clutching them to my chest. "Of course, of course, of course!"

We've talked about it. Dreamed about it. Even if it's nothing more than a small ceremony more symbolic than legal in nature. But between school and work, travel and pregnancies, we've never found the time.

Will I marry them?

I want nothing more in this life than to be forever connected to my cohort in every way possible. *Of course I'll marry them.*

Greedy is closest, so I reach for him, kiss him deeply, then nuzzle my head against Grace's sweet little cheek. Levi finds my lips next; Sione kisses the top of my head.

Spence leans over last, his hand lovingly gripping my throat and then tightening ever so slightly when his lips meet my ear. "Their wife, but still my whore," he assures me.

A shiver racks through my body at the promise of his words.

"When is the wedding, Mommy?" Rowan asks. "Do we get to be there?"

I smile and nod. "Of course you'll be there, baby." But then I look back to each of my guys. "I don't know when, exactly, but I do have conditions."

They all watch me, each wearing a different look of amusement. Good to know they didn't expect anything less from me.

"I'm finishing my degree first," I declare. "And I will *not* be knocked up on our wedding day."

No one says a word.

Though it's clearly not necessary, I double down. "I want to get drunk on our honeymoon and fully enjoy newlywed life. At least for a few weeks."

Greedy shakes his head, grinning.

Levi mutters, "I'm in."

Spence tuts something about drafting a memo.

It's not until Grace chimes in that I remember we have an audience.

"Dunk," she slurs in her little toddler babble language. "Dunk, dunk, dunk." She claps her hands to punctuate each word.

Sione groans—not mad, just disappointed—and Spence rises to call for Mrs. Lansbury.

"Mommy, what's drunk?" Jole asks as our beloved nanny walks into the room.

"Heavens," she mutters under her breath, taking Xander out of Spence's arms and guiding Grace by the hand toward the door.

Seeing her in to cause trouble, Rowan piles on. "Yeah, Mommy. What's drunk? Why do you want to be *drunk*?"

"Okay, you lot. Come along."

The babies have no choice but to be shuttled out of the room. Jole follows dutifully.

Rowan is slower to join her siblings, clearly annoyed by our lack of answers. "Mrs. Lansbury, what's drunk?"

With an eye on me, the older woman tsks. Then she focuses on my daughter. "I'll tell you when you're older, dear." She pulls the door closed behind her.

Once the kids are out of the room, my men pounce.

"Yes?" Greedy asks, his voice gravelly and full of emotion as he plants his forearms on either side of my head and holds plank position above me.

"Yes." I circle my arms around his neck and kiss him fiercely. "A million times yes." I break away and kiss Levi next. Once I've batted Greedy out of the way, I scoot to the other side of the bed and seek out Sione, straddling his lap and peppering his neck and face with kisses as he holds me in a loving embrace.

"We're going out tonight," Spence declares.

When I turn and regard him, his eyes have that deep, taunting tell. He wants to go out. He wants to let loose. My man wants to *play*.

"Dinner. Dancing. Drinks." Each word is a salacious promise. "Then if you're a very good girl, we'll fuck you boneless in a five-star hotel and issue at least six orgasms. Then, tomorrow, we'll take you ring shopping for seven carats."

I didn't think Spence's dirty talk could get any hotter, but here he is, adding diamonds into the equation and proving me wrong.

I'm giddy at the prospect, though the excitement fades quickly.

"Mahina?" Sione nudges me with his nose.

I offer him a reassuring smile. Nothing's wrong, but I have to keep my promises to myself, too, and I marked off this weekend months ago and dedicated it to finals.

"I have to study."

They'll all understand, but that won't stop them from being disappointed not to have a night out together.

"Fine. We can compromise," Spence says casually from the foot of the bed. He's already unbuttoning his shirt.

My heart catches in my throat, and my pussy clenches at the sight of his deft, ring-clad fingers working open the next button on his Oxford.

"We'll go out next weekend. After exams have passed. Drinks. Dancing. Hotel sex. Ring shopping. But we're celebrating today as well. Give us two hours now—enough time to fill all your holes and fully satisfy our future *wife*—then we'll leave you alone to study for the rest of the weekend."

I scoff, but Spence knows damn well I can't refuse that kind of offer.

"I'm in." Levi jackknifes off the bed and whips his shirt over his head. Greedy is on his feet, too. "I'll lock the door."

"I love you," I tell Sione, resting my forehead against his.

With tears brimming in my eyes, I take in each of my men, one by one. "I love all of you, and I can't wait to marry you."

Afterword

Thank you, dear reader, for going on this journey with me.

Reaching the end of this series and giving Hunter's cohort the happily ever after they all deserved has been a highlight of my career. It's also been a "lowlight," if I'm honest, because DAMN, these characters really put me through it. Truth be told, writing these books was so much harder than I ever anticipated. Between the now and then timelines of the first three books and the very intense personalities of the characters themselves (here's lookin' at you, Spence), there were days I wasn't sure I could do this story justice. And then Joey and her men wanted to be included, too. If you thought the Crusade Mansion was getting crowded, just imagine how loud they all were in my head!

But we're here. We made it. No more running. This is it.

I want to take a moment to acknowledge that Hunter's version of happily ever after isn't a one-size-fits-all experience. In fact, it's so closely aligned with a stereotypical HEA, I feel the need to defend it here. Being a parent isn't for everyone, despite what society and the patriarchy want us to believe. I can assure you that Hunter's desires are authentic and uniquely her own. She only fully realized her heart's desire to be a mother once she allowed herself to receive the kind of love she had never experienced in a relationship before. It helps, of course, that she has four partners who were also eager and enthusiastic about growing their family. I know she's young. I know she chose to put her education and career ambitions on hold in the pursuit of motherhood. Ultimately, the characters tell me what they want and need, and for Hunter, motherhood needed to come first.

Some of my favorite moments in this series happen when Hunter and Joey's "cohorts" appear on page together. I will never NOT snort when I read Kylian's line about the armadillo. And can we talk about the bromance between Stats Daddy and Spence? I swear those two could take over the world if they weren't so busy avenging their women and pleasing their partners.

I was obsessed with finding fun ways to incorporate the Boys of Lake Chapel into this series. I hope you caught all the little call backs and inside jokes. If you haven't read Joey's story yet, what are you waiting for!? The Boys of Lake Chapel series is complete, and it's available on Amazon, in Kindle Unlimited, and through Audible, too! Book one is called Too Safe, and you'll see lots of fun moments with Hunter and Greedy in that series as well.

Finally!! Last year, before the Boys of South Chapel series had even begun, I wrote a bonus scene that occurs during the timeline of Too Fast (Boys of Lake Chapel Book Two). The bonus scene features Hunter and Greedy and gives you a peek into their POVs during the Lake Chapel University vs. South Chapel University football game. You can access the bonus scene by signing up for my email newsletter. All bonus scenes are also available on my website. Happy reading!

Acknowledgments

Thank you to every single reader who (legally) reads my stories. I hope you find an escape and also feel seen whenever you visit the fictional worlds of Lake Chapel, South Chapel, Hampton, and beyond.

Special shoutouts to the individuals who made this book (and this entire series!) possible:

Beth—for being my person, in business and in real life. For sticking with me, even when my brain did not want to cooperate this year. For loving my characters, catching my Abby-isms, and always being there to catch *me* when I fall down the stairs.

Megan—for helping me in a million little ways, and for loving this series and these characters so well. You can be the Hunter to my Joey any day (and now we have the matching jerseys to prove it!).

Linds, Mica, Adah, and Jen—for sensitivity and beta reading to ensure this book was the very best it could be. Having your poignant insights, hilarious comments, and helpful feedback made all the difference for Hunter and her men.

Amy @coffeeandbookobsessed—for swooping in and consuming this entire series to help ensure continuity. Your comments and feedback made this story stronger, and I'm so grateful for your perspective.

Mr. Abby—for holding it down at the homestead and rocking the SAHD life this year. This series would not have been possible if I didn't have your love and support behind the scenes.

Finally, to anyone living with Premenstrual Dysphoric Disorder who battles cyclical demons every month—You are not alone.

You are not just a diagnosis. Take care of your body, mind, and spirit, and don't be afraid to seek help when you need it. Never forget that even on your lowest days, you are whole, wanted, and wonderful just the way you are.

Also By Abby Millsaps

The Hampton Hearts series:
interconnected standalone small town romance novels

Golden Boy
Mr. Brightside
Fourth Wheel
Full Out Fiend

The Boys of Lake Chapel:
a why choose sports romance series

Too Safe: Boys of Lake Chapel Book One
Too Fast: Boys of Lake Chapel Book Two
Too Far: Boys of Lake Chapel Book Three

The Boys of South Chapel:
a why choose second chance romance series

So Wrong: Boys of South Chapel Book One
So Real: Boys of South Chapel Book Two
So Rare: Boys of South Chapel Book Three
So Right: Boys of South Chapel Book Four

About The Author

Abby Millsaps is an author and storyteller who's been obsessed with writing romance since middle school. In eighth grade, she failed to qualify for the Power of the Pen State Championships because "all her submissions contained the same theme: young people falling in love." #LookAtHerNow

She's best known for writing unapologetically angsty romance that causes emotional damage for her readers. Creative spicy scenes and consent as foreplay are two hallmarks of her books. Abby prides herself in writing authentic characters while weaving mental health, chronic illness, and neurodiverse representation into the fabric of her stories.

Connect with Abby
Website: www.authorabbymillsaps.com
Patreon: https://www.patreon.com/AbbyMillsaps
Instagram: @abbymillsaps
TikTok: @authorabbymillsaps
Email: authorabbymillsaps@gmail.com
Newsletter: https://geni.us/AuthorAbbyNewsletter
Facebook Reader Group: Abby's Full Out Fiends

www.ingramcontent.com/pod-product-compliance
Lightning Source LLC
LaVergne TN
LVHW03031807 0526
838199LV00069B/6491